Her Artificial Heart

Paths Unknown, Volume 3

Lee Kaiser

Published by Lee Kaiser, 2025.

HER ARTIFICIAL HEART

First edition. November 8, 2025.

Copyright © 2025 Lee Kaiser.

ISBN: 978-1777457723

Written by Lee Kaiser.

Also by Lee Kaiser

Paths Unknown
Sutra of the Pearl
Her Artificial Heart

Watch for more at leekaiserauthor.com.

Chapter 1

C laudia wouldn't dream of pulling this stunt on any of her friends. (Granted, there were just the two unless one was brave enough to count Benny, who had recently learned of her secret debauchery with his nephew.)

Low rumbles pulsed through every molecule of liquid in her gut and head. There was no T-minus countdown. Not even a friendly "Hang onto your hats, folks" before a bone-crunching launch whiplashed her into submission against the passenger ferry's observation windows.

Everyone knows that when the sea is calm and the sun is shining you carve out your perch at the bow of the second deck—unless it belongs to a hydrofoil that reaches sixty miles per hour on submerged water wings.

"Bloo—dy hell." The buttons on Claudia's wool pea jacket split into a flying spike belt against her scalp. Claudia was always up for a spot of intrigue, but this was ridiculous. Her trendy topknot braid at the crown of her head began sagging dangerously close to that of a disheveled French milkmaid.

A simple disclaimer near the gangway would have sufficed: All Passengers Bringing Hairstyles On Board Do So At Their Own Risk.

She battened down her briefcase under one arm and white-knuckled a crumpled letter.

Dated February 10, 2018, it was written on the kind of translucent stationery and gold letterhead often used to telegraph doom in someone's life, but as Claudia reached for the lounge's doorknob her concentration wavered and up the paper flew. It hovered like a fairy with a magic wand before zipping sideways and disappearing over the vessel's railing.

Too stunned to cry out, at forty-seven-years-old she was still as lean as a thoroughbred. Her legs churned across the sleek whale of a vessel in time to see the cursed thing surfing the hydrofoil's wake. If only she could set the chief of surgery and his disciplinary committee adrift at sea.

With four lopsided steps, she was safe inside the lounge and—utterly alone. A sour odor like regurgitated stomach acid had attached itself to the vast, plastic silence of white benches. Curious how ferry seats used the same epoxied waterproofing against vomit and pee-pants common to emergency rooms, she thought.

No doubt the vessel hosted that low-brow form of British entertainment that terrorized continental Europe, and once seen, could never be unseen. From her first and only Stag and Hen party came the image of a man transporting an empty bottle of vintage wine—the uncorked neck lodged securely in his anus.

Except, this wasn't the frothy pedestrian stink of someone who would live to drink another day, but the layered putrefaction of death. Something or someone had been left to rot here before being taken away.

From inside her briefcase she pulled out a weirdly damp postcard which had likely been riding its dockside, brine-encrusted carousel for more years than she cared to know. Maybe this would tell her why she was being summoned to an island she'd never heard of.

Inquisitor's Island, it stated in tiny print in one corner, *is a far-flung promontory with a bloody past. Unloved and unclaimed by any nation, it lies in tortuous seas dead center of the Mediterranean.* Below was a blurry photo of an island and an eight-pointed cross she recognized from the time of the Holy Crusades.

Let's face it, if she was going to perform her brand of miracle then the nipple of rock in the photo didn't look big enough for a needle exchange van—let alone a hospital.

The flip side had a sepia-tone graphic over which one could scrawl a greeting like—*Having a great time on Inquisitor's Island. Wish you were here*—Which would be dandy if the meticulously rendered background wasn't of someone being burned at the stake.

Worst marketing campaign ever.

One hour after the hydrofoil departed Malta, a dark, iceberg-shaped island rose within the balmy Sirocco winds of a Mediterranean spring, and Claudia pressed her desert boots into the pebbled shoreline of Inquisitor's Island for the first time.

If locals wanted to scare off visitors then the postcard might be enough. If not, a sulfurous metallic stench hanging in the air certainly would. Burned fat and singed hair was an odor she knew well from destroying diseased sheep on her mother's farm in Romania. The coppery smell was from the hemoglobin in blood.

Ahead, in a dash for the dock an overfed rat jumped from a beachside bin labelled *Biohazard*. Not the farm girl's first dance with a rodent with a piece of—What the hell was that between its teeth? She'd seen her share of wasted human flesh but never as lunch for a rat. Clearly, something was not up to code.

As her boot sent the thing tumbling, a joyless man with an AK-47 slung over his shoulder crunched forward from the shadows of a palm tree. If he wasn't a Middle Eastern guerrilla fighter of the type often in the news, he sure had the garb down pat. Scarves billowed about his head and lower face. A brocade vest over a Nehru shirt, floppy flood pants, and untied high top runners completed the look.

She stood there doing the three-arm juggling act with her briefcase, backpack, and medical bag, and feeling way out of her depth as to what this guy was here for. Was he supposed to be guarding or protecting her? An indolent movement of his arm toward a concrete pad with an aerial gondola made it clear—he wasn't a welcoming party and she could carry her own damn bags.

He stuck a key fob into a slot and the car, spacious enough to seat a dozen passengers along its plush bench, sailed up the same vertical cliff visible from miles away.

The man paced incessantly, turning their glass bubble into a tilt o' whirl. *For Christ's sake sit down.* She eyed the assault rifle and kept her mouth shut.

It was right after they skimmed over a shack humming with a noisy generator that the unmistakable crackle and roar of fire sprang up. She gagged and yanked her cotton turtleneck over her mouth as the full force of the earlier stench struck.

On a broad rock ledge below, guards trudged between a pile of white oblong sacks and a brick incinerator spewing sparks and soot. The workers hoisted one or two sacks over their shoulders and when they reached the glowing oven, they upended the contents and tossed the sack aside.

As Claudia's car floated directly overhead, a breeze kicked aside the pall of smoke and the two tasked with feeding the incinerator stopped and raised their red, sweat-streaked faces upward. She reared back, struck dumb, because now she could see what they held in their hands—the limp bodies of children.

What the hell was this place, and why was her friend here? Or *was* she? Claudia fumbled her phone from her briefcase only to find neither a cell signal nor data connection.

With her palms flat against the glass, the scene dropped away, but hands soon gripped her shoulders and forced her down to the seat. *Bugger off.* She glanced at the semi-automatic again and bit into her curse.

Before the car had even ground to a halt on the lip of a ridge, the guy hopped out and marched out of view where flagstones dove into a discordant tangle of deciduous and palm trees.

Daphne Technologies. Trespassers Will Be . . . she took a wild guess at the last ammo-riddled word of the sign.

Hyper alert, her pulse still racing from the dead children, she silently bid him good riddance, and with her backpack slung across her back, the rest in each hand, she trudged along the twisted, downward-sloping route until she caught up minutes later. He was smoking and chatting with a compatriot stationed at a ten-foot-high iron gate—the chain link fence to each side decorated with barbed wire and voltage warnings.

A pretty flowering hedge would have been a reason for pause—she passed through and assigned the place extra marks for consistency.

Across a shallow strip of packed red earth lay her final destination; Claudia lifted her eyes to the farthest reaches of an Old World facade carved straight from the face of a limestone cliff. Broad stone steps led to a pair of formidable Hellenic-era pillars which framed a double-sided cast iron entrance door. Engraved into the iron was the same crusader cross from the postcard and the Latin phrase: *Tuitio fidei et obsequium pauperum.*

As she raised her cell's camera to the words, another rat-faced being skipped into the shot, his hand out long before he reached her.

She did a double-take. So this was where he'd been on the lam all these years, Claudia thought.

"Defence of the faith," he said, turning his lab coat-clad frame to the phrase. "And assistance to the poor."

She lowered her phone to find his glad-hand buzzing around her like a biting insect. "Welcome to our institute, Dr. Vlakia. We're honored to—"

Pathetic. How far had this gifted man fallen to be grovelling at the feet of her own obscure career? Nevertheless, finding the disgraced geneticist here on the island finally shed some light on yesterday's threadbare email from her friend:

I know how busy you are, it stated, *but we need you. Desperately. When you get to the Maltese harbor of Birzebbuga, text us and we'll send the Inquisitor's Island passenger ferry to fetch you. Much love and gratitude. Paula, Benny and Maya. P.S. Don't try to phone.*

The first thing she did was try to phone.

The troubling message was not only missing more parts than a Brazilian bikini, it wasn't Protocol Paula's usual intimate style. If Benny was trying to deactivate the gene which passed on his congenital heart disease, he was likely in the right place. If their desperation was about Maya, however, why not simply say so?

Claudia had called the couple's Greek villa first, then Benny's corporate office in India, and was searching in a panic for the number of Benny's infamous nephew—her fifteen-year-old victim now suffering from early-onset middle-aged spread—when Benny's secretary finally came on to say the family was on holiday in Malta.

"Call me Claudia," she told the wayward geneticist. "And why am I here? All I have is this . . ." Postcard out, Claudia grazed his nose with the burning-at-the-stake side, her unease turbocharged by the dead children. " . . . and my friend's email."

"Sorry, but I'm not the one to answer that." His index finger and one eyeball tracked the souvenir's erratic flight path. "I wish they would stop selling that horrid thing on the mainland. *We* think of our island as a paradise."

At almost a foot taller, Claudia easily kept up when he strode off at a determined clip. "Right," she said. "What is the meaning of those children's bodies down there, Dr. Hocking?"

"Oh." The man's bony knees locked up mid-stride. His shoulders drooped, chopping another inch or two from his limited stature.

Those news photos of him must be airbrushed, she thought, her eyes glued to the sharp edge of his ski-slope nose.

"You recognize me." He let his hands drop to his sides. "It's sad, but I'm not authorized to discuss it."

She watched him bounce off, his chirpy indifference to the suffering of children particularly hideous in a man of such intelligence. It wasn't the children he was sad about but his inability to discuss them.

Hocking wasn't high on her list of potential friends. Best to flood the jailbird with a techno-rant to prove she wasn't a lightweight. "Back to stem cell research are you?" she called after him. "Or, perhaps attempting to clone animals now? I believe the consensus on clones by SCNT is that only one to five percent are without abnormalities due to epigenetic reprogramming failures."

Hocking glanced back and smouldered, beak-beady before climbing the broad steps into the institute. "You certainly have a grasp of the latest in cloning." With the swipe of a key card across a blinking terminal the ancient double doors swung wide.

"I try to keep up," she said, careful to keep things vague. "Who's going to need a donor if they can have an organ bioprinted from their own stem cells?" When he didn't ask if she was a transplant surgeon, Claudia feared what else he might know. She was always alert to possible lab leaks.

He stumbled in after her with a forced chuckle. "We're a ways from there. I must say, the Chinese have successfully grown embryos which are part monkey and part human. Those could eventually give us donor organs."

She froze. "Now that's friggin scary . . . *scary* . . . *scary*." Her voice ricocheted across the limestone lobby, empty except for a metal desk and stainless steel elevator at one end—and the four inevitable sentries with the same passive-aggressive side eye.

Hocking swiped his ID fob again inside the elevator before pressing the Level 5 button. She knew of only two types of elevators with locks: those keeping unauthorized people out or those keeping non-paroled people in.

Since it was futile to ask where they were headed she rode in silence, tapping her foot to the rhythm of a flat tire speeding over a bridge—w*hop, whop, whop, whop,* until—*waa-waa . . . waa-waa.* She expected the fire engine charging down the elevator shaft to crash over their heads at any moment.

Dr. Hocking pulled the emergency brake, and glanced at the pager on his belt. "Oh, for Pete's sake. Not again." He swiped his ID and they appeared headed back down to Level 1.

When the elevator shuddered to a halt, instead of finding herself in the lobby, the rear doors behind them opened onto a long hallway. Hocking tapped his fob once more, pressed a button, and stepped out. "I'll be right back, Dr.—I mean Claudia."

The doors were closing.

"Wait." She bashed the heel of her palm on *Open* and when that didn't work, jammed the end of her briefcase into the shrinking gap, suspending it at hip height. The two-inch slit gave her a view of a strip of the linoleum floor.

Better than nothing. No sign of Hocking.

She was about to start shouting for help when the faint echo of raised voices and panicked footsteps filtered from nearby. A young woman in a Middle Eastern headscarf and jeans bolted into view only inches from Claudia, and a door crashed closed behind her. Carrying a bawling toddler in her arms, she ran down the hall then reversed as Hocking stepped from a doorway.

As two armed guards grabbed her and tried to pry the child away, she pleaded, "Please. He's mine. Let me have him." When the child was transferred to Hocking, both the woman and the child went ballistic, screaming and kicking.

"Don't use the elevator," Claudia thought she heard Hocking say above the commotion, and before ducking out a door at the far end of the hall.

The woman used the distraction to break free but immediately collapsed, limp, as one guard tasered her while the other cuffed her arms behind her back and dragged her out of view. A metal door clanged shut. The alarm ceased.

Utter silence.

Leveraging herself with an arm and leg, Claudia yanked the briefcase free and the elevator doors closed. Now what? If Dr. Mousey-face was smart enough to discover how to jumpstart cloned cells, he only had to take one look at her emaciated briefcase and figure out what she'd done.

Claudia plopped her flat rump atop her briefcase and backpack, and scrutinized the vents above her. Was this the part where poison sarin gas pours out? Goddamn you, Paula. Or was this—? Oh, toss it. She'd know soon enough.

It was the timing that was mucking up her life at the moment.

Only Paula could convince the surgeon to forfeit her warm London bed for a red-eye flight—and do so on a day when the wheels on Claudia's career had fallen off and passed her on a hairpin turn.

Hocking thrashed his head in feigned horror as the elevator doors suddenly parted and he saw her sitting there. "Never a dull moment in this place." They flashed each other fake smiles. On the move again, the elevator rose from the lobby and passed Level 2. "I've just found out your host is available. I could take you to your lodgings or—"

"Paula's here, isn't she?"

All she got this time was a sheepish shrug.

Six years earlier, Hocking's stem cell research earned him the King of Cloning moniker—at least, until he ran afoul of UK medical ethics for genetically modifying the embryos of in vitro twins. If Hocking was the errand boy, who was running the place—a cryo-preserved Einstein?

Claudia rose to shove her mangled briefcase into her backpack and out of sight. The scene she'd witnessed was too disturbing to let anyone know she'd seen it while still in what might be unfriendly territory. She toed her "little black doctor's bag" closer, and even though taser-wielding militants were not on her mind when she'd packed it, at least she remembered a supply of number ten scalpel blades.

The innocent excitement of a new adventure was flashing red. Had Maya been kidnapped and Claudia brought in as the go-between? After all, terminally ill children made the best kind of hostages.

Chapter 2

On Level 2, Claudia exited into more of the same airless palette of worn limestone walls punctuated by polished steel doors, where an unseen woman was hollering her head off.

She trailed Dr. Hocking through a meandering stream of sighs and moans from waddling women. Their black robes and headscarves fit so well with the Moorish arches and chandeliers, she wouldn't have been surprised to see a turbaned warrior swagger by, his curved scabbard swinging from his belt.

A blur of men wearing hospital-blue scrubs at computer terminals was the first hint she might be in a medical facility. It was here at a bend in the hall where Hocking parked Claudia and her stained rucksack in the kind of windowless lounge mob bosses and playboy bunnies might like. Still and fresh as a jungle cenote, with sage green walls and cream carpeting it took a while for her eyes to adjust to the speckled light.

Instead of tossing her stuff atop one of two frosted silk sofas, she dragged it into a dark corner, where, fanned across an oak side table like cheese slices were magazines such as *The Joy of Motherhood*, *Ladies' Journal*, *21st Century Parenting*, and more of the same drool she'd never read.

A framed diploma did interest her. It was for someone with a name so long her eyeballs went into fibrillation. The doctorate in virology was, of course, from anywhere but her own obscure alma mater in Bucharest; even if people knew where that was, they certainly hadn't studied there.

She was scanning for other diplomas when a garish freak show poster caught her eye. Heavily photoshopped, a startled wide-eyed monkey embryo stared back from the confines of a test tube. As usual, the caption would have to be so annoyingly tiny as to make you stick your nose into it. She hated this kind of consumer manipulation because, at six feet tall, Claudia was always peering down at one thing or another. She was no long-legged beauty of the catwalk, though—unless one found her horsey facial features endearing.

Are chimeras the answer to the world's organ transplant shortage? the poster postulated. This globally condemned soup of mixing the genes of two species was what the geneticist had joked about outside the building. What the hell was going on here—the joy of motherhood or the creation of Franken-monkeys?

At the sound of a door opening behind her, she jerked her nose from the poster.

"We make dreams come true, Dr. Vlakia." A male voice with a promise of something comforting like Baileys in steaming black coffee, shoved the test tube image to the back of her mind.

She bolted upright to find a man with his back to her. He was unlocking a smoked-glass door into another room and, no doubt about it, the guy had a weakness for silk. Snugged into a blue-striped silk jacket over faded jeans he was the picture of refined ruggedness.

His dust-gray hair was shot through with the blond of a more virile time, but it was the metallic-hued blue braid which clung to the back of his neck that screamed to be noticed. A vain attempt to appear young? she wondered. Normally, anything going against nature's grain left a sour taste in her gut, but this blizzard of shades was a snub to the status quo.

She immediately liked him.

"Do you have children of your own?" He palmed the glass open and stood aside to let her pass.

Eye to eye, his crystal blues held her dark browns easily. They had jumped over pleasantries into what new acquaintances assumed was a touchy topic for her. It wasn't. She liked him even more despite a cautionary amber light whirling like a Dervish inside her head. He was good-looking enough to make poor grooming irresistibly sexy.

"Never went down that road," she said. "Nor marriage. Are you a doctor here?"

"I own and operate the clinic." He motioned to two wingback chairs in a corner. "My name is Papakostopoulou."

Who could forget a name like that, especially in celebrity rags with a penchant for snappy appellations like J. Lo or BoJo? This guy's plump name and its aberration—Papa K—had caught her eye a few years back at a newsstand, but she assumed it was an article about a Greek gangster. An internet search was in order.

She sat, half-assed uncommitted, one butt cheek clinging to the padded arm of the wingback.

"I go by Homer," he said. "I felt if one of my patients was coding, by the time the floor nurse paged me the patient would be long dead." He squared himself into the wingback and, thankfully, didn't so much as smile at his own joke.

"We're honored to have you."

There it was again. She didn't mind being honored, as long as it wasn't based on her research into a bionic heart. If her friends had breathed a word about it to this guy or anyone else including his shoe-shine boy, they'd have to answer for it.

"To be honest," Claudia began, "which is what I always am—I'd feel more appreciated if you could tell me what I'm doing here. Moments ago, your man Hocking locked me inside an elevator."

A look of mock horror wiped the shine off Papa K. "I apologize on behalf of Dr. Hocking," he moaned. "He's an invaluable asset to us, but the incident was a false alarm. Our greatest fear is that someone will kidnap a client's newborn. The guards mistook one of our surrogates for a kidnapper."

"A virtual deluge of kidnappers, is it?" Claudia asked, recalling Hocking's "Not again."

He bristled when she leveled a cold stare at him, leaving Claudia convinced her skepticism was warranted. "Is that what you're up to here? You're a fertility clinic?"

"Among other things," he said. "I heard about your unfortunate view of the clinic incinerator. The cable car is usually reserved for staff only."

"It looked to me like you're burning children—not bio-waste." She tapped her foot through another long pause.

"You're right, but unfortunately the Maltese authorities don't want the bodies of asylum seekers. Nobody does. They wash ashore occasionally. Along with adults, of course. Refugees trying to cross from the shores of North Africa in appallingly crowded boats."

"How do you know their families aren't looking for them?" she said.

"We send digital images to the holding camps and rescue ships. If we get a response we have our cold storage here, but if not . . ." He lunged from his chair with a sharp sigh. "I can answer any question you may have, but first Benny has some news for you."

Would her friends bring her all this way to announce their next child? No.

"He's waiting up top," Homer said. "And Paula's in the ICU."

That shot Claudia to her feet. "Intensive care? Why?"

"She's fine." The warmth of his palm on her shoulder did reassure her a touch. "Do you know I've been friends with Benny for more than a decade?"

To hell with small talk. ICU was never for patients who were "fine."

They were in the elevator, headed *up top*, whatever that meant, when Claudia realized the problem with his explanation—the child she'd seen with the tasered woman wasn't a newborn. "What's in that hallway on the ground level where I was locked in the elevator?"

"You must mean the one behind the lobby. It has our in vitro labs."

Not a bit of hesitation from him this time.

"Our clients are in the top three percent of society. They want utter privacy from the news media and safety from possible kidnappers. That's why visitors and clients are escorted at all times. Even doctors such as yourself have to prove themselves before we give them passes for the facility."

A fine joke that would be—Claudia working inside a fertility clinic where people spent all day micromanaging sperm and ovum. Sending them out on blind dates and hoping for the best. True, she spent all day with sick newborns, but at this watershed in life she no longer had any interest in what preceded the tiny things, or, what followed. At the first sign of an opinion out of the little scamps, she would drop them.

Surely His Dudeness was exaggerating about their hyper-vigilance of his own staff. Oh boy, had this man's face ever gone permafrosty. His clinic wasn't the only thing locked up tight.

———◉———

AS THE DOORS PARTED on Level 5 Claudia caught the unmistakable burbling of water rushing over rocks. She stepped into an oriental garden sheltered from harsh seawinds by a story-high bamboo grove. Ornamental shrubs and delicate willow trees surrounded a pond expansive enough to contain three pagoda-style gazebos at its shore.

The calming tinkling enticed her up a slight incline to a low waterfall and arched bridge spanning the pond's narrowest point.

With arms raised to the entire panorama, a sparkle had returned to Homer's eyes. "This is what passes for the great outdoors on our island."

The rooftop garden seemed to cap the entire clinic which might have been a catacomb of caverns in its natural state. Claudia frowned. "Someone has gone to a lot of trouble, but how—"

"It's not natural, of course," Homer cut in. "We pump the water from an aquifer under the island. It's here to amaze our guests flying into the helipad behind that hillock over there.

"The Maltese Order of Hospitallers fashioned the fortress from the limestone caves during the Crusades," Homer said to her roaming gaze. "And when the Spanish Inquisition took over they dug out a network of dungeons for their punishments."

Claudia's head snapped in his direction at this dark image.

"After I purchased the island outright from the present-day Order of Malta, we bricked over the stairs and ..." His voice trailed off. "We left the torture apparatus as we found it. For posterity."

She wanted to give this eclectic man and his unique island half a chance if only they would stop hurling spitballs at her. Certainly, while the dead children, mad scientist, and tasered woman had made for a rough start—if one ignored the monkey in a test tube, then Homer's office, this lovely garden, and the man himself might qualify as quite likeable. This wasn't the only island with a refugee crisis at its shores.

However, what in the name of Christ on a Bike was a medical facility doing with an interactive Dungeon of Horrors museum? If it was spinal traction they needed, that's what chiropractors were for.

"What do you mean by present-day Maltese order?" she asked.

"They've become a medical charity with the status of a sovereign nation. All I had to do to get one of their diplomatic passports was get baptized in the Roman Catholic Church." His cocky stance quickly dissolved at something behind her.

"Part of the sale, actually," he blurted out before she turned to see a somber Benny plodding across the arched bridge.

"You made it." Benny squeaked this out when he reached her. Somewhere in his fifties, in the satisfied but weary way fatherhood works on men who come to it late, he seemed even more aged than during his daughter's recent heart check-up. Benny hugged as long as she would allow, forever connected through Paula, a Canadian who happened to inherit the Romanian castle once occupied by Claudia's aristocratic ancestors.

Raised in rural India, Benny Musahar had something else she valued—archaic Edwardian English left behind by British colonizers. His organically pretentious vocabulary appealed to her latent arrogance. Not only was Claudia an over-educated type, she'd been raised by obliviously droll parents on a British estate built with "old money"—so ancient, in fact, that there was none left and the place was a wreck.

Something only the tallest of women could manage, she peered off the tip of her nose at him. "Everything okay?"

He lifted his hand to a departing Homer and cupped her elbow. "Let's walk out a bit."

So much for no one moving without an escort.

They circled past pregnant women chatting inside open-air pagodas—their subdued robes and conversations fitting with the controlled landscaping.

"Maya is dying. The infection has returned."

At this, Claudia halted.

"She's on oxygen," he added.

"Take me to her," Claudia said, already on the move to the elevator.

At Level 3 intensive care, they passed a male nurse at a flickering computer screen and doors closed to prying eyes, before entering a room with the rhythmic beep of a cardiac monitor and hissing oxygen pump.

Before Claudia could lower herself into the stillness and embrace her shattered friend, the listless child laid out on sweat-soaked sheets suddenly groaned and bent into violent dry heaves. Paula daubed her daughter's face with a wet cloth as the child lay back, spent.

Here was the one child with plenty of opinions whom Claudia couldn't escape even if she wanted to. Unlike her grimly handsome parents, four-year-old Maya had ended up with a Miss Piggy nose and an overbite to rival the canopy of the Hollywood Bowl.

However, what her goddaughter lacked in beauty, she made up for in brilliance. "Does being beautiful make you miserable?" she had once asked.

"I wouldn't know, pet," Claudia told her, "but that's not what's wrong with your papa."

Inside Maya's ICU room, Claudia focused on the monitor which showed normal blood pressure. Whatever was failing, it wasn't Maya's heart. Not yet, at least. The girl had been thriving just weeks ago, so much so that Claudia gave the go-ahead for the immuno-compromised child to play with the new wolf pups at Claudia's sanctuary in the Carpathian mountains.

Benny entered with the chart from the nurses' station and handed it over. *History of familial dilated cardiomyopathy/recurrent bacterial endocarditis* was written at the top. As she flipped through, Claudia bobbed her head, but as soon as she arrived at the x-rays her hands fell motionless.

The splintered hemorrhaging along Maya's nails confirmed her fears. Working overtime since birth, the muscles and cells of Maya's leaky heart had become exhausted, and with each bacterial infection within the heart's lining, the child was closer to a blood clot and stroke.

Claudia sighed, ragged and long. The worst part was the pneumonia which kicked her off transplant lists. After all the death certificates she'd signed, was this the start of a slow march to the precipice of putting her signature to her own goddaughter's?

In a voice thick with fear Paula rasped, "You'll do the implant?" She lifted her bloodshot eyes, so wild and beseeching Claudia shrank from them.

"There are signs of infection on both her heart and lungs," Claudia said. "I'll ask for an EKG and more blood tests to determine if she's on the right antibiotics, but guys—good news. Maya isn't in critical need of a transplant at this point."

"I refuse to wait until my daughter is hours from death before I act," Paula snapped, Claudia's good news seeming to have no effect at all. "The artificial heart you gave Benny is here," Paula said. "He took it out of storage at his factory and flew it in."

So this was why Claudia had been called. For one sinking moment she wondered if he'd unpacked the priceless thing. She twisted to find Benny staring at his feet, fully aware of the peril he'd put her in by bringing the Thames Heart Institute's stolen prototype here.

Claudia had turned this prototype into a personal souvenir of the world's first successful, albeit illegal, trial of a bionic heart inside a human. She then asked Benny to hide it at his factory in India's hinterland. However, as far as her research institute knew, it was long gone like any other medical waste—replaced by a human heart inside the Johnson baby.

"I'm always here for Maya but—" She moved to Paula's side at the foot of the child's bed. "The prototype isn't ready for humans."

Claudia didn't know it yet, but there it was, the first of many lies between friends. This time to protect her lab's research.

Now she had Benny's attention. He came to sit beside Paula and folded his arms around his slumped wife. Quietly content with the world and each other, ever since Benny realized that he gave his daughter the gene that was killing her, the billionaire had become reclusive, almost sullen.

At the door, Claudia looked over her shoulder at her friends clinging to each other—rich, beautiful, and (as Maya realized) miserable.

"Benny," Claudia asked. "Can I see you outside?"

At the first unoccupied room Claudia came to, she took him inside and closed the door. "What the hell were you thinking by bringing that prototype here?"

He pinched his lower lip with a dullness she'd never seen before. "It was a terribly daft decision on my part. I would not blame you one bit for giving me my comeuppance but—"

"You're a businessman with patents of your own," she said in a whispered growl. "If that prototype falls into our competitors' hands before we have it approved, millions in research is out the window."

Benny squared himself military-style. "My dear friend, you are acting like Homer's clinic is some sort of den of goondas. I thought it could save Maya, why would I not bring it here?"

There was at least one goonda by the name of Hocking, a fact her friend seemed ignorant of. She trusted Benny with her priceless technology, but Hocking? Hell no. "What do you know about this character Hocking?" Claudia asked him.

Benny frowned. "Why? Does he have some sort of checkered background?"

"I'll say. He's a fugitive from the UK's ethics watchdog. Has he restarted his cloning shenanigans here?"

Benny physically dodged the accusation. "I am certainly not abreast of anything so nefarious."

"Obviously," she said. The thought of what other slimeballs might have their sticky fingers on her research sent a silent shriek crawling up her throat. "Don't tell me the prototype is in Homer's hands."

"Of course it is. He has Maya's life in those hands, too."

"That's the other thing," Claudia snarled. "Maya needs to be in a proper hospital. What's she doing in a fertility clinic?"

"If we can't use the artificial heart," he said, "then a transplant will take place here. Homer guaranteed he could find us a donor."

In the world of heart transplantation there was no such thing as a guarantee, especially for a recipient so young. If Benny was buying a heart from illegal sources then the promise she'd made to Paula to save Maya's life—would have to be broken.

"How is a fertility clinic supposed to find a donor heart?" she demanded.

Benny's confusion slipped into shame as he avoided her gaze. If her friends were counting on Auntie Claudia to continue her rebel ways, then they couldn't be more wrong when it came to her biotech breakthrough.

A month from now, when the Thames lab came out of stealth mode and published their research, Claudia planned to be interviewed inside a television studio about the world's first bionic heart—not interrogated in a room with a two-way mirror about her part in organ trafficking.

Chapter 3

It was the shriek he'd been waiting for all night.

From far below came the pitched wail of the hydrofoil docking at Inquisitor's Island. It set Dafnis's cheek vibrating against the layers of palm fronds inside his secret treehouse, and he was on his feet, shoving aside the oak's dense foliage.

A narrow sunbeam crawled across the thatched platform. He'd made it to sunrise without dozing off, his brain a riot of activity. The day was dawning without confusion and what a day it was going to be. He wished it would never end.

Like a barometer stuck on the same forecast, Dafnis started every day in a fog with a trend to clearing in the afternoon. Crisp, starry nights, smooth as onyx were when his synapses sparked to life with the faces, voices, and scenes of the past flashing on a screen only he could see. But the minute he drifted to sleep fierce electric storms moved in to snuff out all that day and more. The who, what, where, and how of his entire nineteen years were once again missing in the icy mists of morning.

The clinic's doctors told him it was a form of amnesia they'd never seen—a pariah of an ailment with neither a cause nor a cure. One named it Leaky Brain Syndrome and since this bloated man smelled like he knew a good lick about his own seepage problem, Dafnis thought that sounded good enough whenever people asked what happened.

Someday soon, Dafnis would prove he was nobody's fool, but for now he was still the clinic idiot. *Homer's* idiot. His son. Fortunately, the sticky slur rolled right off his back most of the time since Dafnis couldn't remember that *he* was the son they were talking about.

Whenever he heard the nurses and doctors calling each other idiots, Dafnis dreamed of a day he, too, would be enough of a moron to fit in with this giggling gang. Six years after arriving, though, he was stuck working the night shift, alone and unseen by all others.

Their ferry sloshed to a stop. At the bow was a tall woman with something like a frayed string of wet rope plastered to the side of her head. She flung a backpack over her shoulder and climbed down the outside stairs to the main deck.

This would forever be known as the day the puzzlingly wonderful Dr. Claudia appeared on his beach like sunken treasure on an epic journey from who knows where, and he dropped those other idiots cold.

A flutter of yellow under the beach palms meant Nabi was creeping around. Since Dafnis was outside the fence without a pass, this shifty-eyed butt-kisser was the last person he wanted to see. Thankfully, he rarely did anymore. Dafnis worked and slept on the clinic's ground floor while Nabi hung around the rooftop helipad's paramedic shack.

You always knew when the black-bearded lecher had entered the nursery to scan the children at lights out. Jaza said he had the kind of scarred, twisted face you didn't want as your last image before drifting into sleep, and smelled like a cross between a cheap cigar and sweaty horse. While Dafnis had no idea what a horse smelled like, he knew from delivering messages to the smoking pit that nothing could be worse than calling someone a cigar, cheap or not.

He wiped the dew from his watch's dial. Half-past six. Jaza would have to show up within the next fifteen minutes for any chance of hiding inside the hydrofoil's on-board morgue.

It hadn't been easy convincing his girlfriend to join his escape plan. All the tears and sadness. *Or, . . . wasn't I the one who cried*? It made him crazy whenever this happened. What was real today and what was just a flickering memory of long ago?

Well, *somebody* had cried and it might have been him.

Inside his treehouse, he kicked at the stray acorns left behind by the overnight storm and thought about how horrible it must have been for his tree to have all those dead people hanging off it. Still, he would have always taken the hanging tree punishment over the iron instruments left behind in the clinic's basement.

"Idiot," he said, and tried to pitch the first acorn out the window opening. "Idiot ... idiot ... idiot." The thatched cubicle was soon a war zone of speeding brown pellets until one smacked him in the forehead and he dumped the lot of them through the opening for the ladder.

Plop . . . plop . . . plop. The damp oak's wood smell sucked the tension from his chest, the leathery leaves like tiny gloved palms guiding the baby acorns to a soft landing on the forest floor. Much like they must have done when he fell through them at thirteen and landed on a pile of palm fronds.

It was a Homer story, of course, but since it was already in circulation before his Jaza arrived, there was no way to check if it was true.

Would his father be freaking out wondering where he was by now? *Nope.* He'd be at the clinic's helipad, giving the Search & Rescue crews hell. It was almost March which meant the horrible work of summer was about to begin. Homer was probably marching into their shack this very minute, yelling and waving his arms, "We're falling behind. I need more bodies. Bring me the ones still breathing but nowhere near alive."

How could someone be alive and dead at the same time? Even crazier was why the boat people believed Homer was their hero. What a pile of dog shit. Of course he knew what that was. There was only one dog on their island, but they had lots of piles.

Before he was able to worry about a single thing more his stomach got grouchy. Jaza said they'd be eating from the streets of

Malta from now on. He didn't know what a Malta was. He kinda knew what a street looked like, but it was still hard to imagine how this might work since Homer's island didn't have any streets—the monster clinic took up the entire dinky thing. He figured the Homer story that it was built as a knight's fortress and used to torture people must be true.

It was time for Dafnis and Jaza to get to hell out of The Republic of Homer—and that was no lie.

He sniffed and cursed at the first whiffs of the greasy-sweet stink from the clinic incinerator. It sat on a rocky ledge halfway uphill between the dock and his treehouse. *Crap.* They hadn't planned on running into the burn crew—their escape was ruined and he needed to find Jaza.

He could almost hear Homer in his ear—*One thing at a time, boy. How will you get back inside the clinic now that it's daylight? The day guard won't be dozing like the one last night, will he? Secondly, how will you account for your absence?*

The image raised a smile just as the tall woman below headed across the beach toward Nabi. Figures he would volunteer for a chance to pat down a female guest.

Nabi was the only other person Dafnis knew who hadn't left Homer's republic in years. The island where their refugees lived was only twenty minutes away by hydrofoil, but neither Nabi nor Dafnis had any reason to go there.

He watched one of their dumpster rats dash for the ferry. They always did this for some reason, but this time a small corner of himself hoped it would make it. Whoa! The woman booted it but good. He waited for her to repeat the trick the minute Nabi laid his hands on her, but they boarded the gondola to the clinic, the pat-down left undone. She must be a personal friend of Homer's.

Minutes later, as one set of boots lagged another on the stone pathway below his tree, a line of rag-swaddled heads also bobbed past. Wouldn't you know the slackers were cutting off early again—not for lack of bodies. Dafnis grabbed one of Jaza's discarded shawls and slid down the hemp rope he kept tucked from view.

He straggled behind, hidden within the undergrowth bordering the path, and just before the gate he wrapped the shawl around his lower face to blend in. The men branched off into their bunkhouse, but Dafnis headed across the dirt yard to the same side exit he'd snuck out of the night before.

With only ten more yards to safety, out of nowhere an ear-splitting alarm started. *Oh shit. Lockdown.* He kicked his dawdling into a trot and patted his pocket—yes, the fob stolen from Homer's office was still there, but he needed to hide before someone saw him. No way the key fob would work in lockdown mode. Flat against the building, he scanned for somewhere to hide. Nothing but open ground between him and the fence.

Just then the alarm cut out. The exit door opened. Don't look too panicked, he told himself and slipped into his room between the door and lab further along the hallway.

There was no lock on his room, but one of the guards had once shown him how to spot anything weird, and how to do something called a *modus operation*—every time he returned. He pushed aside the lumpy sack of pillows he left under a sheet, lifted his mattress and slipped the stolen fob key back between the pages of his secret atlas. About the only thing this place had over his father's penthouse was his very own bathroom (with a lock, too). Why else would someone want to live in a windowless hole just big enough for a metal bed, a dresser, a desk, and hundreds of notepads?

Inside his jacket pocket was the one he'd taken in case he fell asleep inside the treehouse with no Jaza for help. Imagine waking up with no arms or legs—that's how much he needed it to start his day. His medical condition and who he was, the layout and purpose of the clinic, and a description of his night shift job at the lab were the first things Dafnis read each morning.

Normally, he took it everywhere but, hey, today wasn't normal. The mental storms had passed him by for the time being.

He pulled a change of underwear and hospital scrubs from his dresser. His room had a closet, of course, a big one where the cleaners used to keep their mops and buckets, but it was jammed to the ceiling with hundreds of notepads filled with thousands of jotted words. Because he had no computer, television, or phone, these notebooks and the paperback Oxford dictionary which sat on his wooden desk were the only way Dafnis could make sense of the world.

A shower could wait, getting some cafeteria food couldn't. As soon as Dafnis exited his room, the lab door down the hall opened.

"Dafnis, my boy."

Hocking, of course. The old man had a way of appearing at the worst time and leaving behind a trail of bad news. "Homer has been searching for you all morning."

"Mind your own business," Dafnis tried to yell, but rude as ever, Hocking slammed the stairwell door on it.

When he pulled out his pager to text Homer, he found four unread messages. The first one had come in at six that morning when Dafnis would usually be finishing his night shift—*Don't sleep. Let's talk.*

Then a half hour later—*Bed's empty. Where r u?*

Twenty minutes after that—*Not in caf.*

The last one had come in during the alarm—*Very worried!!*

Dafnis shuffled to the scrub sinks at the opposite end of the hall to the elevator and laid his palms against the cold steel edge. Was it possible someone saw him scaling the perimeter fence at three in the morning?

He typed—*Scrubbing up*—and was still staring into the mirror above the sinks when he saw Homer burst from the elevator.

His father trotted in and braced himself against the counter to catch his breath. "You didn't answer my pages."

"I left it in my room and went for a walk," Dafnis said, without raising his gaze from the basin. All Homer had to do to catch this lie was check the sign-in sheet at lobby security. Anyone could go out the emergency exit near the lab, but only his father and the guards had a fob to get back in. He probably thought Dafnis was too stupid to remember the fob in an unlocked cupboard in his penthouse.

"I wasn't avoiding you if that's what you're accusing me of."

"No. No." Homer gave Dafnis's shoulder a tender squeeze. "Considering . . . your condition. I worry."

"Then *don't* worry. I'm almost nineteen now. I was at the helipad, okay?" Dafnis was able to hurl this second lie at Homer with such conviction because there was some truth in it. He'd often sat inside the helicopter in the past when no one was around. Their Sea King medivac was a beauty of a machine, and because Homer called record-keeping "a royal pain in the ass," they got it "off-the-books," whatever that meant.

For years, the dream of his pilot's license was the bait that kept him loyal to Homer long after Jaza argued in favor of escape. Since the helicopter would also have been their easiest way off the island, the two of them stayed—and waited—and planned.

"It's time I learn how to take it up."

Homer looked like someone had him by the balls and for the first time Dafnis saw his father's pity. On the soft underside of Dafnis's upper arm, written with indelible ink, was the constant reminder to himself: *Trust no one but Jaza*. She was right yet again. Homer never intended for him to fly at all.

"You've been lying to me, haven't you?"

"Lying," Homer murmured. "About what?"

Since hitting people was a sure way to lose friends, Dafnis punched the soap dispenser instead of his father. The crash brought a man in a white lab coat bursting into the hall. Dafnis knew he didn't like this person, but he couldn't remember the reason why.

"Get the fuck out of here," he yelled while Homer shooed the man away.

The distraction helped to slow Dafnis's galloping breath and change his rage into a pout. "I'm not feeling so great," Dafnis admitted as a wave of queasiness struck. "Can't we talk in the cafeteria where I can eat breakfast?"

"No. I'm running late for an appointment with a guest."

"A tall woman?" Dafnis asked.

"Tall, I don't know, but yes Dr. Vlakia is female."

His father peered at the surveillance camera above the sinks, then down the hall. "Let's chat in here where no one can bother us."

He was pointing at the one place in the entire clinic Dafnis avoided because it pulsed with the bittersweet memories of a room he shared with Jaza in adolescence. Now stinking of chlorine and piles of sheets stained with every possible color of human waste, raw longing and odd snippets of conversation burst onto his faulty memory cells as he entered this former dormitory room for orphans.

Of all his father's stories, the one about how the clinic began was the most unbelievable to Dafnis because it was hard to imagine their island without patients. Homer said there was a lab and a room he shared with Dafnis. The refugees they rescued during weekly trips to Malta took shelter in the stone landings above. They had a roof over their heads and water from the well—but not much more.

The part he remembered started when Dafnis was thirteen. They rescued eleven-year-old Jaza and she became the first orphan to sleep across from the lab in a room of straw mats and itchy blankets.

During their early months together Jaza tried to explain what menstruation was and what was about to happen to her, but those were girl things, nothing to do with him. The following year, the week of the clinic's first surrogate birth, he woke in the dark to find her pawing through the orphan girls' common clothes bin and weeping. She pulled out new pajama bottoms and something else he couldn't identify.

"Please don't tell them," she said, wheeling around to where he sat upright, slack-jawed on his sleeping mat. A month later he returned to the room to find a new orphan on her mat.

He didn't yet know where they would take her or what they would do to her, but he knew for certain the familiar world of childhood was drawing to a close. His days of being invisible and free to do whatever he wanted were over. He sprang his frustrated pet beetles from their glass jars, and retaliated with the worst thing he could think of—he left his father's penthouse permanently and moved into the staff changing room and shower beside the lab.

What everyone else called the laundry room would forever be the orphans' dormitory to Dafnis. Whenever his leaky brain sent him in search of Jaza inside the laundry room, Dafnis would stare at the machines and wonder what happened to the sleeping kids.

He followed Homer into the circle of thumping dryer drums and turbo fans which created the white noise his father liked. Sometimes they talked in the blue noise at the beach, but never in the green noise inside the treehouse. That was Dafnis and Jaza's secret place to be invisible.

"I've come to offer you the kind of work you've always wanted," Homer said.

It must be the kind of work Homer always wanted, too—he was bouncing around on his toes again. Jaza said Homer was hyper because he had so many ideas that the extras sometimes shot out the bottom of his feet and lifted him off the ground.

Homer didn't know it, but what Dafnis wanted more than anything was a way to escape his father's island. If this new job involved flying or floating, it had his attention. "The medivac?" he asked.

"Something even more exciting," Homer said. "I want you to go into the lab and announce your resignation effective tonight."

"I can't just—"

"Dr. Hocking has a replacement in mind. Get something to eat and then meet me in my penthouse while you're still alert enough to understand."

He wasn't going to do any of that until he knew Jaza was safe. When he asked his father where she was, Homer froze.

So Jaza *had* been caught trying to escape.

Homer shifted into the superior tone he used to hide his stress. "Her latest attempt to kidnap the boy isn't the only issue I'm dealing with this morning. If you want to see her, she's above us in the quarantine room. We had to sedate her again."

"What? Please don't do that. She's my friend."

"The guards do whatever is necessary to protect clinic property." His father braced himself against one of the dryers, as if ready to drop on the spot. "Something I'll never understand is why Jaza wants to keep a surrogacy child with abnormal intelligence."

Although Dafnis had no memory of sequencing the child's genes and discovering this, he knew why Jaza wanted to keep the boy.

"I'll expect you up top. And if you see her—"

Dafnis slumped at what he knew was coming.

"Tell Jaza she can leave, but the boy stays here."

Homer had said this so often it seeped into Dafnis's fragmented memory first thing every morning and made him believe there was a woman called Jaza that he could boss around. Like that was ever going to happen. It didn't stop Homer from trying, though.

His father fancied himself a genius at making people do things they didn't like. If that's what genius looked like, it was better to be an idiot.

As his sixth year on Homer's island drew to a close, his life felt as flat and doomed as the swamped dinghies of refugees floating by—his future, like theirs, in anybody's hands but his own.

Chapter 4

Dafnis stared dully at Jaza laid out across a stiff gurney inside a locked glass cage. One likely reeking of cigarette smoke.

The Homer story this time was that the old knights built the slit window inside this room to pour hot oil over their enemies climbing the rock face below. Since the hospital's smokers took it over, the only thing Dafnis had ever seen pouring out of it was cigarette smoke.

Jaza was wearing what she always wore for their escapes—jeans and a white tunic, but they'd taken her socks and runners. No backpack inside or outside the cage.

Inside the room was the faint sound of something Dafnis knew well—one of their old tango songs.

There was never enough time to be alone, but in the evening Dafnis used to follow Jaza while she powered down the piped-in music, and when they got to this room, if it was empty of smokers, she would pull the remote from a magnetized strip on the wall, up the volume, and cock her ear to the endless loop. Jaza would thrust her arms overhead in a seductive arch while he stepped behind, his palms pressed to the soft sides of her breasts. His hands slowly sliding down to the swell and rise of her wide hips was what floated in his nightly dreams.

Their tango lessons started after Homer agreed to train Jaza as a midwife. It was supposed to be a way for her to escape to the mainland with her son, but Homer outsmarted her once again and brought in a Maltese mentor who happened to be a tango fanatic.

When she swiveled to face him he always pressed his cheek close to hers and whispered, "I love you." They locked hips and swayed with the weariness of Homer's grip on the life they wanted to share. By the time Jaza was fifteen she'd already had one miscarriage and one birth from two different men.

He parted and dipped and when he brought his smiling face in line with hers it did seem to stop the tears. Their feet stalled. He cradled her into his chest and whispered, "*Shhh*. We'll have our chance some day."

He might have floated for hours in this daydream if not for the sudden jolt of approaching voices. The sharp squeal of the entry fob into the janitorial closet next door was enough to prod Jaza to consciousness. He watched her struggle to rewind her hijab and the tight bun she always wore underneath, before nudging one wobbly leg over the edge of the gurney. It dangled in mid-air before her bare feet hit the hard granite and her legs buckled.

Whatever they'd used on her this time must have been strong since she still hadn't seen him across the room. When she did, Jaza surged forward to slam her palms flat against the sliding glass door of the cage. Her wistful eyes spoke to him, but he shook his head. In this moment he was a friend, not a lover. Homer would shut them down altogether if he suspected Dafnis might follow her off the island.

She offered her cheek. "Dafnis. Nice to see you." Then turned her back to the ceiling's surveillance camera and mic, and slid a finger to her lips. Dafnis nodded. They shuffled in unison toward a tangy seabreeze wafting through the window slit on the far side of the gurney.

"What have they done with my baby?" Jaza asked above the roll and crash of waves. "Is he safe?"

"He must be because Homer said he's going to serve the Republic," Dafnis told her.

She tensed and drove a fist into his chest. "Why can't you see this for what it is?" It flew from her, hoarse and low.

It made him want to give up and die whenever she challenged him like this. She was his entire world. Forgetting the cameras, he let a strand of her hair slip slowly through his fingers. "Homer wants you to move to The Squats and work at their clinic."

"Please, Dafnis. It's time to tell them you read the gene sequencing wrong. He's not mentally deficient."

"Homer said it could become a real job."

"There's no way I'm leaving my son behind. How will we escape from there?"

"I'll take Homer's boat," Dafnis said. "I can phone you when I'm ready."

"You know where to land a motor boat on The Squats, do you?" Jaza said.

It was another one of those non-questions people liked to use for some reason. His gaze settled on a vague hump of land in the distance. "Well . . . no."

Jaza squeezed her eyes shut.

Dafnis knew how easy he was to bullshit. He had Homer's eyes, deep and blue as the water around them, but his own father was his worst tormentor. Dafnis was the only person not allowed off the island.

She let out a sad chuckle. "You're his son, but Homer won't ever give you a phone."

This hurt. Everyone said Homer was championing the rights of refugees. What good were rights if only for the few?

"They can keep their silly lives over there," Jaza said. "Homer the kindly father," she snorted. "The thought of it makes me want to vomit."

Dafnis propped his chin against the top of her head. If it wasn't for him, Jaza would have left years ago—and she was always right. How the hell was a two-year-old going to serve Homer's island?

Chapter 5

The panic Claudia felt inside the locked elevator was back, but this time she stood captive inside a guesthouse in a remote corner of the Zen garden.

It was long after her heavily armed bellhop left that she found him still hovering outside her sliding glass door. As soon as he heard it open, he spun around and blocked her way.

It didn't cross her mind at first that he might be preventing her from leaving. After all, lock-ups smelled of unwashed armpits and industrial disinfectant, not apple blossoms and Red Cedar siding. Neither did they have sunset-hued shoji panels of longlegged cranes airborne around Mt. Fuji.

Traditional Japanese ryokans such as this were supposed to be the drafty, paper and wood weaklings of the construction industry—not fortresses of one-inch-thick riot glass likely picked up during a fire sale at a medium security prison.

In the sitting room, she rifled through a shelf of well-thumbed books of the kind one sees at old-age homes. Graying, their spines broken and slumped with abuse, some parts unrecognizable or missing altogether. The plot lost long ago; it made her think she might be here for days—even weeks.

She scanned the living room for something to threaten the guy with. Not that she was stupid enough to use it. Large-screen televisions had proven themselves fine battering rams during civic conflagrations the world over. This two-story structure, however, was the definition of unadorned utilitarianism—the living room was nothing but a cluster of rattan tables and couches, and a sunken brasier nook. The upstairs bedrooms were also bare except for a single futon mattress and closet in each.

In the end, she settled for an iron coal poker beside the hibachi grill.

Thwack. Thwackity-thwackity-thwack.

Trailed by an arthritic beagle, a lethargic guard dragged himself to the glass door, blinked once or twice at her animated fist and poker, then turned and lit up a smoke; the beagle flopped outside the door, chin on paws with a bleary-eyed stare of utter empathy.

Late in the afternoon she found the beagle still there, the guy still chain-smoking. What an asinine set-up. First thing tomorrow she was out of here and the sooner Paula and Benny knew, the sooner they could evacuate their daughter out of this backward hospital. Benny, at least, had the foresight to choose Claudia for Maya's transplant rather than the kind of incompetent charlatans inside trafficking rings.

She was well into stringing together an escape rope of starched sheets for the upstairs balcony when the glass door downstairs squealed.

"Claudia?"

It sounded like Homer. She charged down the spiral staircase and sidestepped the beagle at the bottom. As it lifted a paw onto her foot, it raised a smile in her and lanced much of her fury.

"I was giving you time to settle in before I disturbed you," he said.

"You've disturbed me by putting me under house arrest. Am I a guest here or a prisoner?"

Homer motioned to the rattan settee where an armed guard elbowed his AK-47 out of the way to pour cups of tea atop a delicately lacquered coffee table.

Claudia had her own elbows out as Homer dialled up the charm. "Think of the clinic as our state capitol building. Your freedom will depend on your future role here."

"From what I've heard," Claudia said under her breath, "I doubt there'll be one." If this news irritated him, he didn't show it.

"By the way, I want my prototype back. Immediately." The cutting-edge technology was secure inside an aluminum container and vacuum-sealed pouch of alcohol, but until proven otherwise she had to assume he was capable of grand larceny.

He tilted his head as if he had all day. "Regardless of what you may think of me—I'm not a thief. I doubted that the contents of Benny's box could help us, but I didn't want to take the wind out of their hopes." Homer again raised an open palm to the couches. "Please."

She stood her ground. "I'll have a double scotch over ice." The guard on the receiving end of her command glared before Homer sent him out with a few sentences of what sounded like Arabic.

"I tried English on the other guy," Claudia said, "since we *are* off the coast of Malta. I guess the hired help only speaks Arabic, do they?"

"Maltese is a Semitic language closely related to medieval Sicilian Arabic. We all default to English here." His quick smirk seemed intent on proving he wasn't oiling his ego but simply trying to be helpful.

This mini-tyrant with boarding school manners was certainly intriguing. Trail-worn and unshaven in faded jeans and a combat medic's green lab coat, he seemed ready for battle. Claudia was so far down this tacky tangent that she didn't notice when the docile mutt snuggled beside her on the couch.

Homer pointed. "You don't mind?"

"Hardly. I have a refuge for abandoned wolves in Romania."

He leaned in with fascination. "I'm looking forward to learning more."

"Yeah, not gonna happen. You found my London hospital profile. Anything else?"

"Nothing except your position as clinical research coordinator at the Thames lab in London. I don't suppose you want to tell me what you're working on?"

It was obvious he didn't mean it as a real question, more a waltz around the room with Homer letting her take the lead.

"You never know," Claudia said. "Why don't you go first?"

They traded slow grins.

"I'll be googling you, too," she added. If only she had the courage to catch him off-guard by calling him "Papa K." Mafia, if that's what he was, rarely liked surprises.

"I'm no more forthcoming than you." He planted a furtive palm on the table between them and added, as if it was the first item on an arduous to-do list, "We have that in common."

Then it was back to Daphne Technologies' Tips For A Pleasant Stay. "As far as the internet, we don't have any for guests. Nor cell phone service."

Claudia shook her head through the clinic's growing mound of mystery.

"There's an unreliable satellite phone," he added.

"Well then," she said, "I should be starting my goodbyes for an early morning flight to London. I have a meeting tomorrow afternoon. Missing it could jeopardize my career."

The first time Claudia had a vision of a vulture flying off with her future Nobel Prize in its talons was days earlier when Bags, nick-named for something other than puffy eyes, woke her from a dead sleep around noon.

Her arm shot out on the fourth ring but came up with nothing until she remembered her bedside phone was no longer on the cardboard box which had served her well for over a year, but an actual table.

It was almost criminal what some people considered to be trash, so when she first spied the green felt mahjong table at the wheelie bins out back, she thought it would go swimmingly with the lawn chairs in her kitchen. Somehow it had ended up beside her bed.

Propped on her elbow, Claudia glanced at the call display and lifted the handset. "You're a Dead Man Walking. I got home at seven this morning from a twelve-hour double transplant."

"Good afternoon, love of my life," her caller said.

Bags hadn't been anywhere near Claudia's now extinct love life for at least four years, but it didn't stop him from leering at the legs of her Pup Patrol flannel pajamas whenever he caught her at home on days off. He was the last man allowed time with what one of Claudia's old boyfriends had called "two fine works of art." No doubt he still dreamed of her long legs emerging from the black lace bodysuit now rotting in a landfill somewhere.

"I take it you haven't seen your latest disciplinary letter?" Bags asked from the dry soulless depths of a true research manager.

"Can't imagine from who," she said, the words disappearing into a yawn. "I haven't taught those whinging brats since last semester."

Insubordination be damned. As far as Claudia was concerned protocol and procedures were distractions, created for dummies who couldn't think on their feet. Much-reviled by the clinical rotation students, she prefaced her bullying the same way every year—"Unique from all other organs, the heart isn't dependent on the brain to function."

In the sterile landscape of her life, Claudia would agree that the opposite was also true. Was she not proof the head could function without one speck of input from the heart?

"Listen to this, Bags. That double last night is the last transplant I'll ever have to deal with." Claudia used to think that nothing could compare with holding a beating human heart in one's hands—the coppery aroma like the coinage which she had in the millions.

"The hearts in my future are coming from a shelf, not a body," she said.

"The letter is from the hospital, not the university," he replied. "They want a performance review."

There was a slight delay while she changed mental channels. "Those bastards. For what?"

"It doesn't say, but do you think it's the implant?"

"Couldn't be," she said. "It was done in the hospital's private wing and Jeremy was the only one in there from the lab. We were both super careful with our conversation. And the rest of them trust me. Completely. In fact, the anesthesiologist said working on it was an honor and a story for his grandkids."

"You're right," Bags said. "Not exactly the words of a man who suspects he's doing something illegal, are they?"

"Anyway," she said. "Who'd be daft enough to complain after I saved the kid's life for God's sake?"

"I know," he whined.

The bed groaned as she fell back and stared at the spider webs dotting the plasterboard ceiling. Who could have blown the whistle on them? she wondered. And why? Were the Johnsons planning to get rich from her genius effort? Give someone a hand and they'll bite it off and sell it to the highest bidder.

"It has to be the parents," Claudia told him. "Fine. Go ahead and sue me."

"Claudia, wake-up. A complaint like this will give Hackney the perfect reason to cancel your hospital privileges. If it goes to court it won't be easy finding a new hospital for our human trials."

True. Too true. Like a relay runner handing off a baton, any delay between publishing their patents and the start of human trials would allow competitors to get their own version of an artificial heart to market first.

"Let's not get ahead of ourselves," Bags said. "I can think of any number of things Hackney's chief of surgery could be hauling you up for."

He chuckled. She didn't. The fuck she would let five years of ball-breaking research at the Thames lab get away from her like this.

"I've got to dash," Bags suddenly said. "But remember, February fifteenth is the hearing."

"The fifteenth?" she murmured as he hung up, her mind still circling their closest competition. Bollocks, that was the day after her flight to Inquisitor's Island.

Inside the Japanese guesthouse, Homer jumped on news of her imploding career and video conference like a snoopy schoolboy. "What's that all about?"

"Wouldn't you like to know."

He most certainly did, she thought. His eyes downcast, a self-conscious streak of red climbed above his collar. "You could use my personal laptop inside my penthouse for the meeting."

"Thank you, but the meeting is confidential." Not at the risk of becoming cornered inside your living quarters, was what she should have said. "Why don't I conduct it on Benny's satellite phone, right here in the guesthouse?"

He shook his head. "No electronics up top. Security reasons," he said, sliding effortlessly into the voice of authority she would hear many times. "We're under our own flag, you see. The men serve as both security guards and armed forces and are so dedicated they work solely for room and board."

It might explain the military-grade guns inside a medical facility, but otherwise, voluntary militants hinted at fanaticism. On her mother's remote farm, Claudia had carried a firearm against predators, but the only time she had to fire it was to protect herself against organized criminals poaching timber. If not for young Maya she would have cut and run at the first whiff of the burning bodies.

"Is this some kind of cult?" she asked.

His chuckle sounded genuine and playful. Rehearsed ones often did.

"The men are here for their families and other displaced people, not me," he said. "Our profits go to settling them into a new life in a peaceful country. My original plan was to set up a lab and continue my research into a vaccine against pneumonic plague, but when I saw the boat people's plight—"

"If you're talking the Black Death that killed 200 million," Claudia cut in, "then I'm sorry to break the news, but you're over six-hundred years too late."

"You have a brilliant sense of humor, Claudia. We need more laughs around here."

If so, she couldn't see them rolling out of Homer anytime soon.

"Actually," he said, "I discovered a vaccine that kills the pneumonic bacteria. It was too late for my wife, but I figured it might save the millions who might die if someone weaponized the pneumonic plague."

Her mirth stalled into silence, first at the news he had found a cure for the most deadly strain of plague, then at the word *wife*.

"Unfortunately, I had to abandon the cure when I realized one of the side effects was severe dementia." He pointed to the beagle. "Ten helped me see that. He's a grumpy one."

It was nothing but morbid fascination that drove her to ask, "If he's number ten lab beagle, what happened to the other nine?"

"They died in a pool of bloody vomit just hours after I injected them with the Yersinia Pestis bacterium. It's the speed of the pneumonic strain that kills those unlucky enough to catch it today."

That image of the miserably caged, dying dogs laying in their own waste weighed on her while Homer went to check on the drinks. When he returned and handed one glass to her, she noted he was also drinking whiskey over ice. Damn, but it was a good glass of scotch. "Bourbon cask finish?" she asked, raising her glass.

"You know your whiskies, do you?"

"I rarely drink," she said, "but when I do, I only drink legal-age single malt, over seventeen-years-old. Prefer the Oban brand."

"Then you'll be happy to know this is a seventeen-year-old single malt."

Right when the flame of interest sparked again, he uttered the two words she dreaded.

"Transplant tourism." He set his whisky aside. "You're aware that in some parts of the world it's legal?" he asked.

Claudia downed her drink and let the tumbler clatter onto the lacquer. Her sneer was answer enough, but Homer waited until "Go ahead" burst out of her.

"We source from the Philippines and Iran. Sometimes we buy organs from the black market in China and Africa. Rare blood types, of course, and—"

Up to this point she'd been making eye contact, but now she looked away because she knew what came next.

"—Organs for the youngest of our children," he said. "I oversee every transaction to ensure none of our organs are harvested without the consent of the seller or their family."

She bolted from her seat. "I call bullshit on that. The entire transplant field knows the Chinese are harvesting organs from executed prisoners."

He straightened but said nothing as adrenaline sent her on a march around the room. "I have no doubt impoverished families in Africa are willing to put their child's life on the line for a big enough payout." She halted in front of him. "It's immoral."

"I can only act on what I'm told," he said, drawing near, his voice now soft and low.

Had someone snuck in and let all the air out of him?

"The Republic of Homer is the latest country to make transplant tourism legal," he explained.

Before she could laugh at the absurdity of naming a country after himself, or break into "Hail Homer," the supreme leader fell into an infomercial tone. "We offer a safe and professional venue for the transaction, under fees set by our health ministry. I'm not getting rich off this."

"I hope not," Claudia said, and hurtled to her feet, "because this gold mine of organ harvesting is going to blow up in your face when artificial ones come to market."

"Not in time to save your friend's child though."

Truly, he had the advantage and the cruel comment hit her full force. "Screw you." If he was running a do-good non-profit then why was he only helping multi-billionaires?

The chuckle she expected from Homer never came.

They locked glares; the nostrils of his straight Roman nose quivered before he stomped to the sliding door and flung it open. "Ten, let's go." He turned to her while the dog trotted out ahead. "You're the only cardio-thoracic surgeon here. Do you think Paula is going to sit and watch her child die? She'll be the first in line at one of those risky underground transplants you loathe."

He stepped out and slammed the glass so hard it bounced out of the catch mechanism and it was then she realized there was no way to lock the door from the inside.

⸺⬦⸺

SHE MOPED A WHILE, mired in his arrogance, but a damsel in distress Claudia was not. Inside the guesthouse she double-checked to see if Homer was lying about no cell signal, then powered down the blank screen, and opened her glitter-green doctor's bag. In adolescence she'd never joined the Black Goth scene, instead becoming enraptured with Elton John's glasses. The bag was much easier to spot in a dark chaotic accident scene.

Here, laid out across her futon, was everything she might need to save someone's life, including her own. She had hydrocortisone for anaphylactic shock and asthma attacks, glyceryl spray for a heart attack, glucagon for diabetic shock, and all the syringes she would need. Since the classically aloof surgeon couldn't stand to see any being suffer needlessly, she also kept an over-abundance of morphine.

She dug through to the sharps which could open an airway—or some other vulnerable parts of the body—locked one of the blades into a scalpel handle, then sat back with a self-satisfied grin and finished the scotch Homer left untouched before he stormed out.

The only witness to this clandestine operation was the beagle. Content, he let his rigid front legs collapse, and promptly dozed off outside the door.

Chapter 6

An unholy clatter inside the guesthouse tugged Claudia out of the mental cradle of a steaming hot bath. Someone was howling in pain downstairs while upending the kitchen's fork and knife drawer.

She threw on the guesthouse's kimono-style bathrobe, grabbed the scalpel from her side table, and took the stairs two at a time. Crouched in the open doorway, both arms shielding her head—was Paula. At her feet lay a jumble of metal utensils.

"Oh, shit. It's only you. I thought . . ." Claudia laid her weapon aside and rushed to help her dazed friend stagger to the couch. "Here. Let me take a look." Standing over her friend's scalp, she tried to brush aside Paula's hands.

"Where did all that cutlery come from?" Paula moaned.

"I stuck it along the top edge of the door jamb to alert me of intruders."

Back to rubbing her head, Paula glanced over her shoulder toward the kitchen. "Thank you for leaving the steak knives out." She tossed a key onto the coffee table in front of her. "It's for the guesthouse. Detaining you without cause is a breach of civil rights."

Claudia scoffed. "Not in The Republic of Homer, apparently. I can't even make a simple phone call without passing it through this man's throne room."

"His heart is usually in the right place," Paula said. "He wants his clients to feel safe. That's why surrogacy couples don't have to come here anymore. The clinic brings in frozen embryos instead."

Claudia recoiled in confusion. "Embryos from where?"

47

"He gets them cheap on the black market because they're tagged for destruction. After the births he flies the babies out."

The so-called fertility clinic wasn't fertilizing eggs at all but merely running DNA sequencing on embryos stolen from other fertility labs. Claudia shook her head at this new thievery. "He's quite the penny-pincher, isn't he? This clinic is looking like a police state."

Paula rose in silence and turned away. "Do you think I could get a glass of water?"

Only now did Claudia notice that Paula's alabaster complexion was as sickly dull as her daughter's. "Of course."

When Claudia returned, she handed Paula the glass, then slid in hip to hip with her friend and said, "I want you to know what you're getting yourselves into. Homer's black market transplants aren't some kind of do-good largesse. They're a bullshit excuse to prey on the world's most vulnerable."

Paula sipped the water and jerked her listless torso to life. "As long as they can save Maya, I don't give a shit what they are."

Hell. Homer had warned Claudia that Paula would use any means to save her daughter.

Paula raised the remaining water to her lips, the glass rattling against her trembling teeth. "Please tell me you haven't changed your mind about saving Maya. Everytime her heart gets infected, I'm terrified she's going to have a stroke and die."

"I'd be within my rights to change my mind. You tricked me into agreeing to do an illegal transplant."

Paula hung her head, avoiding Claudia's reprimand. "It's just that . . . Well, you told us you were retiring."

"From transplants, yes, but not from my research."

A mother fearful of losing her only child wrapped her chilled fingers around Claudia's and pleaded, "Nobody is going to give us a donor heart while Maya's lungs are infected. I'm through with false hope. We need to act."

Mere inches away, as their eyes locked on each other Claudia knew she would have to break the worst news. "Do this now with the infection raging and you'll need to replace Maya's lungs, too. We won't have any control over where her organs are coming from. They might be diseased or damaged in transport. She could suffer terribly and end up dying just the same."

Paula wobbled to her feet, hands on hips, rocking within her sleep-deprived exhaustion. "I want you to understand what Homer is doing for the refugees he rescues," she croaked. "Asylum on a private island with proper houses. A clinic. Schools for the children."

"Sit down before you collapse," Claudia said, guiding her friend onto the couch.

"But the ones that still want to enter Europe," Paula persisted, "can make money as organ donors. The families are paid $250,000 US dollars for a kidney. In some European countries that's more than enough to buy a home and qualify for residency."

Claudia whistled. "Are you sure?"

"Lots of families have left with up to a half-million. What could be wrong with both sides getting what they want?"

Claudia sent her friend the most earnest smile possible under the circumstances. "We might be taking the life of a perfectly healthy child at the other end." When she tried to place her hand on Paula's shoulder, her friend pulled away—"Don't."

"Look. I'll consider it."

"No, you won't. You're always up in your head." Paula reached over with three sharp raps to Claudia's temple and said, "You might think it's okay to abandon your own child, but I'm not going to give up on Maya so easily."

These words from Paula were such a breathtaking betrayal they sucked every molecule of oxygen from the room. Never could she imagine that her best friend, someone who avoided confrontation at all costs, would turn this confidence against her. There they sat, speechless in the glassy silence of the guesthouse while Paula wept softly.

"Here," Claudia handed Paula a box of tissues when she sensed things winding down. "I can promise to stay until Maya's fever breaks and she's out of danger. Now, go sit in the garden. It'll make you feel better."

When Paula rose obediently, Claudia looped her arm loosely around her friend's waist and aimed for the exit. In a more alert state, Claudia's uncharacteristic intimacy would surely have raised an eyebrow from Paula.

Odd how her friend was now the rebel. Protocol Paula was stealing keys and tossing ethics aside. Where Maya's heart would come from and whether it would be at the expense of another child's life, Paula could care less. An involuntary shiver rattled through Claudia—was she the only one to find it disgustingly convenient to bring discarded embryos into a facility in dire need of organs? A bit of after-dark reconnaissance might lead to the tasered woman and some answers.

———◦———

THE WINDOW TO RESCHEDULE her disciplinary hearing was closing fast—heavier by the minute.

It had been well over an hour since she'd sent the breakfast delivery guard off with a request to find Benny and his satellite phone. Where the hell was the guy? Her door sentry was missing, too. This one, neither a chain smoker, nor depressed, was hip-hop dancing through the ornamental shrubs—earbuds in.

"Hey, comrade Snoop Dog," she tried yelling. Inmates in the movies got their jailor's attention by dragging a dented aluminum cup back and forth across their cell's bars—but Claudia had neither. Bashing a broom handle against the bamboo framing of her upstairs balcony ended up sounding more like the percussion section of a Sumatran folk group than a call for help.

Through gaps in the trees she caught glimpses of her pregnant fellow inmates circumambulating the pond. For a quarter-million dollars these surrogates undoubtedly had less freedom than she did. Interesting—at the trill of a referee's whistle the women gathered, not at the elevator, but in front of an emergency exit beside it.

Just then, she caught a glimpse of Homer striding up the path to the guest house. How best to look the most miserable? She dashed downstairs, unlocked her door, and grabbed a random book from the shelf. Slumped across the rattan couch, she was trying on a variety of sour pouts as he entered.

"Ah, Claudia. There you are."

She ignored him and kept her nose in the book.

"They brought your breakfast, I see. I've come to escort you round the garden. You must be sick of the dead air in here and our dusty collection of books." Hovering above her, he pinched the book's cover with brazen delight. "I've reduced you to reading the Koran for entertainment." He grinned at Claudia's indifference. "I'm also hoping for a fresh start between us."

After an adequately snooty look she walked over and tucked the book into its slot. "What Paula's been telling me about your payments to the refugees *has* brought my blood pressure down a notch."

"I thought it would."

Homer, the master manipulator, had somehow managed to recruit a former teacher with unwavering integrity into his Bootcamp of Deception.

Two guards on the left, she noted as they wound down the path. *Armed, sitting under a mature willow.* Something she couldn't have seen from the angle of her balcony.

At the pond, Claudia broke with habit and clung to Homer's arm. While 21st century women no longer had to worry about snagging their whalebone crinolines on a patch of invasive barberry, a tumble from a plastic flip-flop blowout was possible.

"First of all, I don't want you to miss your video conference," he said. "As for me, I'll be in my office two floors down. There's a laptop and wall monitor. When you're done you can call my office extension from the intercom inside my penthouse."

Truth was, if she postponed her critical performance review with just hours to spare, the hospital would surely pump her for a reason. The less they knew, the better.

Today, arm in arm with Homer she wagged her head in a slow arc to show she was warming to his penthouse offer. "It wouldn't start until five in the evening here."

"That's fine."

"Well—I suppose it makes sense."

He flashed a grin so cheap it could have been pulled from a cereal box. "And whenever you're ready, would you care to observe a liver transplant?" He cut off any possible refusal with a wave of his palm. "I know you haven't agreed to Maya's transplant, but I thought you could see our surgical suite."

She didn't appreciate being manipulated in this way, but found herself a captive of two piercing blue eyes under hooded brows.

"I'll give you a *maybe*."

"You might be interested in how the male nurses and surgeons interact. Unless you're here in the garden or on the maternity ward, nothing but male company I'm afraid."

"Except for wandering surrogates the guards mistake for kidnappers, I suppose?"

Homer cocked his head and blinked, utterly oblivious of her impromptu interrogation.

"Oh . . . That. Yes. They get attached to the newborns sometimes."

The man was flat-out lying about the tasered woman. "But I'm sure I saw someone with a toddler yesterday."

"We have a nursery, of course, for the older children, and a midwife who looks after them."

Claudia trotted out a ho-hum nod to keep the small talk flowing. This woman could be key to understanding what Homer might be hiding.

"She arrived here as an orphan," Homer said, "and has since become a valued member of staff."

Since when did Homer's Employee Appreciation Day include a complimentary tasering?

"At the moment," he said, "we have a client's toddler back here for a congenital defect."

"I'd be happy to go to the nursery and do a thorough exam of the child."

Was it fear she saw darken Homer's face? "Infants are my passion," Claudia quickly explained. "More interesting than someone's old liver."

"A kind offer," he said, "but it's a minor case of undescended testes. Anyway, the nursery is a bit chaotic since it underwent a move closer to the surrogates' dormitory."

There was her clue to finding the nursery and midwife—a place so off-limits as to make him turn down the services of a pediatric specialist.

Chapter 7

I t took a twisted kind of cynicism to find fault with saving the life of a one-year-old infant. If that's what this disciplinary hearing was about then good riddance to the now-soggy letter from the hospital board—birthed as it had been days earlier while she squatted in the lobby of her building.

Instead of having her hands immersed in someone's thoracic cavity that particular afternoon, Claudia found herself on her haunches, the ends of her sloppy bathrobe splayed across the worn vinyl while she rifled through her bloated mail slot for the missing reprimand from Hackney University's chief of surgery.

Like dried paste from a tube, the clumps of glossy flyers at her feet had been crammed tighter than an intestinal tract bunged up on a year's worth of junk mail. Nothing but time-limited offers admonishing her tardiness. She'd missed the End of Summer swimsuit blowout. Hadn't worn one in fifteen years. And the Yuletide sales. Nothing to someone who spent every Christmas and New Year's inside an OR. There was still time, however, to buy a *two-fer* Valentines dinner cruise on the Thames—surely the most useless promo of all.

While Claudia rode the clinic elevator to what might be the most pivotal meeting of her career, she also wondered what awaited her on the top floor of Daphne Technologies. This crusader fortress turned slapdash-transplant-center left her thinking Homer's penthouse might be another dark ursine hole, or squat dusty attic.

Despite her spartan lifestyle and manure-infused flat across from the stables of a London racetrack, she still expected her workplace in the halls of medical excellence to be efficient and sterile.

"Hot one out there today, wasn't it?" Homer said inside the elevator.

For an opinion junkie like Claudia, even the daily weather report was a potential landmine of bickering about the effects of global warming. Fortunately, she'd spent the day inside Maya's windowless ICU room while waiting to shake down Benny on the clinic's midwife. He didn't show and Paula was clearly not up to concentrating on anything but her ailing daughter.

"My penthouse shares Level 4 with the staff suites," Homer said, unlocking the polished oak door. "It's basically directly below the Zen garden."

Rather than the rodentia-like hovel she imagined, Claudia wandered into an open-plan mansion—a dreamscape plump with the luminescence of cathedral windows facing the sea on three sides.

"If you drilled through this plaster ceiling and continued on through the natural limestone you'd emerge close to the helipad." Was he hinting at a secret escape route or merely orienting her? Claudia was starting to attach veiled meaning to almost everything Homer said.

"The laptop is on the coffee table down there. It's already connected to the web and the tv monitor." He pointed past a divider of potted plants to a sunken living room with a wrap-around sectional couch and gargantuan television monitor. "Shout if you need anything. I'm popping into the shower, then I'm out of here." He ducked down a hall to the left of the entrance where she assumed his bedroom and ensuite must be.

In the opposite direction, through the open door of another room she could see one of those dysfunctional types of desks utterly bare of everything except a pen and notepad lined up in perfect symmetry to each other. Why even have a desk if you're going to act like that?

She spied a satellite phone left on a leather office chair, and for an instant considered grabbing the thing and phoning Bags to tell him—What? That she'd discovered the bail-jumping Dr. Hocking? That Inquisitor's Island had legalized the buying and selling of organs and Claudia might use one to save Maya? Unless Homer was doing something truly evil like birthing children to be spare parts for rich people, the less Bags knew the better. Anyway, his phone would already be on mute inside the London boardroom.

Before descending into the living room, she passed a galley kitchen on one side and a sit-up bar on the other. The wall-size monitor connected to the laptop made her feel like she was in the White House Situation Room, about to watch a Navy Seal raid in real time. In fact, this ambush by hospital administration was feeling like a full-on assault from the land, sea, and air.

While she scoured the half-dozen seated around the boardroom table, Claudia screeched to a halt at the hospital's lawyer, Barb. This woman, who was always on the hunt for someone she could pander to, had outdone herself in the category of—The Most Garish Hospital Stooge to Walk the Halls. Between the blue and yellow feathered boa wound around her neck more times than a hangman's knot, and her hook nose and shifty eyes, the hospital had their first avian mascot. Every lawyer was a stooge at one time or another, but Barb also had an unspoken vendetta against Claudia.

The sight of Bags next to her was comforting, though. The man was a keeper.

He had a butt flatter than a beggar's wallet, and from their first meeting during ad hoc deals brewing inside the bar at a healthcare symposium came his nickname and a weekend fling.

Bags had his own share of boardroom tediums at the Thames institute, but she understood why he wanted to be here today. He shared Claudia's obsession with getting their heart approved for the marketplace.

She flashed him their secret two-finger salute which meant *bullshit straight ahead*. Stone-faced, he seemed to be having one of his curmudgeonly days. She knew them well from her own, hence the reason their fling went nowhere. According to Claudia, men were either too intimidated by her ambition, or were needing a woman who was occasionally around in the evenings to "service" them.

The chief of surgery examined his watch. and turned to the boardroom's video feed. "Dr. Vlakia will be joining us remotely. Can I assume everyone knows each other, including the representative from the UK's medical licensing body?"

Ah, she thought, the grim reaper cometh. Breaking something-or-other subsection of the hospital's useless manual was one thing, but surely the council wouldn't have the nerve to suspend her medical license when no harm had been done.

The man smiled warmly and waved.

"I'd like to start the performance review, then." The chief cleared his throat. "Four months ago, I received a formal complaint from the family of Dr. Vlakia's infant patient, Heather Johnson. Surgical records obtained from the private wing of Hackney University Hospital showed the infant's diseased heart was functioning through a ventricular assist device known as VAD. The Johnsons have accused Dr. Vlakia of taking their daughter off this, and excising her entire heart before implanting a totally artificial one from the Thames Heart Institute—a device not yet approved by the regulatory agency here in the UK.

"Dr. Vlakia, do you agree with these facts as reported?"

"Yes, except it's not accurate to call the Thames heart a device. It replaces all four chambers. There are no hoses and no pumps external to the body, either. It's the world's first stand-alone bionic heart."

"But not yet approved for the market?" the chief asked.

"No. But we expected to start human trials within—."

The licensing guy cut her off. "Excuse me, but I'm a bit lost. Artificial hearts for grown adults are still dependent on external pumps, as far as I know, so how is it possible to make one without . . . I mean, we're talking about an infant, aren't we?"

Claudia answered with a cocky nod. "That's right. There's nothing outside the baby's body except the battery pack which sends wireless pulses. It was a successful implant of a bionic heart robust enough to sustain millions of beats without deteriorating. Our closest competitor has only managed three-thousand."

The chief aimed a pained sigh at Claudia. "We're discussing Dr. Vlakia's questionable surgical practices today, so if you please—. Was there anyone present other than the surgical team?"

Claudia groaned inwardly. She had begged Jeremy to steer clear of the unauthorized implant. If the heart malfunctioned, they could leave the baby on the bypass machine and call him in.

"Yes. My lead scientist, Dr. Jeremy Ames." The chair didn't make a note which meant he had already pumped the team for info.

"Did the patient's parents approve this change of device?"

"Again, it's not a device."

To his credit, he jotted a note.

"Not directly," Claudia said. "Heather's heart had never fared well on the VAD. She was starting to have multiple strokes so when I told them she might be dead within seventy-two hours, they told me to do whatever I could for her."

"Any witnesses to this?" the chief asked, his pen poised over his notepad.

"No. Why does it matter? The child is alive and thriving." Claudia thrust her face at the monitor knowing how grotesque she would look. "Heather was no longer hooked up to the VAD's two-hundred-pound unit. The family was free to go anywhere they wanted while we waited for a donor heart."

"However," the chief countered, "I understand the patient stayed in hospital for the duration."

Only now did Claudia remember the Johnsons' three-month-long bedside vigil. At the far edge of her screen Bags slumped as she explained: "We decided not to risk a battery pack failure."

The hospital's lawyer piped up. "The family is seeking four-million pounds in damages for the stress of having their child used in an unauthorized human trial."

"What?" Claudia gasped. "That's bullshit. It's just a money grab."

The woman unfurled her farmyard neck. "They're suing *us*. Not you."

"The disciplinary committee feels it's best to suspend your hospital privileges until the case is resolved," the chief added.

Claudia froze, too stunned to believe what she'd just heard. If the hospital was upset with her rogue implant, Bags would soon set them straight. Only fools shoot holes in the world's first successful bionic heart for infants.

She stared at her longtime friend who had said not a single word so far. The laser fear in his eyes brought back the night of the implant when he'd pleaded with her to put her raging ambition aside. Let the child die, he told her. This was not the time to test her 3D-printed creation. If it was charitable beneficence one wanted, the Thames research institute was not the place to go looking for it.

"Bags." Claudia stared into her monitor. "Your institute has spent tens of millions on this pediatric heart. Now that we're about to make medical history, are you not going to defend it?"

"The investors are still committed to its commercial potential," he said. "It's just that . . . without an OR the human trials are stalled."

Her limbs had gone liquid. "They're pulling the funding, aren't they?"

"Until there's a settlement—yes."

"That could take years," she shot back. "And what are my team of scientists supposed to do in the meantime? Go on the dole?"

Just then a brash circus-tent ringtone pounded through their meeting. All eyes scanned the boardroom, but Claudia knew it was coming from inside Homer's den.

The politely curious licensing rep ignored the jangling Big Top tune and jumped in. "The council feels it's best to suspend your medical license until resolution."

She could do without the shitty university hospital's facilities—but not her license to practice medicine.

She sat slack-jawed—for a few seconds, anyway.

"All of you—" Claudia raked a boney finger across her monitor. "Are missing the point. Transplantation cannot be the solution to end stage heart failure. While you sit in here and dither over bloody nonsense, you're handing a death sentence to hundreds of children.

"We've been at this for thirty years, but more people than ever are dying while they wait. Technology is the only solution." Her hands flew to each side of her skull as if to contain an imminent eruption of gray matter. "Gawd—We're so close."

She looked up to find everyone, including Bags, ignoring her rant while they tracked something in the background of Claudia's monitor.

A gander over her shoulder revealed a towel suspended above two hairy legs. The white square bobbed within Homer's row of ornamental Japanese trees—the painfully trimmed foliage not the greatest camouflage for a half-naked man scurrying to answer his phone.

"Excuse me, Dr. Vlakia," the hospital's lawyer said, "but may I ask what venue you're conducting this hearing from?"

"No, you may not. I'm your coworker. Not your daughter." Suggesting the forty-year-old stooge was an entire generation older than Claudia was a fortuitously timed smackdown.

She winced. "It seems highly inappropriate, is all."

"For God's sake, Barb, you've already thrown me under the bus. Go ahead and shove me in another foot. If you don't want one of Europe's most progressive heart surgeons to sully your retrograde institution, then let's be done with this sham of a performance review."

The lawyer's mouth snapped shut as she scouted the panel for how to respond.

"Are we in agreement to conclude the hearing?" the chief said to a domino of rusty nodding. "As you wish, Dr. Vlakia. We'll draw up the terms of your staff termination at Hackney University Hospital. The council can include the suspension of your medical license. If you could provide us with a fax—"

"Hey Benny," Claudia roared as the low murmuring of his phone call halted. "Can I give these stiffs your fax number?"

A faint but emphatic—"Yes"—came back.

"I'll leave it with Barb's receptionist," she told the chief. In one forced groan Claudia felt like the toxic frustration of five years had let loose. "Could I be the one to break the news to my Thames scientists?"

The chief looked at Bags who nodded.

"I guess that's it then?" she asked. With the first hint of a nod, Claudia jabbed the monitor's End Call button.

She was still motionless, regurgitating bits and pieces from the meeting to the soothing humming of a distant fan when she heard: "That sounded intense."

"And final," she said over her shoulder as a fully clothed Homer exchanged a wild-eyed nod.

"I heard."

There was no sense keeping anything secret, not with the civil case about to blow up in the media, but the thought of her competitors swarming every detail of her bionic heart like a school of piranhas, still felt like a vise behind her eyes. This was a research lab's nightmare.

"I'm not one for wretched diplomacy," she said, "but I can usually keep my tongue civil. Too much, maybe?"

He shrugged. "Feel like a drink?"

"Double scotch on ice." She slid herself onto one of his bar stools. "Same brand from last time, thanks."

While he lined up two tumblers under the bar's automatic ice dispenser, she eyed his pricey liquors. "For a non-profit clinic, that's quite a larder of libations."

"The clients have sensitive palates," he quipped over the chugging dispenser. "However, no liquor allowed within the staff quarters on this floor. But this here—" He killed the ice machine and hauled something from a cupboard below the countertop "Is too special for clients."

A squat, green bottle she instantly recognized appeared before her.

"It's a thirty-year-old Tobermory from the Isle of Mull. Limited edition. I paid three-hundred and twenty pounds for it but could probably get three times that at auction today."

Her hand covered his as he was about to crack the top of the unsheathed bottle. "Shouldn't this be saved for a celebration, not a funeral dirge?"

Snap! The corners of his mouth lifted with mischief as he cracked the cap and let the golden liquid splash onto the ice in both glasses. "To you," he said, sliding her drink over. "And all the other wayward surgeons who have made my vision a reality."

The leathery taste of berries and spice tickled her tongue. "Ahh." She closed her eyes. "Oloroso sherry cask."

"The surgeons here have run afoul of their hospitals," Homer explained. "Sexual misconduct with patients or theft won't get past me, but some of them have a single drunk driving conviction or an indiscretion with a married staff member. One guy was charged with billing fraud. In reality, he was being framed by a competing surgeon."

He poured her second drink and folded his arms across the countertop, a suspiciously hungry twinkle in his eye. "What'll you do now?"

Claudia might be a surgeon without a license to operate, but she could still join her team in the lab. For the Thames institute to shut them down a month away from patent approval made no sense unless... They were looking to replace her. This was always what hung over the heads of inventors who sold their ideas to biotech labs. She downed her drink and coasted the empty back with a fill'er up finger tap.

More fortunate than most workaholic surgeons, she could always return to her wolf sanctuary in Romania, the site of many happy months for Paula and her before Claudia took up her London research, but she knew the futility of trying to resurrect the past. She'd watched her own aristocratic mother try to return to communist Romania to reclaim the respect she felt due her after decades of exile in England, only to become the butt of jokes.

Homer grimaced. "Sorry about the towel caper. I knew the call was coming in, but I forgot my phone."

Claudia slapped the counter. "That was priceless. It'll get around that I finally got laid. My research team will be so happy I'll just let them run with it."

"You're safe on this end. I put a stop to any vulgar gossip about the women here."

She tossed back most of her new drink and noticed Homer still sipping his first.

"I have to be cognizant that I'm not just a CEO, but the figure-head of a country."

"Don't forget your Order of Malta diplomatic post."

"Right you are." Their eyebrows twitched in unison.

"Aww, come on," she drawled. "Surely, you must be the archbishop, too." She tipped back the dregs of her drink and rattled the ice. "I've never seduced a man of the cloth."

Homer planted his elbows directly in front of her. "At the moment I'm your bartender, and about to cut you off. If I convince you to perform Maya's transplant you might not remember your promise in the morning."

Claudia helped herself to the bottle and winked. "Take advantage of me and I promise I'll remember in the morning."

Chapter 8

W*hoosh. Crack. Crack.* Claudia woke to a flutter of bent branches outside her bedroom window.

Before the surgeon remembered that she no longer had a medical license nor a research lab to return to, she pressed the tips of her fingers into the bongo drum inside her frontal cortex where bits of the previous evening had calcified—hairy legs, the silky aftertaste of sherry, and her boozy suggestion around an archbishop's uniform—which in the glare of morning landed limper than a training bra.

Her libido had burst its banks inside Homer's orderly penthouse. *Why do I do that with someone I'm not even interested in?* Old habits dormant since she had Bags half a decade ago. Homer could have laid on the drinks until she agreed to Maya's transplant, but chose not to. He was the impartial ear she so badly needed. Maybe even a friend.

Hold on, girl. Why would you trust someone who not only allows his guards to taser women, but lies about it? I asked for privacy. Instead, he hangs around and talks me into observing a transplant today. Are these not the tactics of a manipulator?

Claudia scooped her watch from the side table; just after four in the morning. There would never be a better time to snoop around for the woman she saw being tasered. With neither light nor civilization for hundreds of miles, the dark garden outside was a hinterland of possibilities. A pathetically dim line of solars between her and the emergency stairwell might be the only hitch, but even the moon was staying out of sight behind a shelf of clouds.

WITH DOUBLE-STRENGTH coffee and a cold shower out of the way, Claudia dumped her meager wardrobe onto the bed to separate out everything in black. By cutting holes for the eyes and mouth, a ski hat became a hood. Black socks went over white runners.

However, if she got caught, a believable story would be tougher to slap together. She could say one of the guards had taken a shine to her and let her out. Oh hell, no one would believe that. Claudia demanded loyalty, not sign-ups for a fan club.

Outside, a firefly-like spark flew. Then two more in ragged succession. Must be the glow from the guards' cigarettes. The fuckers weren't dozing at all, but the shadows cast by the encircling bamboo fence would get her to the stairwell almost as fast as the path.

By clutching the sliding door's cumbersome handle in both hands, she inched it aside and side-stepped out. No matter how excruciatingly slow she shut it, though, the final metallic *click* reverberated across the drowsy night like a sonic boom.

She was off, but was this circuitous route enough of a head start to slip inside the same stairwell the surrogates had filed into?

It took thirty seconds to dodge a tight field of decorative boulders and shrubs—more than enough time for the guards to stub out their cigarettes and lumber up the path.

A slog through waist-high grasses brought her to the bamboo wall.

They would be at her door by now. Would they dare enter a woman's private space without Homer's permission?

A final sprint and Claudia popped up from behind a gazebo, the neon Exit sign just steps away. She squinted at white lettering on the metallic door: Emergency Use Only. Alarm Will Sound.

"No. No. No," she muttered before—"Ouch . . . Shit." Instinctively, she yanked her hand off the ledge and pressed it to her chest. Blood bubbled from two puncture wounds on her left wrist.

Thud. Whatever had sunk its fangs into her slid out of sight inside the gazebo and soon a canine snarl brushed away the fear it might be a poisonous snake.

"Ten. Take it easy, boy."

Those useless words flushed out a waddling silhouette of swaying ear flaps and snapping jaws which attached themselves to the cuff of her jeans. What in hell had got into this thing, a breed so docile they weren't easily startled? Was it rabies? She pulled the sleeve of her black turtleneck over the trickle of blood and pushed the idea aside, because—pounding footfalls were closing in.

Her beagle ballast turned Claudia's dash to the exit into a halting limp. She flung the door wide and with one robust swing of her leg sent Ten skittering off-balance into the top landing. She wasn't going to let this damn senile dog sink her plan. The heavy fire door clicked closed, the squealing alarm cut out. Yips faded and in the sliver of renewed calm it came to her that she could just as easily lose the guards by holding back.

From behind the gazebo she watched them charge into the stairwell, but before the door snapped shut, she caught it and silently slipped through herself.

Illuminated by strips of LED lights, the staircase clung to the clinic's stone like an interior fire escape. She could almost hear the condemned souls of the Spanish Inquisition rattling their leg irons down these very steps to the torture chamber—if that's where they led.

She waited and listened while the guards and their unglued canine had rampaged far enough down the cast iron scaffolding.

Creeek. Creeek.

Yip. Yip. Yip . . .

"Shit. Fuck off dog."

Yeowl. Thud. Thud. Thud.

Finally, a door far below banged closed, followed by an uncertain silence. The stairwell was hers while the Keystone Cops ran amok in the lobby, trying to figure out where she'd gone.

On the way down, she passed doors which accessed Homer's penthouse, the ORs, and the maternity ward, but at the one leading into the Level 1 lobby, she paused. Beside it was one more door which could very well lead into the hallway where the tasering took place. Hardly the time to investigate, though.

Rather than end here, the stairs continued down—outside to the playground, she wondered, or into the dungeons? It had to be one or the other.

At the very bottom Claudia eased the heels of her palms onto the cold steel lever of a metal door. No alarm. Only the creak of hinges right before a puff of fresh air and moonlight seeped into the dank stairwell. She angled out into a quarry as flat and wide as a baseball diamond, and where a half-moon poured light down its gleaming limestone sides.

At the far end, faltering light cast spidery shadows onto a boxy brick building, both floors in darkness.

She inserted herself into the lonely stillness of the quarry, and laying down a trail of sneaker squeaks in her wake she headed for a vague jumble of angular shapes which turned out to be a playground. There, obscured at first by a jungle gym, was an expansive but dimly lit window so close to the ground she dropped to her hands and knees to peek inside.

Murky light from a solitary wall sconce fell on the mats of a dozen sleeping children. Along a far wall was a sink, overhead cupboard, and a bin of the type that might hold toys. Nothing more except a plastic play table and chairs.

Claudia ducked when the back of a rocking chair swayed into view and a figure in an ankle-length black robe and headscarf rose with a baby propped against one hip. The person crossed to the sink, unhooked a drop-down change table, and ran a hand across an overhead shelf. With the baby safely on the floor the figure crossed to an intercom beside the door.

It emboldened Claudia to peer over the windowsill in time to see the baby flip onto its stomach and crawl between the motionless children. At first, Claudia thought she was looking at a blue bruise on the child's thigh. In her varied medical career nothing came to mind as to why a baby would have a string of numbers tattooed on its body. The bizarre sight sent her backwards onto her butt.

It was when an armed guard entered with a bundle of diapers that the woman lifted the child off the floor and turned. Here finally was the same young woman she'd seen tasered.

After the guard scanned his fob key and left, she watched a toddler with a plastic cup totter to the corner sink and reach for the water tap. Forgetting herself for a moment, Claudia craned closer to the pane for a clear view. Etched into the child's tender white thigh were more numbers.

Not only would a masked woman tapping on a window in the middle of the night scare the bejesus out of the midwife, but Claudia needed more time to find out what these freaky tattoos were for. One thing was obvious. She had caught Homer at yet another lie—this possible employee didn't seem to be free to move around at all.

Claudia raced to retrace her steps across the quarry and into the unlocked stairwell, the list of questions fomenting in her mind longer than ever. Break into a sprint, she wondered, or keep up her creeping tactics? Even for a hospital the place was unnervingly quiet. Where might the two guards have gone?

When she reached the final door into the rooftop garden, instead of bursting through and making a dash for the guest house, latent anxiety froze her hand on the handle. Shouldn't she immediately tell Paula or Benny what she'd seen? One of them was bound to be awake in Maya's ICU room. Together, they could invent the perfect

story: concerned about Maya, Benny went to fetch her but finding
no guards had let her out with their old key.

Claudia backtracked down two landings, squeezed past the ICU
door's nerve-rattling alarm, and stepped into the deserted hallway.
With nothing to give Claudia her bearings, she crept around a corner
and there, feet away, was the elevator.

Maya's room was the door beside it, Claudia thought. Or was it?
Let's see . . . I stepped off the lift yesterday, turned to my . . . Ding. The
elevator's shining doors began to part.

Crap. She ducked inside what seemed to be a storage room, eased
the door shut, and turned to a troubling scene. The antiseptic odor
wafting from a tray of bloodied clamps and retractors meant those
who had used them were likely still around.

Footsteps approached, then faded.

She cracked the door, listened, and as she stepped out and
swiveled to press it shut a deep voice behind her said: "Don't move.
Get on your knees and put your hands on your head." She was happy
enough to do so since the cheerful singsong voice apprehending her
sounded like it was leading a game of *Simon Says.*

An automatic curiosity brought a gun barrel into her ribs. "I said,
don't move . . . Benny. Cover me from the front."

Did this guy say—Benny?

The minute her knees hit the floor, someone tore the rough-cut
burglar mask away. A handgun came into focus in a direct line with
her face—behind it lay Benny's dumbfounded expression. His raised
handgun plunged to the side of his pajama bottoms.

"Claudia. What the hell are you doing?"

For one weird moment she almost said, *Practicing my ninja skills.*

The guy behind stepped into view. A youth in his late teens, he
kept his handgun raised.

"You know this person?" he asked Benny.

"She's a friend and a guest doctor here."

The arm holding his weapon drooped a bit as the youth's striking blue eyes roamed across Claudia's features. "So she is."

Both men flicked the safeties on their guns and shoved them into their waistbands. In Benny's case, the hunk of metal bypassed his manhood and slithered halfway down his leg before he fished it out and handed it to the other guy.

The youth's ruddy cheeks and chunky build made her think he'd popped in from a rugby pitch. A typical jean-clad teen with full lips on a pleasant-enough face, and short wavy hair of an equally nondescript dusty color, she felt an instant affinity with him.

He grinned at Benny, who was military-parade rigid—and more pissed than she'd ever seen the man. Whether friend or foe was irrelevant—a masked intruder had gotten within feet of his dying daughter. Critically ill hostages were the best kind when negotiating.

"I was practicing my ninja skills," she said, casting a side-eye at the beaming youth. "Can I have my wool hat back? I might need it."

"No," Benny said. He snatched it from the teen's hands and stuffed it under his armpit.

"What's a nin—ja?" the youth asked. Obviously, his ignorant state wasn't from living *under* a rock but rather *on top* of one in the middle of nowhere.

"You are lucky Paula is sleeping," Benny scowled. "She would not be giving you the benefit of the doubt like I am right now."

"How do you spell nin—ja?" the teen cut in once more.

Claudia turned. "N-I-N-J-A, oh yes she would. Who do you think gave me a key for the guesthouse?" Claudia waved her forefinger between the young man and herself. "Aren't you going to introduce us?"

"Not until you tell me why you were sneaking around the clinic."

"I'm your daughter's doctor. Isn't that reason enough?"

The new guy jumped forward, his palm out. "My name is Dafnis. I'm Homer's son."

"His *son*?" Homer had made it clear to her that there was no wife on site, but she hadn't considered he might have children. Claudia pumped Dafnis's arm to show she appreciated his forthrightness. "You look much too young. How old are you?"

Before he could answer, Benny marched between them. "He is a lot older than Maya. Still not over that, Claudia?"

Claudia had tried in vain to warn her two friends against starting a family so late in life. Maya's congenital disease had nothing to do with worn out eggs or sperm. Nor had she ever wagged an I-told-you-so finger at them, yet, here they were stressed out of their minds with a critically sick child.

With one eye on Homer's son, the other on Benny, she said, "I can explain everything." If surveillance cameras had been tracking her the entire night, the dark wind-lashed helipad might be the safest place to disclose what she'd seen. "Let's go to the garden."

"Great to meet you," the teen said. "I'll tell the guards Benny is with you. He's one of us." The Dafnis kid headed toward the elevator, then turned and waved as the doors opened.

This was his home, he had a right to question her, but there wasn't a speck of enmity in him. Rather than the angst and suspicion of most teens, this one radiated such open-handed cheerfulness she immediately felt lighter in the midst of the night's disturbing discoveries.

———⊙———

AT THE HELIPAD, A SAGGING moon cast the horizon in an anemic glow. Claudia raked the hair from her face and tried to defrost Benny with small talk. "Setting a chopper down in this wind must be a bitch."

He gave a ubiquitous head wobble which Paula once told her meant many things including India's version of: *Yeah, whatever.*

"It took my pilots awhile to get used to it," he said. "We watch the weather and never approach from the fenced side over there." He pointed to a chain-linked drop-off Claudia now knew formed one side of the quarry below.

They fought the wind all the way to the center of the concrete pad where she cupped her hand against his ear. "Are there cameras on us?"

"Most certainly," he shouted. "They can't hear us, but the guards are monitoring our every move from their control room next to the lobby."

"I'm really freaking out here, Benny. Did surveillance see everywhere I went tonight?"

"I do not know, but probably. Not inside the guesthouse, of course, or private suites, but there are cameras in every room and hallway of the clinic except the public bathrooms. Only mics in there."

"Oh, sounds cosy."

"It gives me comfort to know my family is protected. What were you searching for tonight?"

"The surrogates' dormitory block." Claudia pointed to the fence. "From over there, you'd be looking down on it four stories below. To get there, I entered the clinic's stairwell from the garden but continued down past the lobby and exited into a huge quarry. That's where the dormitory is. Have you been there?"

"Certainly not. You've got me thoroughly bamboozled."

"The day I arrived," Claudia explained, "I saw the guards taser a young woman and take a child from her arms. When I asked Homer about it, he blew the incident off. Said the guards mistook one of the surrogates for a kidnapper."

"Well, it seems plausible, does it not?"

"Not to me. Did you know the clinic has a midwife?"

"Yes, I have met Jaza on a number of occasions."

"Well," Claudia said, "She's the one the guards tasered, and the child they took was no newborn. I found her tending the children tonight inside the dormitory's nursery. Tell me, Benny. Why would the guards attack one of their fellow employees?"

All she got out of him was a shrug. "Was Jaza able to shed any light on it?"

"I didn't talk to her. Not after I saw numbers tattooed on the children's thighs."

"Tattoos?" he asked, his placid face darkening. "If that is indeed what you saw, then an interaction with Homer is in order." He rubbed the back of his neck and said, "I can go to Homer and play dumb. Ask him where you went tonight. If there is nothing untoward going on, he will be the one to bring it up. But Paula is right—you're a doctor here. I will demand you not be detained inside the guesthouse."

"If he refuses?" Claudia asked.

Benny stood silent and wide-eyed. "He would not refuse me."

As he turned to leave, Claudia grasped his arm. "How will you explain our meeting up here?"

"The truth is always best. I escorted you from the ICU floor, and brought you up to show you the view and discuss the challenges of flying in."

"And me wandering around?" she asked.

"The truth again," he said. "You are a peculiar woman who thought it would be fun to play cat and mouse with the guards."

———— ⊙ ————

THE MORNING AFTER HER ninja search, Claudia stood outside one of the operating rooms, flipping through the chart of the liver transplant she was due to observe. The patient inside wasn't the rich old alcoholic she expected—his or her family unwilling to be a living donor to keep their relative alive. Instead, the diagnosis was

PH1, a rare hereditary disease which could destroy both the kidneys and liver.

Only the sex—male—was visible on the chart. The patient's name and age had been blacked out which seemed irresponsible in the extreme. Who knew if this was the right guy on the table? She flipped to the next page—it had better be the right guy since both his kidneys and liver were coming out, and hopefully the new ones had already come down from the helipad.

She scrubbed and entered well into connecting the blood vessels of the new kidney. Surprise. The OR was as modern and bright as any other she'd ever worked in.

As an onlooker, the simple procedure held no thrill. No race against time like her heart transplants. Kidneys were so viable outside the body that they could extract the donor kidney, go home to a meal and good night's sleep, and return the next day to finish the job. Not that anyone did that, of course.

The Russian surgeon she'd met at the scrub sink jerked his thumb in the direction of the anesthetist at the head of the table, but Claudia knew he meant the patient. "Recognize this guy?"

She peered at the youthful face behind the ventilator tubing and arched her eyebrows to their limit.

"Good," he croaked. "That's the way we like it."

The patient could be anyone from a famous rapper to a gang member, but even that titillating possibility wasn't enough to sustain her interest. The room's monotonously neutral colors slow-danced with the hissing ventilation. "Suction . . ." a dreary voice said.

The liver would be even more mind-numbing. Once the ureter was joined with the bladder, she saluted the surgeon and walked out, peeling off her outer gloves as she trudged toward the elevator. They were dreaming if they thought she'd wait patiently for an escort back.

She was bent over, struggling with the gown's paper ties at her back when someone yelled, "Watch out!"

Crack—the crown of her head exploded in pain.

Homer's son stepped from behind the swinging door of an operating room. In white scrubs, a red plastic organ bucket in hand, he flashed a timid smile then brushed past her. Quite the versatile young man, able to both wield a gun and assist in surgery.

Through the OR door's window she glimpsed a team lifting the corpse of an adolescent into a body bag. It was always painful to see someone so young die during their transplant.

Moments later, Homer's son appeared beside her at the elevator, this time pushing a gurney with the same body bag.

"Got far to go with that?" she asked, sensing an opening to befriend this cooperative teen. Where else would Homer's son be taking a body if not to the infamous "cold storage" which likely held her captive bionic prototype. She could retrieve it herself.

"Level 1," he said, quickly adding, "Do you want to come with me?"

Chapter 9

H ere was the ninja doctor they'd caught sneaking around the ICU in the middle of the night.

Dafnis was well into his surgical shift, but it was only noon when Dr. Claudia ran into him, or, more correctly—into one of the OR doors while he was leaving with the kid's liver.

A lady doctor anywhere on the island was so weird that he froze up. There he stood like an idiot when he should've been taking the guy's liver and his own ass down the hall ASAP. When her face went all scowly, he knew it had to be the scrubs. Nobody paid any attention when he put on the doctors' white ones by mistake. But she was new. And really odd. The first doctor he'd met who wanted to go down to see the dead people in cold storage.

Since his brain needed another three or four hours to get up to speed, it wasn't until after the woman removed her surgical cap at the elevator that he remembered who she was.

"I wrote *ninja* in my notebook," he told her while they waited for the elevator. "Thanks for helping me spell it. What's your name again?"

"Claudia."

He scribbled it into the notepad, which also held all the steps for both his old job and the new one.

"That's *Claudia* with an *A-U,*" she said, fingering the page. "And cross out the *Dr.*"

Now that Dafnis thought about it, this lady didn't look or act anything like the other doctors. He'd never seen them chase rats or practise ninja skills, and they definitely didn't have sprouts of hair coming from the top of their heads.

He flipped through to the People section of his notebook and asked: "Are you a Chinaman coolie? That's what one of the nurses said you looked like."

He jumped when her laugh blew up the hallway. She told him *coolie* was a rude word he should erase from his notebook. China was a country. Not her country, though. She was from somewhere else.

Days later, she showed him both places on an internet map, which was such an amazing thing, because, for the first time in his life he saw their island—a tiny dot at the center of a big blue blob. That, she said, was the Mediterranean Sea. Their home.

When the doors parted, Dafnis snugged the gurney in after her and reached over to press Level 1-Rear.

"Are you both a guard and a porter?" she asked.

No one had ever looked at him with a good kind of curiosity.

"Sort of everything. Like the night we caught you, security told me to go guard the ICU with Benny. Usually, I work the night shift in the fertility lab." He tucked his chin against this lie that Homer told him to use if anyone asked about his job.

Also, he wasn't supposed to tell her something else, but he wanted to this time. "My gun's never loaded." He shrugged. "They don't trust me to know who's bad and who's good."

When the elevator bounced to a halt at Level 1, the rear doors parted onto Dafnis's world. "This is *my* hallway. Do you want to know why?" People never did, of course.

Claudia gave him a toothache of a smile.

"That door down there with the window is my fertility lab, and past that is the room where I sleep." A sharp tug cleared the gurney's rear wheels from the elevator. "Mostly—" Dafnis rotated the gurney for pushing and smiled at Claudia. "I help make babies inside the surrogates."

She backed away, her mouth sagging like she was going to throw up.

He'd mucked it up again.

"I meant that I do—" Dafnis jammed his foot against the closing door and flipped through to the description he needed. "I do preimplantation genetic testing on embryos prior to transfer." He pocketed the notepad and leaned into the moving gurney.

"That's a relief," Claudia said as she trailed alongside him.

"What kind of work do you do?" he asked.

"I implant artificial hearts into babies. Do you know what that is?

Dafnis didn't, but it sounded mind-blowingly cool.

"They're made of gelled seaweed which comes out of the stylus of a 3-D printer."

"You mean there's not a single bit of human in it, but it's a real heart for kids?"

"You got it. Once a human heart leaves the body, it will soon deteriorate into nothing but a rotten hunk of meat. My artificial one is ready all the time."

He skidded the gurney to a stop and screamed, "Are you serious? I can't wait to tell Homer about this."

Up ahead, a dreaded nose appeared from a gap in the lab's doorway and Jaza's words came to mind. *Hocking is a snitch. Avoid him.*

At cold storage, he scanned his fob and stepped inside to let the body bag slide from his shoulder onto the steel floor. Damn. He'd never seen the place so jammed up. They were just little kids, but there had to be more than thirty of them.

"If you help me," Dafnis said over his shoulder. "We can probably swing this one to the top of that pile over there."

He turned to see Claudia shuffling in a tight circle; eyes wide as if she was trying to memorize every detail. Something about one particular pile grabbed her attention because she marched to it and reached over her head to draw down two tiny body bags, one after the other. She unzipped the first one, stopped, and cupped a hand over her mouth, then repeated the same actions with the second.

Strange, because he couldn't smell them at all from where he stood.

"What is this?" She wheeled to face him. "Why the fuck are these kids carved up like Swiss cheese?"

He wished he knew. Homer said they were in a "twilight between life and death," but the surgeons called them cadavers. Dafnis liked to think of these limp bodies he sometimes wheeled from the helicopter as *half-drowned.*

Too tired and confused, he asked her, "What's Swiss cheese? How do you spell it?"

She smacked the notepad from his hands. "Answer me." She was shaking but her voice was still kind. "Sorry, I should be asking Homer, not you."

He scooped his notebook from the floor. Trying to explain his father's decisions always made Dafnis sound even stupider than he already was, but he liked this new person and decided to try.

"These guys in here are all boat people we saved from drowning." When the doctor shook even more, Dafnis realized how ridiculous that sounded. "What I mean is they never—"

"That youth you brought down isn't a transplant patient?"

"No. Homer doesn't want any more dead customers down here. Not since an old guy got burned up by mistake and his family was so pissed off they tried to close the clinic. "But—" Dafnis shrugged, "No body, no record. Not much they could do. Homer says record-keeping is a pain in the ass."

While he stood there chuckling Claudia stomped past with a murderous scary face.

"Don't you think it's funny?" he called after her, and hopped over the body bag before slamming the door on his way out.

"I wrote about it in my notebook of funny stories," he said when he caught up with Claudia at the elevator.

A voice echoed throughout the hallway: "Paging Dr. Vlakia to Level 1 lobby. Paging Dr. Vlakia."

"Uh-oh," Dafnis said. "I hate getting paged. I'm always in trouble."

Outside the elevator, he watched her punch the crap out of the call button and huff like she was trying to blow out fifteen birthday candles.

"What do you suppose that bastard wants now?" she asked him.

A safe distance behind her, Dafnis answered with the only bastard that came to mind. "I bet Hocking reported us for shouting in the hallway."

"Homer," she said, and whacked the call button again.

That was the day Dafnis found out Claudia could growl like a dog. Eventually, Dafnis and almost everybody would also realize Claudia had lusted after his father's blue ponytail long before she liked the man himself. Dafnis had always assumed they suited each other because they were both so stinking old.

Chapter 10

Claudia didn't need to go *up* the clinic's elevator but simply *through* it to get inside the lobby. Waiting for her were the three people she least expected to see at that time of the day—Homer, Paula, and Benny.

The lines on Benny's empathetic face had cratered during the night, and he shot his old friend the squinty-eye when Homer dumped a truckload of condescension on her. "My staff tell me you have a special interest in seeing where our surrogates live."

Claudia would take angry Homer any day over this slick version of himself slowly circling his prey.

"We're having lunch in their cafeteria," Homer said.

Throughout history, wining and dining one's foes had worked to conquer them—but not this time.

"And—" He fished something from his pocket for her. "I want you to feel free to go anywhere. This is the same key fob the guards receive."

She pocketed the card with a grunt and defaulted to the impervious mug she carried into all her surgeries. It wasn't until they arrived at the surrogate block and she buzzed them in that she knew the fob was genuine.

"You'll still need an escort for the dormitory."

Why give her the key to a locked building, then turn around and order her to stay out?

When they passed by the hall which Claudia calculated held the nursery room, she lingered until she noticed Homer's eyes on her.

Predictably institutional, their corridor led into a cafeteria every bit as bland with white-washed concrete walls and sandy-colored lino. Wall to wall windows opened directly onto the sort of claustrophobic view only a hard rock miner could love. It was the chalky limestone cliff she'd discovered the night before.

Surrogates were already lining up along a cafeteria counter common the world over, but the succulent aroma of roast lamb was anything but ordinary. Plate after plate of it appeared on their table along with what looked like Greek moussaka and stuffed grape leaves.

"How do you like the lamb stew?" Homer turned to Claudia, his elbows planted in anticipation of a compliment. "I taught the ladies my favorite Greek recipes."

She chewed on the meat first, then the question, surprised at how suspicious she'd become since arriving. "Oh, but I'd love to try some African dishes."

In an apparent defense of his republic's gastronomic statutes, Homer answered with, "Let's not ruin a good thing, shall we?" She imagined the Republic's first amendment might be a fail-safe recipe for phyllo dough.

"Now," Homer announced. "I'm going to explain some things I should have covered earlier."

To hell with being preached to, she thought. "Why are there children in your care with numbers tattooed on their legs?"

"They're the offspring of widowed surrogates," he said without hesitation. "We don't allow them to live with their mothers and, of course, the tattoos are temporary, the kind children use for fun. It helps us identify them."

"The mothers don't know their own children?"

"Of course they do." All heads turned to Paula's bloodshot eyes, ablaze under the fluorescent light of the hall. Benny's hand sought out his distraught wife's. Her friend had every right to be frustrated.

If only there was something I could do, Homer's eyes seemed to say. It was a feeling of helplessness she'd also known as a doctor, except this time the solution was within her power.

"The nursery has a vulnerable population," Homer said. "The tattoos help the guards retrieve the children for visits with their mothers in the playground or elsewhere."

As much as she craved an ambush, his answer was watertight enough to be the truth, but only if the children belonged to the surrogates and not what she suspected.

One of the African surrogates, a sturdy woman creeping up on the final years of childbearing, arrived with a platter of food.

"Saania," he said, "is from Sudan, but her English is excellent."

Eyes downcast, her broad grin and zippy yellow smock and headscarf inserted some life into their bleak table.

"You have a child in the nursery. Do you remember her number?" he asked.

The surrogate frowned, either offended by the question or concentrating. "Six, dash, two, one, six."

"How often do you visit?"

Saania slid the dish in her hands to the center of the table and poked him in the ribs. "You forgot already? She lives with my brother's family over at The Squats. It was *your* idea."

This titan of a woman hovered over him, locked in a staredown until, as if out of nowhere, Homer's neck disappeared under one of her thick forearms. Benny looked ready to spring until both the woman and Homer shook with belly laughs.

Her free hand mussed his hair. "This Homer's always looking out for me," she cooed. "He's—My—Big—Brother." With each word, the woman tightened her grip, Homer lost in the gleeful squirming of a boy.

"See the family resemblance?" Saania asked, finally releasing a happily gasping Homer from the headlock before trundling back into the kitchen.

Claudia sat, the serving dish poised in her hand while Homer picked up his fork and dug in. What *was* the story with this Laughing Buddha of a woman?

"Do all the surrogates treat you like that?" Paula said.

"I wish they would. I want them to feel that this is their home, not a workplace. The guards' cooking never quite caught on."

The wave of snickers signaled to Claudia this was as good a time as any for her next volley. "I have a question about the refugees in comas. Are you harvesting organs from them without permission from their families?" The only smile which remained was Homer's.

"Claudia. That is an unfair insinuation," Benny said, leaning toward Homer. "Forgive us."

Homer brushed off the apology. "It's a valid concern. Shall we visit the bodies in cold storage after the meal?" he said to Claudia.

Homer barely acknowledged Benny when he asked to tag along, but at some point the sneak must have winked because Benny's face broke into a mischievous smirk. Raised in India, a land of arranged marriages, was he naive enough to think this odious side trip was about courtship? Last time she checked, morgues were not on a list of hotspots to seduce women.

Go ahead. Wax benevolent for your old friend, Homer. Claudia knew the calamity that awaited her inside the cold storage, and before the day was done she would make sure Benny did too.

———◉———

DESPITE THE BITING cold inside the cold storage, Homer slammed the steel door shut with a decisive *clank*.

"Is this a date?" she said, expecting sly Homer but getting an entirely new version.

The vapid remark spun him around, his black fury sending her a step back. "What I'm going to say is for you only, so shut up and listen." He wagged his thumb between the two of them. "You and I are more alike than you think. You're not the only one with grandiose plans."

This hit her like a blast of fresh air. The meal's superficial civility didn't suit a man of Homer's confidence—it was for the fawning mediocres of the world.

His breath hung in chilled puffs around her face. "You'll find very few organs missing. Go ahead and open every bag. "

"To be honest," she said, "which is what I always am—I'd rather not."

Homer eyed her with a wary admiration, obviously knowing only the most pathological of liars would claim something so impossible.

He stepped over the new body bag and planted himself in front of her. "We sell the organs of those who don't survive the crossing from Libya," Homer said, looking her square in the eye. "Unfortunately, a lot of the dead are children."

Head bowed, Claudia pinched her nose against this rank fact.

"We try to rescue as many as possible, but last year alone almost two-hundred children perished," he said.

Claudia jabbed a forefinger at the body bag between them. "You call what you did to this poor boy a rescue?"

"Like the rest, he was brain dead."

"By what criteria? Are you at least conducting brain scans?" she asked.

"We did—before we lost our neurosurgeon. I decided it was too time consuming so after six hours we disconnect the ventilator. They either breathe on their own or . . ."

She gaped in disbelief. "People have emerged from comas weeks or even months later."

He bent to the cadaver at his feet. "Whether a donor comes from the black market or a refugee boat, Paula and Benny are going to stay here until a match is found for Maya. It's a transaction that works for both sides."

She rubbed some warmth into her upper arms. "Did it work for the family of this kid now missing two kidneys and a liver?"

He bolted up and flung the body over his shoulder. "He didn't have one."

How convenient, she thought. Without families or criteria for brain death, it was open season on refugees in comas.

"Our clinic and rescue vessels are no different from any of the other non-profits out on the water."

"Then why lie about bodies washing up on shore?"

They both knew why. He wailed the body bag onto the nearest pile and turned to her, the fight suddenly gone from his voice. "I'm sorry about that, but humanity didn't get where it is by always doing the right thing. Somebody has to make the hard choices."

She looked away when he said, "Why don't you come out with us on the next search for stranded boats?"

As worthwhile as most of Homer's hydrofoil rescues might be, she couldn't risk connecting herself to his black market transplants. "Watch you save the dying just long enough for you to sell what's left of them? No thanks."

"Okay, then. Can I ask you not to tell Benny about the orphans. It's just . . . it sounds like we're preying on people already vulnerable."

His sour smile followed by a carefree shrug chilled Claudia to the core. "You disclose the immoral practices of this clinic and expect me not to tell its main benefactor? Why tell me in the first place?"

"Benny doesn't need to know that his daughter's organs are coming from the clinic's comatose orphans," he said, "but *you* do. I can't risk him finding out and pulling the medivac helicopter he donated. It gives us almost one-hundred percent of our organs for children."

"All the more reason to shut this down."

Under eyes flat-lined as the corpses underfoot, a slippery smile oozed from the corners of Homer's mouth. "I wouldn't if I were you." His eyes skimmed over the surveillance camera above them. "We have you on camera during a transplant."

"I should've guessed you'd try to blackmail me."

All of it lined up so perfectly. The lie about bringing Maya's organs from Africa served to keep his reputation with Benny. The blackmail explained why Homer trusted her with his confession.

"I hope you're not planning to use that taser on me, too."

He tightened, probably wondering how she could know this. She finally had him.

"Why would I harm you when I need you to save Maya's life? You now know more about my clinic than a friend of twenty years. Keep that uppermost in mind."

Was this supposed to make her feel special? Before escaping that cold hell, she left him with a final threat. "You're not off the hook with Benny. You keep *that* uppermost in mind."

———◆———

SIX A.M. WAS STILL the middle of the night for Claudia and she intended to let the wanker who was playing tunes know that. Until now, early mornings in the Zen garden outside Claudia's guesthouse had been thankfully lifeless, along the decibel level of bingo night on a geriatric unit.

Before she could haul herself outside, the music stopped, replaced with *ka-brick, ka–brick* and a harsh rasp identical to an old drunk clearing their throat. When the crisp tones of a flute deep inside the garden interlaced with the annoying birdsong it was easy to imagine a youth dancing a jig at an all-night party. Ah, but weren't those school pals of hers lusty lads. To be so carefree and happy again before life's sad tricks snuffed out all that and more.

It couldn't be one of the Muslim guards with the flute, nor Benny, a non-practising Hindu. Paula, a former primary school teacher, was the type to own a flute, but Claudia had never seen her with one.

She dragged a sweatshirt over her head, pulled on jeans, and left in search of the sound—whether for an altercation or a chat depended on who she found. It might be a Westerner, maybe even a client of Irish descent.

Pondside, a flurry of tiny gray and yellow Flycatchers flitted between the high-stepping legs of two great white egrets. Homer's garden was their stopover on their long migration home to Europe. The bone-white wings of one statuesque bird parted, and from its dagger-like beak came the jarring rasp.

Off it flew to land on the railing of the arched footbridge. There, with feet dangling above the pond's shimmering waterfall, lips going to and fro across a flute, sat Homer. The scheming body-snatcher inside the cold storage had become a moonlit minstrel in a pastoral painting.

When she tried to retreat into the night's shadows, Homer gestured with a curled palm to join him.

"Sorry. Did I wake you?" he said and scooted to one side as Claudia mounted the bridge. "There's so rarely anyone up here at this time. It's my sanctuary for solving the world's problems."

Claudia flashed a tired off-kilter smile and pointed to an outrageously long, conch shell-encrusted flute.

"It's an African tambin of the Fulani people." He reached behind his back and pulled a lacquered stick and ridged can from a duffel bag. "I've finally got my rhythm section. Now, when I give the signal, pretend you're peeling potatoes. Like this." He ground the stick across the ridges, then picked up his flute and signaled for the rhythm section.

"Don't stop."

They finished the wonky tune in giggles and grins.

"Did one of your refugees teach you that?"

"There's more to me than ruling over an island-nation." He cocked an eyebrow as if bracing for a snarky reply. "I was still a virologist in Syria when I brought this back from a medical conference in West Africa."

After the horror of finding so many tiny bodies yesterday, she didn't think Homer could ever redeem himself in her eyes. How could there be such a soulful side to a man who preyed on unconscious children?

"Before this flute," he said, "I didn't have a musical bone in my body. Or a thought for the suffering of others. The have-nots were simply too lazy to work for what I had. When I saw this gorgeous thing in Senegal I had to have it. How hard could a three-holed instrument be? I planned to amaze my colleagues back home, but after two days I pitched it into the bowl of the first legless beggar I came across.

"The next day, that guy had quite a stash of money. When he saw me, he insisted I join him."

"Each day I rushed back to the hotel to show my wife what I'd learned. We met at medical school in Athens and I was so enamored I followed her back to Syria for twenty-five more years of bliss, but those were my last days with her."

A tender memory seemed to pass through him.

"I felt like a school kid again."

Claudia grinned. "Your trash was his treasure."

"That's how I see every refugee in my republic. Like my friend, I'm not giving up on them." Homer raised her hands, pressing the tender pads of his fingers into her palms. "How can I ever repay them enough for opening this closed heart of mine?"

This was no act. "That's quite a confession," she said. "Did you ever go back to see what became of that beggar?"

"He's here at The Squats. He runs quality control at the flute-making workshop."

"How great is that?" she said.

It wasn't clear whether they hugged before they laughed or after or who grabbed who first, but her usual wooden resistance broke down. Claudia abandoned herself to Homer's warm body—his arms tight and confident; despite his horribly scratchy beard on her tender cheek. Claudia had felt accepted in Bags's arms, but Homer's ardent embrace signaled so much more—which was precisely why it scared her.

As far as Homer's wife, she didn't ask and he didn't offer. While he tooted hallelujah on his flute in Senegal, the woman came to some kind of tragic end.

If this was a made-up story to gain her trust by hinting at his own human failings—it worked. Curious about the flute player, she agreed to tour his refugee island called The Squats.

Afterwards, Claudia sat on the bridge until the rustling apple blossoms mixed with the hushed chatter of the surrogates filing off the elevator. As they circumambulated in twos and threes around the pond, far from Syria's bombs or African sex trafficking, she thought about Homer and his hard choices.

Chapter 11

Claudia was minutes away from exploring the low-lying island for asylum seekers which was visible from Homer's penthouse.

While it was too late to rescue the North American municipality of Smashed-In-Buffalo-Head, a name makeover for the nascent settlement affectionately called The Squats was still possible.

Homer thought the name cute, but to her it brought up squalor and tattered tents awash in a field of mud. Consider London, she tried arguing. Had its ancient residents not been proactive, they would still be calling it Plewnejd, which, granted, was still better than The Squats—no matter how much Dickens would have loved the name.

The morning Claudia arrived for her tour she found Homer and his son already side by side at the clinic's helicopter.

"It's not leaving without her," Homer said.

The slowly rotating blades must have masked her footsteps because neither man turned around.

"I stayed awake inside the nursery all night to make sure she didn't run off and hide," Dafnis said. "I thought she was okay with it so I brought her bags up here a half-hour ago."

Obviously, the *she* in their conversation was not Claudia. Considering Homer's neurosis over spies and state secrets, she was also surprised father and son weren't using Arabic or even Greek.

"Now she's crying," Dafnis said. "It's the kid. She doesn't want to leave him." Utter silence from both until Dafnis said, "Why don't I take him to The Squats on my days off? Just for a few hours."

"Absolutely not," Homer shot back. "You won't have time. Not until we get the first one in the air and you know what you're doing."

"Oh. Claudia. Good morning," Homer said when he turned to check the elevator. He patted his son's shoulder. "I'll think of something. Go down and tell her there's good news."

With Dafnis gone, the two of them exchanged smiles. "If I'm finally going to have some female companionship in this testosterone-sated facility," Claudia said with a haughty nod, "then it is indeed a good morning."

"I would love to show you around over there, but we're starting a new enterprise today."

"Oh?" Claudia tried to mime Homer's deep voice. "What's that all about?"

"Wouldn't you like to know." His belly laugh dissolved at the sight of something behind her. Claudia turned to see the midwife with Dafnis. That Homer would pair her up with the very person she wanted to pump for information surely meant he had nothing to hide.

"She was already on her way," Dafnis told his father.

The young woman was morose and red-eyed as she squared off with Homer. When he tried to greet her with a hug she turned away.

"Jaza, this is Dr. Claudia, she's going to tour The Squats and observe a sea rescue aboard the hydrofoil." The two women nodded at each other before Homer tried again to catch the young woman's attention. "As far as your transfer, you can return to the clinic on your days off whenever you want."

Homer's idea seemed beyond anything Jaza had hoped for. She snapped to attention, her hands pressed in prayer mode. "That means I can sleep in the nursery with my son?"

"No. We've hired your replacement. If you prefer, you can sleep in Dafnis's room beside the lab."

Jaza gawked and pivoted to Dafnis, her cheeks ruddied.

"It's obvious you love each other," Homer said. "I should know, I had more than thirty years of happiness myself. All right, let's get going. Kiss your sweetheart goodbye, son."

Still wide-eyed with wonder, Dafnis crept closer to peck Jaza's cheek and brush away a single tear there.

Dafnis and Jaza a couple? Homer's attack on the midwife and seizure of her son made even less sense.

"Try that again, son." Homer didn't watch the passionate kiss but grinned and nodded at Claudia instead. Given everything she knew about the midwife, Homer's toothy matchmaker performance shot to the top of the creepiness scale.

The minute father and son left to fetch the pilot both women duck-walked under the rotors and clambered inside the helicopter where they sat to each side of a portable gurney and attached IV pole, facing the rear. At the head was a built-in monitor and oxygen tubing. She imagined the metal lockers under the gurney held more portable resuscitation equipment, but other than a few duffel bags secured by ties to the floor, the rest of the interior was uncluttered.

Ten minutes tops was likely all Claudia had as she leaned over the gurney and said, "My first day here I saw you being tasered."

Jaza whipped around with an expression of bewilderment. "Wha—?"

"They locked me inside the elevator," Claudia continued, "but I propped the door open enough to see you with a child. Why would the guards use such force on their own staff? Aren't you the midwife?"

"I—" Jaza squinted in the direction of the helipad gate beyond Claudia. "Not anymore. Homer's sending me to The Squat's clinic so I can't try to escape with my son again." She leaned across the gurney as if she too realized they had only minutes left. "Please, help me find out where they're hiding him and what they plan to do with him?"

"Why would they keep a mother and her child apart?"

"They think he's clinic property, to use however they want. But he's Dafnis's son."

"Dafnis?" Claudia asked, not sure she'd heard right. "Surely Homer wouldn't harm his own grandchild."

"He doesn't know Dafnis is the father." Jaza checked the helipad gate again, her voice edgy and rushed. "Years ago I agreed to be a surrogate. Then I thought going to school on the mainland would be a way to escape but they brought—."

Claudia cut in. "Why are you still here? You must have made a quarter-million dollars as a surrogate."

Jaza gave her head two robust shakes. "That's what I'm trying to explain. I was already pregnant when it was time to impregnate me with the client's embryo. Dafnis made it look like the in vitro transfer went ahead."

"Did the client find out it wasn't his child?"

"No. We invented a chromosome sequence to pretend the baby had retarded intelligence."

"How in the world could Dafnis—?"

"He's not stupid. His brain injury is a medically unexplained phenomena."

"I wondered if that's what happened to him," Claudia said.

"Dafnis starts every day as the adolescent with a head injury," Jaza said, "but the longer he stays awake, the more he matures because the memories start returning. His brain is like an engine warming up. Some nights, he's brilliant. That's the Dafnis I fell in love with."

At the sound of voices Jaza reached across the gurney and grabbed Claudia's arm. "You mustn't tell Homer I've been lying about my boy. Please. He might force another pregnancy on me. Or send me away for good."

Claudia winced as the girl's fingers dug deep into her forearm.

"They admitted two children this week for transplants and suddenly my boy is missing.

"I don't trust Homer," Jaza said to Claudia's gaping jaw. She wagged her finger before Homer and two other men climbed aboard. "Neither should you."

Homer's hand lighted on the shoulder of the same guard from her arrival at the dock and then the words: "Nabi the rescue swimmer." Claudia was staring at Homer's moving lips but reliving the moment Hocking lifted the shrieking toddler from Jaza's arms. Harvesting vital organs from comatose children was bad enough, but taking them from healthy children incapable of defending themselves was madness.

Before heading to the copilot's seat, the Nabi guy directed a searing glare at Jaza, but she seemed too immersed in thought to notice.

Minutes into the flight Jaza slipped her a note with four jotted numbers and patted her own thigh. The familiar row of numbers jolted Claudia back to the shock of seeing them on the children.

Worse was the dreadful fact that Jaza's son and Maya were close in age.

The medivac helicopter suddenly banked sharply to the right, sending both of them clawing the air for a handhold. "Why are we turning south?" Jaza yelled in Nabi's direction. "The Squats are straight ahead."

Nabi appeared from the cockpit crouched on his haunches and giving the thumbs down.

"Detour," he shouted above the whirling blades. "Swamped inflatable." He pulled a wetsuit from one of the duffle bags and started to strip off his outer clothing and boots.

Was this for real? Had Claudia not made it clear to Homer she was only going to observe, not participate in any search and rescue of potential organ donors. He assured her there would be more than enough paramedics on board the hydrofoil, yet here she was the only medical personnel on the way to a rescue. She eyed the portable ventilator and defibrillator not with the respect they deserved, but with contempt knowing they might revive someone just long enough to hand them a death sentence at Homer's clinic.

The midwife, too, seemed to descend into smoldering resentment as she hauled out a trove of medical supplies and equipment from the hidden cubby holes inside the medivac.

Claudia found herself shoving aside her better judgment and powering up monitors.

"Don't feel you have to help. This isn't my first time on Search and Rescue," Jaza said.

Claudia nodded but knew once the casualties were pulled aboard, everything would change. No decent doctor could ignore a victim's suffering. She shifted herself to the window seat closest to the main bay door.

After a half-hour of zigzagging, the chopper slowed and turned. If the land on the horizon was Libya the refugees didn't get far at all. Something dark and round in the distance bobbed on the cresting waves. A closer view revealed a swamped dinghy, one end completely submerged. About twenty survivors clung to the end still above water while dozens of dark-skinned bodies dotted the water, most facedown and unmoving.

As soon as Nabi slid aside the chopper's bay door a tsunami of screams hit. Far below a tangle of limbs flailed and reached for the skies. The oh-so-familiar shrieks of babies cut to her core, the screams silenced only when a wave crested over the tiny heads.

Suited up, Nabi slipped on flippers and jumped feet-first off the chopper's skids into the sea below. Jaza lowered the line of an electric hoist and attached harness, and minutes later, Nabi reappeared dangling from the harness at the opening and clutching the limp body of a young African boy with the bluish pallor of hypothermia. "I don't think he's breathing," Nabi said.

Using the handheld remote, Jaza swung the harness inside so Nabi could unbuckle the boy for the transfer to one of the stretchers.

"Send me down," Nabi said before pushing himself clear of the skids. "And lower the basket for two babies." He disappeared from view once more.

Jaza was already taking the child's pulse. "Nothing," she said to Claudia. "Start CPR. I'll get the oxygen bag and defibrillator ready."

While Claudia peeled off the boy's wet shirt and positioned the heart pads Jaza continued bagging oxygen into the boy. Claudia sent the first jolt from the paddles. No response at first.

"Come on, sweetheart. We've got you," Claudia pleaded. On the second defibrillation the cardiac monitor opposite the gurney sprang to life. "Okay. Got a rhythm and a pulse," Claudia said and turned to ask for an intubator but found Jaza already feeding the tube into the boy's trachea.

IV bag in hand, Claudia turned to hang it, surprised to see Jaza maneuvering the rescue basket to clear the skids. Down it went to the chaos below. For a teenager, the midwife not only knew the rescue routine inside and out but was fast and organized under pressure.

Claudia stripped off the boy's remaining wet clothing to encase him in heated blankets and soon the color returned to his face. Oxygen saturation levels looked adequate. Pupils were reactive. This little angel was going to make it.

She was about to insert an IV line in her patient when the helicopter lurched sideways. The stretcher remained locked in place but the boy shifted to the edge and would have slid off had Claudia not snatched hold of the blanket encircling him. "Well, shit. As if we don't have enough to do already."

Jaza rushed over to help cinch down the straps and just as they got the job done, the helicopter swooned again, even more violently. "What in the . . .?" The midwife rushed to peer out the open bay. "Oh. No. No. No."

From far below, Claudia heard Nabi shout what sounded like, "Cut the line."

"What's going on?" Claudia said.

But Jaza was too preoccupied with muttering to herself to hear Claudia's question, let alone answer it. "No," she muttered. "I sure as hell am not going to lose those babies."

Where Claudia kneeled clutching the stretcher, she eyed the floor bolts. If not for those, her and the boy would have both been jettisoned out the open bay. Another jerk flung her so close to the seat near the opening that she pulled herself into it and buckled in. Far below, a swarm of bodies came into view around the sides of the floating oblong basket. Some clung on while others tried to claw their way atop the metal ribbing.

Inside the bobbing metal basket, safe from the throng, lay two infant bodies.

A fearless Jaza lunged to dash an armload of lifejackets out the open bay. "The basket is getting swarmed by—" She jumped back as a tethered Nabi appeared, rocking like a metronome in and out of the opening.

"Cut the fucking line." His legs cycled wildly, trying for a foothold on the skids. On the next swing inward he got a grip on one of the seatbelt straps around Claudia and with his other hand grabbed a tool off the wall above her. When Jaza tried to block his path he pushed her out of the way so violently she bounced off the fuselage onto her knees.

Claudia could see why he'd stayed clipped to his harness. With one unstable foot on the skids, he grasped hold of the basket's line and slid the tool around it. Seconds later the helicopter jumped at least a foot, bouncing Jaza into the air only inches from striking her head.

As Jaza scrambled around the stretcher to a seat, Nabi was once again clawing his way inside off the skids. He untethered from the line, then shook the tool in Jaza's vengeful face. Back the tool went into its wall holder. With a final "Homer will hear about this," he crouched and duck-walked his way into the cockpit.

Claudia leaned forward, expecting to see the basket and survivors clinging to its sides but the watery space where the throng fought for their lives was now bare.

The engines roared, the medivac rose and far below, gone from sight, two babies and a dozen refugees had failed to find asylum. They drifted below the waves.

⎯⎯◉⎯⎯

NO MORE THAN THIRTY minutes later all four of them were back at the helipad, no closer to her planned tour of The Squats. Too weary to shift herself, Claudia had intended to stay onboard while they unloaded the boy, but when the refueling hoses came out the fumes drove her into the Japanese garden.

Supine on a bench inside one of the gazebos, she heard footsteps enter the garden and stop.

"What happened out there? I only saw one gurney going down to the OR." It was Homer pumping somebody for info.

"The dinghy was completely swamped. Bodies everywhere." Nabi's voice.

"Why leave, then?"

"I tried going back down for two babies but the basket was getting swarmed on all sides. We had to cut it loose."

Thud. The gazebo shook as something slammed against the wood siding.

"Dammit," Homer said.

Nabi's voice. "Search and Rescue probably saw us in the distance but—"

At this, Homer snarled, "I could care less what they think. It's those babies I need."

"Stop worrying, Homer. There'll be hundreds more tomorrow. And that boy down in the ICU is a score. We'll get a lot of mileage out of him. Everything's working—except his brain."

What the hell was this idiot talking about? Claudia thought. The boy had reactive pupils. He'd be off the ventilator within days.

Footsteps faded. Homer must have left because the next voices she heard were Jaza's and Nabi's.

"I don't want to hear that out of you again," she said.

"Hear what?"

"Score. Mileage."

"*Tsk*," Nabi guffawed. "I take my orders from Homer. Leave if you don't like it. Can't go without your loverboy, can you? Well, he might be the first one gone. I hear Homer has plans for Dafnis."

"Shut up. Who'd be stupid enough to tell *you* anything?"

Footsteps faded in opposite directions.

This doe-eyed teen was feistier than she thought. Hell, Claudia herself should have spoken up when she heard Homer talking about babies like they were items on a grocer's shelf. The man had a ruthless side he kept well hidden.

When Claudia climbed back into the helicopter, they were minus Nabi, but Jaza's face was red and puffy.

"This is a lot of responsibility for someone as young as you," Claudia said even though she knew the botched rescue wasn't what had upset the midwife. How painful it must be knowing the man you love and the father of your child was withholding information about his future. "There's nothing you could have done to save those children."

A tight sniff from Jaza. "It made me think of my family. I'm the only one left."

For someone so young, worry lines told of an indelible exhaustion. The death of her entire family, forced labor and the loss of her freedom, a miscarriage, a missing child, and now—a lover's betrayal. Jaza had been through more heartbreak in seventeen years than most people experienced in a lifetime.

Whatever Homer had planned for Jaza's son couldn't be good, either.

Chapter 12

From the air, The Squats looked like a chubby dessert spoon turned upside down—not a single row of tents in sight. At the elongated "handle" end of the island the midday sun glinted off the roofs of a few dozen shipping containers surrounded by a line of vineyards at the shore. Whether these metal dwellings were still occupied or not, this had to be the original camp.

They banked toward the main town. Except for a few bicycles crawling along a ring road at the shoreline, and a construction site looming ahead, the medieval blueprint persisted with a labyrinth of stone structures tumbled together and spiraling up the rocky sides of a wedding cake-shaped hill. The entire settlement would fit snugly into the racetrack outside her apartment building in London. .

At the apex of the island they skimmed over cranes swinging above the makings of either a hospital or a school, before settling onto the vast flat rooftop of a stone tower nearby.

Uniform-free and gunless, a young man in jeans carried Jaza's pathetically small leather suitcase down a stone staircase on the outside of the tower to a jeep parked in a cobblestone laneway. There stood not only Benny, but Dafnis.

"What in the world are you two doing here?" Claudia looked at one then the other, but Dafnis was already fixated on Jaza's stormy eyes and downturned mouth.

Benny attempted to hug Claudia but this was never a given. "My helicopter brought us over here from the clinic." He tucked the suitcase into the back of the jeep and flipped a thumb toward the churning argument between Dafnis and Jaza. "Lover's tiff. Poor

Dafnis is having quite a day. He just realized vehicles not only travel through the air and across water, but on land, too."

Here was the relaxed and upbeat Benny she knew before his daughter's tragedy hardened him.

"The boss told me to shake a leg and he warned me you might be in a foul mood." He raised an eyebrow at Dafnis as the teen jogged in, minus Jaza.

"You heard he put me to work this morning, then?" she said.

"I heard," Benny said. "Go easy on the poor chap. He was taken unawares by the diversion. Regardless, you managed to save a young life."

"Yes. As long as the boy isn't . . . " Remembering Homer's warning that Benny might pull his chopper if he knew it was used to harvest organs, she checked herself and said, "too traumatized" instead of—*carved up for parts*—. "You and Homer are working on me harder than a couple of used-car salesmen."

Shopkeepers anywhere along the moral spectrum were bound to flummox Dafnis. "Is that good or bad?"

"Ba—ad. Don't worry," Claudia said to the teen's defeated slouch. "I'll explain it later."

Dafnis brightened. "Next to Jaza, you're the nicest person I've ever met."

With cheeks hotter than a blast furnace, she tried to scurry away but ran straight into a beaming Benny who turned to Dafnis. "Claudia is in need of more friends. *Many* more."

"Are you really?" Man-On-A-Pogo-Stick wheeled toward her. "Pick me. Pick me."

This geyser of genuine affection from Dafnis shouldn't have come as a surprise to anyone. Claudia was the one who said his life was a story worth telling. So, one day while they sat side by side at Homer's penthouse bar, Dafnis cracked open a new notepad and wrote: *I Am A Jeep* as a title, then the first paragraph: *Until Jaza jumped me, I was stalled, unable to start the life I wanted.*

She explained the double meaning in unflinching detail. It was still a perfect first line, though, and said he should carry the notepad everywhere to remind him that Jaza was his girlfriend.

"Where's Jaza?" Claudia said. Anything to deflect attention from her friendless life.

He stood, open-mouthed. "What?"

"Jaza." She raised empty palms.

"Oh. She's taking the stairs to the water. I guess that's where her clinic is," he shrugged. "She's mad at me because she thinks Homer's going to send me to work outside the Republic." He studied his shifting feet. "Yeah. Right. If only."

Poor Dafnis—simple information eluded him yet he couldn't wait to talk about feelings which should stay private. Benny patted Dafnis on the back and slid in behind the wheel.

"I'm learning to drive a plane," Dafnis announced from the back seat to more raised eyebrows from the two of them.

A wave of heat heavy with road tar and pounding jackhammers blasted through her open window while the jeep bounced downhill along barely distinguishable dirt switchbacks. They wound through the construction site and past road crews laying down a byway so narrow their tires sometimes scraped the steps into the one- and two-storey stone cottages lining it. Peasant-rough, cramped and no doubt dark inside, the dwellings, however, had proud shutters freshly-painted red, yellow, or orange.

"Wow." Dafnis craned around in his seat. "Are these little buildings ever weird. Do people live in them or—?"

"Most of them are dwellings, but some might be stores," Benny said.

"You mean like storage rooms in the clinic?"

While Benny patiently answered Dafnis's questions the boy's sad ignorance of the world off-island punched a hole inside her.

"Remember when I showed you some money that time?" Benny offered. "You can take that into these businesses and exchange it for things you need. We could try it if you like."

"What a day this is going to be," Dafnis said, pushing himself erect with a bounce.

Claudia winked at Benny. "I too have a question for our all-knowing sage. What are they building back there near the helipad?"

"A hospital. I retained the engineers and tradespeople from India, but eventually the residents themselves will take over."

At the next hairpin turn the CEO billionaire skidded the jeep to a stop for no other reason, it seemed, than to drink in the otherworldly kaleidoscope of the Mediterranean at high noon. "Like the fortress we landed on, the island was built by the Knights Hospitallers to grow food and make wine. They terraced this hill here where the town is, but of course that was long before the leper colony moved in."

"The what?" Claudia asked.

"Lepers," Benny said. "In large part, these stone cottages date from the island's nineteenth century leper colony."

"Do you mean animal leopards?" Dafnis asked him.

"No. I'll explain it later tonight."

They continued until the dirt lane funneled them across a cobbled ring road and onto a strip of hard-packed beach at the island's dock.

"Sorry," Benny announced, opening his door and hopping out. "There's no way around it. It's quite a jaunt up to the town square, but we must alight here and continue by foot. That there," he said, pointing to a low stone warehouse with a Red Cross ensign, "is where

Jaza will work. The construction crews will undoubtedly keep her on task with broken bones and accidents with the saws."

Like compact islands everywhere the main road at the water buzzed with bicycles and scooters around a hardware depot and bike repair shop. Similar to Homer's island, meandering cliques divided themselves into the billowing robes and headdresses of the Middle East, or the twisted turbans and batiked skirts of Africa.

As if summoned, Jaza wandered down from the clinic's covered veranda to ask if Claudia wanted to take a look. From the girl's intense gaze, this was no mere invitation but a repeated plea for a private chat. With Dafnis on Homer's side, Claudia realized she was this desperate mother's only tenuous link to her missing son.

"Later. For sure." A nod from Claudia put a secretive smirk on Jaza's face.

"Dafnis. How about you?" Jaza asked.

His eyes caught Benny's. "I—I don't think I can. Homer told me to stay with Claudia and keep her happy."

Claudia hooted.

"Come on, my friend." Benny gave Dafnis a back pat laced with manliness. "You are in charge here. Act like it. One day this island will be yours."

"It will?" Dafnis frowned. "Yeah, I guess."

Jaza linked her arm through his and smiled before sending a thin grimace in Claudia's direction. "I'm not very hopeful, but when the hydrofoil docks I can try to find the parents of the boy we rescued."

They left Dafnis at the clinic and wandered briefly through a tight stone tunnel which skirted the waterfront. If the thick defensive wall she saw from the air encircled the entire medieval fortress at one time, foot traffic through this tunnel with heavy iron gates at each end may have been the only way in and out.

At the top of a steep cobbled stairway was a young African woman in jeans and a t-shirt. She was filling a five-gallon jug at a downspout jutting from a squat stockade-like structure which Benny said served as both a city hall and solar power station.

"The first public works project Homer tackled . . ." Benny said, straining to catch his breath, " . . . was getting an electricity grid and water lines into these old dwellings.

"The water originates from a cistern the knights installed under the tower we landed on and to date about ten thousand families have paid for the utility."

Benny returned the woman's wave and said, "The rest depend on community taps like that and latrines on every street."

"You know the families here?" Claudia asked.

"My workers are training her husband in welding." He plodded upward, wheezing louder by the step but managing to squeak out the rest of his story. "Homer is adamant that everyone pays their way. The Squats is operated like a town. Even the widows are put on task at the orphanage, cooking and cleaning while their own children are in school."

The stairs ended at a tight treed square ringed by market stalls and a few storefronts, and which residents called "The Colony" after its former lepers. They branched off down a side alley filled with shoppers ducking in and out of cottages selling clothing, bread, shoes, and haircuts. Up another staircase was The Colony's newly built school where Benny pointed out the spot for a future water park for children.

"Homer's priorities are building the school and hospital. Only then will he allocate land for houses of worship."

She halted. "The residents let him get away with that?"

"Homer has nothing against religion, in fact, he was a leading member of his Greek Orthodox church in Syria. Having the Muslim and Christian congregations share the school's gym is his way of forcing them to cooperate with each other."

What Homer was giving, she had to admit, was the cliched hand-up rather than hand-out. "And what's going up over there?" Claudia asked.

"Three families have pooled their money for a new block of flats. You could call them the island's first property developers. Homer pays residents to be donors, but what they do with the money is up to them."

"Then you know about the organs the refugees are selling?"

"Of course. It seems perfectly sensible to want to improve one's lot in life." He stopped and eyeballed Claudia. "How could *you*, of all people, object? You are undoubtedly one of the most practical people I know."

"I have no problem with adults who want to be living donors," she said. "Sell a kidney or even part of their liver, but a child . . ." Claudia shook her head at the thought of Homer's comatose victims and zeroed in on Benny. "Are you waiting for someone to sell you their child's heart and lungs to keep Maya alive."

Claudia's unadorned question raised a gasp in him. "It would be an unbearable decision for any parent," Benny said. "But if the child was truly dead and the parents agreed, then why not? I would give them every penny I had in gratitude."

"What if the child was only in a coma?"

"That is ridiculous. No parent in their right mind would kill their child for money."

"Maybe so," Claudia said. "But a lot of these refugee children are orphans."

Benny made a grand sweep of one arm. "Then we can be thankful Homer is a man of integrity. Any doctor attempting this would be gone from here in the blink of an eye."

So it's true, she thought. Benny has no clue how his rescue helicopter is really being used. And Homer wants to keep it that way.

"Speaking of survivors," Benny said, peering out to sea. "Is that not the hydrofoil coming in from the rescue you attended? Shall we crack on down to the dock? I can show you the medical equipment on board."

At the dock next to the clinic, survivors straggled off the rescue vessel and into two tents on the beach. Claudia tucked aside the flap of the one labeled *Medical* to find a glittering wave of shiny survival blankets all huddled around laptop monitors broadcasting animated faces at the other end.

She straightened. "There's public internet here?"

"Yes. Via satellite," Benny said. "It was one of the first services Homer provided for the original camp. The laptops are still free to anyone who wants one. Residents can use the satellite phone at the new clinic, too."

Of everything she'd seen so far this was an unexpected slice of freedom and astounding generosity at the fringes of Homer's autocracy.

Orange-jacketed workers trudged from the ship, bringing row upon row of white body bags to shore. There must have been more than a hundred of them strewn across the sand but only a few survivors wandering bag to bag.

Two wee bodies, side by side, stood apart from the rest. The crunch of Jaza's body hitting the medivac's fuselage was all Claudia could think of as she trudged transfixed on the tiny bundles—until an equally tragic sight grabbed her.

At the far end of the dock, an adolescent girl, dressed in a long tunic and hijab, wandered alone, methodically crouching, unzipping, then closing each bag in turn until she found what she was seeking. She knelt, removed her headscarf, lifted the tiny gray corpse to her lips, and wrapped it ever so lovingly in the scarf. Claudia was now close enough to see her cradle the baby as if it yet breathed. A single tear spilled from her dead eyes while she shuffled to another row of bags, bent, and tucked the infant into the crook of a dead woman's arm.

What pain had this child already experienced to have no tears left to shed?

The girl pressed her lips to the brow of both bodies in turn, tugged at the zipper, and trudged, without stopping, to the processing tent on shore.

"I'm going to see if Jaza has found the family of the boy we saved," Claudia told Benny when he caught up with her marching off the beach.

"Do not get your hopes up," he said. "Some days we can save everyone if we get there in time, but today . . . Homer told me only about fifty made it out of two hundred in the raft. The refugees do not tend to know how to swim. And of course, the smugglers never give them lifejackets."

"Bastards." Claudia cursed under her breath all the way to the clinic door. Expecting chaos, an eerie pall of low moans lay over the reception room, the only patients a handful of pregnant women, slouched across chairs or stretched supine on the floor in utter relief or exhaustion. Not a sound came from two unconscious men hooked to life support.

When Jaza saw Claudia, she finished drawing blood from an adolescent boy and hurried over. "I've already asked everyone here." She shook her head and pointed. "That Nigerian woman over there remembers the family. There were two other young children and their parents. She didn't see them in the screening tent and they're not here."

"That means his entire family drowned," Claudia murmured.

There existed surgeons Claudia knew who, over time, became emotionally invested in their chronically vulnerable patients. They were the flakey and unprofessional types. Yet, here she was—clinging to the boy as if he were one of her wolf pups abandoned and alone in Romania's harsh ranges. She had to know he was safe and cared for.

"What can I do to help?" she asked Benny.

"Nothing," he said. "The boy you saved will come here and join the other orphans. He'll be fine, won't he, Jaza?"

"Probably. They say the orphan's dormitory is where the lepers used to live. It's not bad. It's behind the clinic if you want to take a look."

"Do I have time?" she asked Benny.

He raised his eyebrows in place of a nod but told her they needed to return before dark. "No more than an hour from now."

Claudia trotted at Jaza's heels through a back exit of the clinic and into a playground which fronted a two-story brick building, both freshly painted the same gaudy lime green.

"That's it there. I'll be busy with blood work all day, but can we talk when you're done?"

"Of course."

Jaza pressed her lips together and left.

Sitting on a bench and watching some children on a merry-go-round were two African women. Had they or someone in their family been a donor? About to speak with them, she heard Jaza calling. The midwife waved from the clinic's exit. "Could you come and help us, please."

Inside the clinic, the midwife led the way down a hall and into an examination room where the same adolescent girl from the dock sat, no longer stoic but stiff with fear. "This girl is eight weeks pregnant," Jaza said. "She wants an abortion but none of the doctors here will do them. They're from Malta where it's illegal. Can you do it?"

"Wait a minute. Why would a girl so young be pregnant?" Claudia asked. Knowing how strict Muslim households were with their daughters, Claudia immediately assumed incest. The girl must have grabbed onto the frustration in Claudia's voice because her lips began to tremble. She grasped the neckline of her tunic and hid her face, rocking to and fro.

Jaza stepped forward to wrap her arms around the girl and whisper something. "She's ashamed because she was raped by their Arab smugglers while they crossed the Libyan desert. The transport trucks stop for the night and then the drivers do what they want. They carry guns so . . ."

Stunned at the thought of what this child had endured, Claudia lay her hand on the girl's lap. It seemed to calm her as she let the tunic fall from her hands and said something to Jaza.

"They shot her papa when he tried to stop them," Jaza explained. "They had to leave his body behind in the desert. I've heard these same things many times. They tell me there's no protection for them in that country. It's run by gangs fighting each other."

Bereft, the girl stared into space. This unwanted pregnancy wouldn't be the last tragedy this adolescent would have to face alone.

"I'd do it myself." Jaza said. "But my trainer was also from Malta and never taught me how."

"Then you're going to learn how to perform a D&C right now. The entire procedure shouldn't take more than thirty minutes." Claudia caught Jaza by the hand. "Get someone in here to prep the room and this child. You need to show me what you've got for instruments and local anesthesia."

The procedure was almost complete when someone began pounding on the door as Claudia took up the curettage. "It's Benny," Jaza said when she returned to the room. "He says you have to leave right away. Something about your friend's child."

Claudia stretched and sighed. "Oh, bugger it. We're almost done."

Jaza settled onto the stool beside Claudia but leaned into the surgeon's line of sight. "You're going to find out what you can about my son. Right?"

"I–I'll try. Now pay attention to what I'm doing."

Minutes later, Claudia rose to yank off her gown and surgical gloves. "That's it. Keep this child comfortable for the next hour and monitor for any irregular bleeding. You can remove the speculum yourself."

But Jaza also jumped up. "Trust no one except Dafnis. Call me here on our satellite phone," she said as Claudia yanked open the door and barged through to find Benny pacing at the front of the clinic.

"Is it Maya?"

"Yes. We have to hurry. There's no time to track down Dafnis, either."

The return flight was a mere twenty minutes but it seemed much longer with Claudia speculating on critical scenarios for Maya. Benny flipped through messages on his phone the entire time they were airborne. At one point she asked for Maya's status but he brushed her off. "Nothing from Homer. These are all to do with my factories."

As CEO of a multinational, Benny knew how to deal with pressure, but this was beyond bizarre considering his young daughter might be breathing her last.

At the Zen garden's elevator, Claudia swiped her fob and paused to catch her breath, only to find Benny sauntering around the pond, still scrolling through his phone. "Benny, hurry." She held the elevator door but he waved her on. Claudia let the doors close and exited onto the third level ICU and operating rooms.

She scooted past the deserted ORs, the floor morbidly quiet. No activity outside Maya's room, either. Paula looked up from her book as Claudia burst in and focused her attention on one beeping monitor after another above the bed.

"Did you enjoy your tour?"

"What the hell is Homer's problem?" Claudia hissed. "There's nothing wrong here."

"No change since you left this morning, but I heard you had an awful start to the day."

Claudia collapsed into one of the chairs. "You didn't call Benny in a panic about Maya?"

"Why would I? Is he back, too?"

"What kind of trick is that bastard Homer trying to pull?" Claudia snatched up Maya's chart, flipped through and tossed it aside. "We'll talk later." She stomped to the elevator, swiped her fob and plowed the heel of her palm into the Level 2 button.

Slam. Claudia charged through Homer's reception room and burst into his office without knocking. He looked up from his satellite phone. "I'll have to call you later," he said to his caller and lowered the handset into its charger.

"You're back."

"Stop with the games, Homer. I had a shitty morning no thanks to you and now you've sent me into a panic for the second time today. Why?"

He picked up a pen and began jotting notes on a pad and talking as if she wasn't there. "I'm a man of great talents, but I don't control what happens out there on the water. If only I could." Fake smile and a sweeping invitation to sit, which she ignored. "You have my unending gratitude for helping us save lives this morning," Homer said.

"Oh, piss on you and your organ thieves."

His attention drifted back to his pen and paper. "Here I thought you were coming to tell me how great your visit to the refugees' island was and that you've decided to do the transplant."

"Why did you get Benny to lie about Maya?"

He bolted from his chair, his eyes blazing. "Because I could. I answer to no one."

"Then you better make an exception or I'm out of here in the morning."

Her threat tapped his brakes no more than the time it took to wince and then the dark bravado was back. "How did it feel to see all those bodies? Were you able to look at the drowned babies and feel nothing?"

The room spun with memories of a time decades ago when she *did* choose to close down.

Claudia lowered herself into a padded chair at the desk as Homer continued to ambush her conscience. "I want you to know what it's going to feel like when they lift Maya into one of those body bags because it will be nothing compared to what Paula and Benny will face."

"You *are* a piece of work, aren't you?" she said.

He finally set his pen aside; his nostrils flared. "I could care less what you call me. Nobody deserves an organ which has been allowed to deteriorate needlessly." Homer swivelled his chair to a counter behind him, lifted some pages from a tray, and tossed them onto his desk.

"There." He raked an arm above them. "Maybe that will convince you."

From the way his voice drifted aimlessly downward, she knew this wasn't the brain scan she wanted. It was the results of two separate heart EKGs and a chest x-ray for Maya.

"I'd say she's been having those arrhythmias off and on since she arrived," Homer said while she examined them. "You can see how the infections are feeding off each other."

"Then we try a different antibiotic," Claudia suggested.

Homer rose from his seat and towered over her; she knew what he was about to say.

"Sit on your hands and your goddaughter could die from a stroke tomorrow. Do the damn transplants. I can find you a set of lungs and a heart within days."

He held her gaze in a stand-off until she rose to clasp his free hand in hers. How could he miss the torment she felt at not being able to save Maya?

The problem was the corpses—she liked hers cold, gray, and pulseless, not the warm, pink, and breathing variety Inquisitor's Island stockpiled. Homer was wrong if he thought she would get used to these new creatures of the organ transplant world.

She let her voice go soft with compassion; it was the one she used to tell parents their child had died. "I want to believe we're in this together. That your heart is in the right place, but in my world, taking someone's life before verifying brain death—is immoral."

She begged him, "Help me. Get me a flat-line brain readout."

Homer sat staring into his hands as she backed away and clicked the door behind her.

He was considering it, that much was clear.

Chapter 13

The pregnant girl flings life jackets from the helicopter and jumps out after them. Bags balances on the runners, the cutting tool poised in his hand. "The problem is you, Claudia," he yells, "not the bionic heart." Paula appears from nowhere. "Yes. The problem is you."

Lunging at Bags, Claudia tumbles out of the helicopter to the sea below, black to the horizon with bodies. All dead except one. The African boy extends his arm to her as she falls and just before she smashes onto his head . . . Claudia wakes, gasping, drenched with sweat, her head throbbing.

Probably the result of dehydration from climbing stairs at The Squats, she thought, tossing the duvet aside and stumbling downstairs to where she'd left a bottle of water on the coffee table. Homer must have let himself in during the night, because beside the bottle lay the fruit of her constant pleas, shaming, and threats since arriving. She scooped the faxed neurological report to eye level while she chugged the entire bottle.

When it came to brain activity, she was no expert, especially for the detail-heavy EEG she held in her hands, but the lines did look awfully flat. It concluded the scalp electrodes confirmed electrocerebral silence adequate to declare brain death. Claudia had her proof of irreversible brain damage in a donor for Maya. Had Homer gone on an all-night search for a donor through his black market contacts and got lucky?

The attached report also showed a perfect match with Maya in every criteria except sex and race. It was the donor's country of origin and age that got her thinking. *Naw.* She'd been dreaming about him. That's all it was.

Sure enough, when she went to check on Maya hours later, the African boy she'd saved wasn't in any of the rooms. She imagined him happily settled inside the lime-green orphanage.

It was not a good morning for her goddaughter, though. One look at the monitors and Claudia knew—the infection was spreading, driving down the child's oxygen levels, forcing her kidneys and liver to work overtime.

"Don't tell me." Paula held up a weary hand. "I can see what's happening just by the color of her skin."

"Have you had any sleep?" Claudia asked.

"Not much. We were both in here last night." She latched onto Claudia's arm. "Please—the truth."

No one could accuse the surgeon of dancing around a prognosis. "She could have a stroke at any time."

Paula lay her head at the foot of Maya's bed, clung to her daughter's legs, and shook.

"I'll do the transplant."

At first, Paula didn't appear to hear Claudia's soft announcement. "I'll do it."

"What?" Paula raised her head a few inches, then bolted upright. "You'll do the transplant? They have a heart and lungs for her?"

Before Claudia could even nod, Paula had wrapped her arms around the surgeon, her flood of tears managing to mine a smile out of Claudia. There were so many reasons not to celebrate, including the possibility that one day she might regret it. Even if Maya's heart and lungs came from a nation where the buying and selling of organs was legal, the UK ethics which Claudia practiced under would still see her transplant as an illegal act. What she was about to do went far beyond her misadventures with the Johnson baby.

And then there was the ticking clock of a new lung. Lungs were the most difficult transplant of all and doomed to fail far more often than a heart.

———●———

CLAUDIA AWOKE EARLY the next morning to find herself enveloped in a peaked weariness from the landmines of indecision going off around her. Inside Homer's suite she found him on his sectional couch, drinking coffee and watching a satellite news program. He peered off the tip of his nose at the EEG report in her hand as she entered, then clicked off the screen.

"I'll do Maya's transplant," Claudia said as she dropped to the couch and spun the report at him across the coffee table. "How long will it take to get the heart and lungs here?"

Unmoved, he blinked a few times, not that she was expecting balloons and party horns from such a shrewd management style. Logistics were likely already in place.

"The team I have in mind is available early tomorrow, but—" He cocked one brow. "You don't look one-hundred percent."

"Indeed." Claudia slouched. "I get on best with afternoons."

"Don't forget you'll be doing both the procurement and the transplant."

She straightened. "But the donor is in Africa, isn't he?"

"No. He's here. It's the boy you revived in the Medivac."

She froze. "I didn't see him on the ward."

"We've got him on life support in one of the surgeries."

"You mean . . . You conducted the brain scan here?"

"Isn't that what you wanted? Pulling our EEG machine out of storage was the easy part. I had a helluva time finding our former neurosurgeon and faxing him the scans, though."

What should have been a victorious moment for Claudia, whimpered and died on her distracted scowl. "It's not ethical," she muttered, too tired to even raise her voice. "He was my patient *and* I have a personal stake in Maya. I shouldn't decide whether this boy lives or dies."

"You're not. *I* am."

Claudia shut her eyes but felt Homer getting to his feet.

"Screw ethics," she heard him say. "You can trash your hospital's rule book, but you're going to let Maya die because it makes you uncomfortable. Is that it?" He bent at the waist to grasp her shoulders. "*This* is the miracle we needed."

Claudia shook off his hands and dragged herself to one of the bar stools where she lay her head in her arms.

"You think I'm sleeping any better than you?" Homer said as he approached.

"*Shush*. I'm thinking."

Then it was Homer's turn to pace.

"Okay." She tilted her head to exhale every drop of air from her lungs and turned to Homer. "What time tomorrow?"

He strode forward to lay an affectionate peck on her forehead. "It's your call. Name your payment, too. There's no family to collect the half-million compensation."

"*Pff.*" She waved the idea of compensation aside.

"But what are you going to live on now that you can't work?" he said.

"Let Benny know that I might show up with my hand out later. Or send my share to The Squats."

She smelled the sweaty relief pouring off him as Homer crouched at her feet, his eyes moist. "It was wrong of me to say you're uncaring."

If only you knew, she thought.

Chapter 14

U sually raring to get on with her transplants, Claudia lingered at the scrub sinks, memories of the helicopter crowding out all other thoughts. How was it going to feel to reverse all that, stop the boy's heart with a cold flush, and remove his heart and lungs while keeping him *oxygenated* on organ support? Don't call it *life* support—the boy on the table was nothing but a grid of oxygenated parts and dehumanized semantics.

On any other day, no single piece of found treasure could put a glow on Claudia's face faster than a delightfully reusable heart. Of course, the tactful organ procurement teams were never as gleeful. Just as well, she thought, to keep all the mournful business curtained off at the back end. Human forms wilting under a neurologist's voice: Your child will never have another conscious thought as long as they live.

Dr. Claudia could then enter at the sweet end of the deal with a nurse bearing the infant heart in a stainless steel basin—scrubbed clean of any face, name, or river of tears. After which they could all sing Happy Days Are Here Again, and congratulate each other on another young life saved.

Neither had the donor and their agonized relatives ever entered her mind much. Today, the family room would be empty.

Inside the OR two male nurses chatted to each other in between the *clink* and *clang* of stainless steel instruments landing in mesh trays. Their accents sounded African.

Claudia was the intruder in this intimate atmosphere—all strangers to her except the inert boy on the table. Peaceful, but so vulnerable the child seemed in a nest of tubes and monitors, the soft hiss and clunk of his ventilator seeming to count down the final minutes of his life.

She clasped his limp hand, the lifeforce pulsing strong and warm through her latex glove. These delicate fingers were the same ones she'd used to clip on the oxygen monitor inside the helicopter as he lay safely swaddled in warm blankets. Today, his bared torso was a vulnerable bullseye in a mass of surgical drapes.

She guessed him to be around nine and for the first time noticed third-degree scar tissue running the length of his arm—a childhood fall into hot coals or an overturned pot of boiling water? His oversized head above spindly arms also told of a painful march to the brink of starvation.

So many battles won only to lose his life today in OR 3.

Claudia nodded to the anesthetist and studied the monitors which showed normal readings for both pulse and oxygen saturation. She'd heard some transplant teams didn't anesthetize brain-dead donors but across the table this man was drawing a vial of painkiller into a syringe.

"Thank you," she said to him before gazing on the boy's face and murmuring, "Sweetie, I'm sorry."

"His name is Iniko."

Still clutching the small hand, Claudia turned to the closest nurse. "Why does his chart say 'John Doe?'"

"We take turns giving the children a name if they don't come in with one. It was my turn so I gave him my brother's name, Iniko. It means 'born in times of trouble.' My brother was about the same age when he died of diphtheria in Nigeria."

This man's kind act shattered her impression of the surgical staff at Daphne Technologies as cold fugitives running from their past. She watched the anesthesiologist search for a vein for the intravenous line. At the poke of the needle, the boy's arms jerked from the table; his fingers clamped around her own.

"Stop," Claudia commanded and glared at the anesthesiologist. "Pass me your penlight." Light in hand, she leaned forward and pulled one eyelid back, certainly not expecting his pupils to constrict.

"Shit. No one does anything until I speak to Homer." She turned to the nurse closest to the door. "Get Homer on the intercom and turn on the speaker."

"What the hell's going on?" Claudia boomed from where she stood at the operating table when he came on the line. "This boy is showing signs of life. He just moved his arms and there's pupillary reactivity. We need to talk in your office."

"No. Don't you dare step out of the surgical field. We don't have time for you to scrub in again. I'm on my way down."

Homer burst into the OR, having donned a surgical gown, cap and mask, and carrying the same EEG report. "What's your problem?" He stood, hands on hips, just inside the door.

"If this patient is brain dead, why was there a pain reflex when the intravenous line went in? I don't have the skills to read that EEG and neither do you, but I'm starting to doubt the neurologist's conclusions. Or is this just a continuation of the lies you've been spinning since I arrived?"

A few members of the medical team shuffled out of position as if getting ready to bolt.

Homer squared his jaw. "I'm surprised someone of your caliber would be asking such questions." He stepped closer to scrutinize her features. "Are you alert enough to continue this transplant? I don't want any fuck-ups today."

"Excuse me?"

"Had you given the anesthetist time to administer neuromuscular blockers, there wouldn't have been any involuntary movement. Residual reflexes from the cadaver are due to spinal signals, not brain activity. As for his pupils I doubt it was anything but minimal."

"That may be, but you're going to have to prove to me this donor is really brain dead."

"Claudia, there's no activity in either the cortex or brainstem. All we can do is try to save Maya. Make the best of it."

"Would you want someone to do this to *your* child without your knowledge?"

"No parent wants to see a child they brought into this world whole, leave the world unwhole," he said. "It would be excruciating for me, but I'd do it because I know that's the way my daughter lived her own life. Devoted to helping."

It was terrible to see him holding the grief in. He *had* lost a child.

"Be brave," Homer challenged.

In all the decades since they'd taken her baby she hadn't allowed her mind to go there, but now she saw the tiny pale face from her past.

Homer's voice broke into her thoughts with a present day scenario almost as painful. "Are you willing to let Maya die when you could have saved her?"

The man sure knew when to give the knife a half-turn. A world without Maya and Paula would sever her last link with the tenderness others took for granted in life.

Homer stood his ground, slapping the rolled EEG report double-time against his palm. "I don't want the patient brought in from the ICU if you're not going ahead with this transplant." His hands fell to his sides. "Are you going to tell the parents or should I?"

How could she look her friends in the face after getting their hopes up?

"Remove the ventilator," Claudia finally said. "If this boy really is brain dead, he won't survive more than a few minutes."

But Homer easily saw through the uncertainty in her voice. "Do you need a break, Dr. Vlakia?" he asked matter-of-factly.

She shook her head, but Homer's eyes drilled down on her. "We've had to defibrillate his heart once already. If you get your way and it stops again, it may not restart. Are you willing to sacrifice Maya's life for this boy?"

Oh, God. This she knew only too well. The powder inside her surgical gloves was sticky with sweat.

It's ridiculous what the NHS is spending to keep patients alive who have little chance of regaining consciousness, she'd once told a BBC reporter. Not so easy to fight for when the donor heart in front of her had a face and shared history.

Homer was right—dithering to prove brain death could make the heart unusable, but the chances of Iniko breathing on his own again was not zero, either. Patients misdiagnosed as brain dead had been known to start breathing on the operating table.

A high-pitched whirring yanked her back into the moment. The electric sternal saw which would split the boy's breastbone glinted in the hands of the nurse testing it. Claudia latched onto the vibrations, as familiar as an old friend's voice. Her feet landed on solid ground.

She had to stand up for Iniko because no one else would.

"All right." she said, her gaze anywhere but on Homer. "Before we remove ventilation, a moment of silence for Iniko, please."

As soon as the oxygen feed was cut, Homer began pacing and counting. "One minute," he announced.

In common with construction sites, ORs often had the clanging and tapping of steel mallets, grinding retractors, buzzing saws, and nurses barking for instruments from stores. Raucous giggling sometimes competed with someone's favorite Top Forty. Claudia didn't like it, but she tolerated it because there was no getting around it.

Today, when Homer said, "Three minutes," the loudest noise was the squeal of the heart monitor flat-lining.

Claudia jumped in with the first jolt, but after the third attempt to restart the boy's heart someone behind her suddenly cut the charge.

She stood, paddles still in hand, as Homer leaned in with his ominously phlegmatic tone. "And then there were none. Fabricate whatever story you want for Benny and Paula," he said before leaving, "but let me know so I don't get caught up in this disaster."

People began to file out and still she stood motionless until one of the nurses took the paddles from her hands.

Claudia brushed past another team coming for the rest of the boy. There was no death certificate to sign in Homer's lawless republic, but she slid the chart from its slot on the gurney which would soon carry his hollow corpse to cold storage. Had the nurse at least remembered to record Iniko's time of death?

No, but along the margin someone had scrawled, *Iniko—Born in times of trouble.*

That was it, then. The only thing left to do was come up with a story to avoid Paula's wrath. Since lies between friends were high maintenance, Claudia would soon find out one was never enough.

Chapter 15

S he should have known by now that Homer would do this.

Just four weeks into resuming the brain scanning, Homer halted the chopper searches. There was no financial gain in rushing out to save the comatose children if all it accomplished was jamming up his ICU. Instead of ending their life inside an OR, he let them die out on the water. For days, she moped around the rooftop garden, fighting the urge to confront him. Homer's world, an assembly line of never-ending transactions, felt dark and hopeless to Claudia.

That all changed the morning she followed a child's gurney into one of the ICU rooms. While the nurses transferred the boy onto a bed, she noticed two other patients also hooked up to life support—both teenagers. All three were alive because of her. A kernel of light inside Claudia began vibrating. Maya, too, was still alive, the infections clearing, and as far-fetched as it would have seemed when Claudia first arrived, that was the day the clinic felt like home.

However, her offer to serve at The Squats didn't sit well with either Paula or Homer. With the surrogates and female clients off-limits, Claudia easily saw that he didn't want to lose her female company. Her searches for online news of the Johnson case sometimes ended in scotch-on-the rocks at Homer's bar stool and dinner from the surrogate cafeteria if he happened to turn up. No man had ever given her a key to their apartment. She could come and go as she pleased and if she fell asleep while cruising the internet late into the night Homer cooked breakfast the next morning while she showered.

It was during one of her internet check-ins that Claudia found Dafnis on the sectional couch, mesmerized with the tilt and flash of a music video. Homer wanted to give his son more exposure to the "real world," but what was playing out on the screen probably wasn't what he had in mind.

Dafnis's eyeballs swiveled a nanosecond as she flopped down beside him. The teen's butt clung to the edge of the couch, his frozen outstretched arm reminded her of a future wax figure inside Madame Tussauds—perhaps labeled *21st Century Man With A Remote.*

This was likely his first view of both a music video and plethora of bouncing, barely-clad breasts. An African-American in a pink fedora and baggy pants somehow suspended just above the knees—sang while leaping from the edge of one dumpster to another in a graffiti-smeared alley. Two women below him with green and purple dreadlocks took turns shimmying their boobs and butts during the chorus.

Each time, Dafnis inched forward in anticipation of the jiggling body parts. Either the song would end, or he would fall flat on his arse at the next chorus. To his credit he clicked off the screen when it was over and trained his sunny mug on Claudia. Since the guy was long overdue for contact with females of the free world, other than Jaza, Claudia was likely his only female friend since leaving Syria as an adolescent.

At the click of a door, they both looked over their shoulders as Homer threw some documents onto a side table and kicked off his shoes. "What are you two up to?"

Like a schoolboy about to launch into his day, a naive Dafnis twisted his torso, but Claudia managed to cut him off in time. "Just watching a program on the latest American craze of dumpster jumping."

"Good. Good." Homer settled across from them. "He's allowed two hours a week of satellite television. It's time Dafnis knows what other teen boys spend their days focused on."

Dafnis bobbed his chin and grinned until all of them were smiling—each with their own separate reason, but the teen soon bolted as soon as Claudia switched to her usual all-news station.

Claudia and Homer's eyes met as what she'd been dreading appeared on-screen in the form of her official hospital headshot. "In a civil court filing today," the presenter said, "the family of an infant patient at London's Hackney University Hospital is seeking five-million pounds in damages for implanting an experimental prosthetic heart into the child. The surgeon in question, Dr. Claudia Vlakia, has had her medical license suspended. Neither the hospital nor Thames Heart Institute would comment. The alleged incident took place—"

Claudia clicked the program off. "Idiots pronounced my name wrong," she said, beating a path to Homer's liquor cabinet. "Fuck it. The Johnsons' lawyer is trying to get ahead of our patent announcement so he can bury it under the hospital scandal.

"Better to keep me looking like the crazy bitch who carves up sick kids than the inventor of the world's first bionic heart."

"Poor Claudia." Homer tried a side hug when she returned to the sectional. "I know how you must feel. The media aren't interested in my paradise at The Squats. They only want to dig up dirt on the organ trade."

It was worry enough that he was gazing at her as one would a stray kitten in a downpour. She eyed the lambswool throw on his lap with the suspicion he might want to use it on her.

"The lab won't want my besmirched mug around," she said, "But I might be able to get Maya reinstated on the transplant lists when I return. Least I can do. Right?"

He looked on with utter commiseration at what had become a hands-off topic for them—Maya's failed transplant. "What about surgeries from The Squats that aren't transplants? You could stay and do those."

"No. My place is back home in the lab with my team," she said. "Since it's my bloody-mindedness that put them out of work, I should be the one to go on bended knee to the Thames institute."

A long half-hour later she coasted the television remote across the slippery leather as one would a naughty puppy gnawing on shoes. Now that everybody in the world knew that her bionic heart worked and the Johnsons were blood-sucking scum, it was time to move on to other good news.

"How do I find something fresh and easy on the nerves like *Mongolian News Round-up*, or, *This Week in the Amazon*," she asked Homer, who was chopping onions in the galley kitchen.

He paused, and with a glimmer of amusement wiped a tear from his eye.

Where was Bags in all this? she wondered. The little turd was avoiding her. She downed her latest whisky shot and moped off for another, continuing her mental list of backstabbing scientists smart enough to replace her.

The dregs from the bottle dribbled out. "What the hell? This bottle's empty," she said.

Nothing but a shadow shrug from Homer. "All that's left is the cheap stuff, which is hardly what I'd call cheap."

"I'll go without."

Back at the sectional, Claudia put her feet up and closed her eyes. Soon, a metronome of hot breath played against her neck. It was Homer, his forearms propped against the couch. "If you could live anywhere in the world, where would that be?"

She opened one eye. "Wherever my work was, of course."

Homer skirted the end of the couch and joined his hip with hers. "You wouldn't follow a lover to a strange place as I did with my Syrian wife?"

That pumped some oxygen into her brain. "Do I look like that kind of girl?"

The quip seemed to go unheard while his chin bobbed to the beat of something more profound. "I have a proposal for you."

Claudia went rigid.

"Not that," he chuckled. "While you wait for the case to be heard, why don't you bring your entire research team here. I can find the children for your human trials. In return, when their bionic hearts start to fail you could repay me by replacing them with the real thing. There's good money to be made from congenital heart disease."

It was Claudia's *can-do* optimism that seduced her into the most trouble, but this particular too-good-to-be-true idea fell into her lap with more stupefaction than a blazing Hindenburg blimp.

"The Thames institute owns the patents and every piece of equipment," she reminded him.

"You must have copies of your research, though."

"Yes, and it's called patent infringement if I get caught using it. The commercial value of this bionic heart is in the stratosphere. The lawyers would go so berserk it would make a malpractice suit look like time out at a kindergarten."

"Rubbish," Homer said. "You're advancing their research on your own time."

"You do realize it will take six months alone to optimize the lab. That's the entire team working flat out with no screw-ups."

Homer raised his eyebrows. "It would be faster to source black market equipment. So, what do you think?"

"Are you kidding? My own lab with no one on my tail? My lead scientist is a lone duck. He'd follow me anywhere, but the others—especially the ones with families . . ." She unfurled palms clean of familial attachments and left the sentence unfinished.

"I can give your team free room and board, but someone else will have to pay for the lab construction and salaries."

Yup. Always a catch. "Such as who?"

"Benny," he said.

"No way. It's too sci-fi for him. He already turned me down years ago before I sold the idea to the Thames board." Before Benny, no one in India had dared to try and build a multinational empire from a bunch of bleating goats. He started as a dairyman who latched onto how much women were willing to pay for ayurvedic face and body products. Claudia had a whole closet full of them, but she used nothing but cold cream.

"Anyway, you know as well as I that he won't invest in anything he thinks is illegal."

Homer planted hands on hips. "Yet, he's willing to purchase black market organs."

"That's because Maya's transplant is personal. This is different. It's a business venture," Claudia said.

"Claudia dearest, then make your business offer personal. Tell me, was it the money that motivated you to build a bionic heart?"

"Of course not. That's not how inventors think. I wanted to see if I could make it work—Mostly, I wanted to save infants."

"Then let's go save some children. Promise him you'll put the first heart you build into Maya. What have you got to lose?"

"It's so risky," she said as a way to stall.

Chin on his chest, eyes burning into hers, he knew her argument didn't make sense. "You've lost your livelihood, your life's dream, and your reputation. You've proved the thing works, so what else could possibly be at risk?"

Claudia had always assumed a heart would come available for Maya long before her artificial one was ready. Telling Benny and

Paula that her bionic heart could save their child— would be a cruel lie. Far worse than the one that already existed between them.

What did she have to lose? Two dear friends, and probably Homer, too. But since she couldn't tell him the truth, she said the first thing that came to mind. "I'm thinking of my team of scientists."

She wasn't, of course, but loyalty was something Homer understood. The topic was closed, she told him, all the while knowing the lab idea wasn't going to be easy to root out.

Chapter 16

S luggish body, sluggish mind.

Claudia was on a brisk jog to the gondola for the first time since arriving more than a month ago when she rounded a corner to find herself already there. *Damn.* That couldn't have taken me much more than—she raised her watch—ten minutes. She eyed the gondola but immediately remembered the crematorium. Bushwhacking to the beach it was, then. How could she possibly get lost on such a compact island?

She stepped off the path into a forest infused with the musky, sweet aroma of milky orchids, and headed for a sunny clearing, which would be useful to get her bearings later on.

"Claudia."

The hushed female voice wasn't Paula's, nor could it be any of the surrogates who weren't allowed outside the gate. She was squinting through the subtropical gloom, when, behind her a *whoosh* and *clatter* sent her flat on her rump.

A hemp-runged ladder swung madly as if thrown down from the heavens. "Hurry. Get up here," the voice said.

She scrambled to her feet and mounted the wobbly rungs because the urgency in this voice told her safety lay above, not below.

Climbing the thing was like trying to get a handhold on two snakes; each tug sent the hemp ladder spinning. When her fumbling palm hit solid wood instead of the roping, one final thrust sent her face first onto a thatched surface. Her pounding heart synced to the rhythmic grinding of the ladder coiling into a heap beside her.

She rolled onto her back to find herself staring into the face of the midwife who then scooted cross-legged onto a piece of thick matting in the corner.

Other than a large open-air window, the sides and ceiling of this cramped treehouse were of entwined palm leaves, brittle with age. Hidden from the ground and accessible only by retractable ladder, this was one formidable hideaway.

"You can sit over there." Jaza pointed to an untidy pile of gray blankets, army surplus thin and scratchy.

Unless she wanted to look like a duck straddling a squat toilet, standing wasn't an option for Claudia. "What is this place?" she asked while crawling on all fours. Other than the blankets and a two-liter bottle of water, the space was empty and not much wider than a king mattress.

The midwife leaned in. "You're still here." The quiet delight in her eyes quickly turned into an embarrassed slouch. "But you didn't call me."

Oh, crap. The promise to find this woman's son was one Claudia had intended to keep, if not for the battle to save Maya. It simply slipped her mind.

"It's a long story."

The midwife responded in the knowing tone of a fellow sufferer. "A Homer story, I bet."

She understood what Jaza meant. With Maya out of danger, her botched transplant made poor ammunition for Homer. Claudia was finally out from under his thumb, but every last person on both islands was in some way beholden to their president and CEO. Homer held the ending to every story.

"Surely you've seen your son by now?"

Jaza shrank from Claudia's astonishment. "No. I've only been back once, but I'm not allowed to go anywhere without Dafnis."

Why would Homer, a man Claudia thought she knew by now, do such a thing? "This is bullshit," Claudia said. "A boy needs his mother."

"I tried to sneak out of Dafnis's room one night," the midwife confided, "but he caught me. The door was locked from the inside."

Their eyes met, Jaza's suddenly hot with indignation. Since Claudia knew what the boy looked like, it occurred to her how often she'd seen him inside the nursery or on the playground with Dafnis.

The treehouse trembled as Jaza surged to her feet. "Dafnis has always been difficult to deal with, but now . . ." She scanned the intimate space. "I sit here sometimes and try to imagine what he was like before his brain injury.

"The story is that Dafnis fell out of a tree right after they moved to the island. It's cruel, isn't it, that the treehouse he built to escape his father might have granted his wish so completely?" The midwife closed her eyes and slumped against the palm fronds. "But it's also taken from him everything that makes life worth living. Can you imagine waking up every day and not knowing a single thing about *where* or *who* you are?"

Claudia felt her compassion meter flicker. "What a trial for him. And you, too," she managed. "Does he know you're here on the island?"

Jaza shook her head. "I like to give him extra time to remember who I am." She leaned forward in a panic. "You won't tell anyone about the treehouse, will you.?"

"Of course not. I'm sorry I haven't helped as I promised, but I'm going to make it up to you—and no one is going to stop us."

———◉———

CLAUDIA'S THEORY THAT the guards now saw her as part of Homer's inner circle, proved true. They marched through the main gate and into the lobby, eyes tracking their every move, but unimpeded. With the nursery in sight inside the quarry, Jaza sped into a trot, but Claudia caught up, "Go slow. Don't bring attention to us."

From behind came a man's voice. "How did *you* get in here?" They turned in unison as Dafnis grabbed Jaza's upper arm and pulled her backwards off balance.

"Settle down," Claudia said. "She's with me. Is there a problem with that?"

Dafnis glared. In this moment, the carefree youth Claudia knew was no more.

"I'm responsible for Jaza. Homer is going to freak out."

Out of nowhere, Jaza gasped, shook off Dafnis's grip, and dashed back toward the stairwell.

Swaying hand in hand from the exit were two figures, one an adult, the other a boy.

"Mummy," the child shrieked as he broke free and ran into Jaza's arms. They were both sobbing when she swept her son into the air. Overwhelmed with hugs and kisses, Jaza lost her footing and dragged them both to the quarry's hard, dusty surface.

"Why did you leave me?" he cried, struggling to say anything at all in the crush of his mother's arms.

Claudia reached the pair at the same time Homer caught up with his runaway companion.

"We've been playing Ride the Horsey up in my suite, haven't we, son?" The boy gave a curt nod, still too focused on his mother.

Claudia couldn't imagine the high-and-mighty Homer volunteering his time for child's play unless—Did Dafnis tell him the boy was his grandson?

"The two of us have had quite a morning." The look of a kind elder flipped to entrenched bitterness as Homer's gaze fell on Jaza. What problem could Homer have with this powerless young midwife, already barred from contact with her son?

"I—I'm sorry, Father," Dafnis began. "I didn't know—"

"Yes." Hands on hips, Claudia squared off with Homer. "And *I* didn't know I was committing a crime. I went for a walk, ran into Jaza at the gondola, and suggested we visit her son inside the nursery."

"*Tsk. Tsk.*" Mischief shone in Homer's eyes. "What shall we do with such rebels in our midst? Unlock the torture chamber?"

Dafnis gaped and bolted forward. "Father?"

"Oh, Dafnis. I'm only kidding. Why don't the four of us go to the playground before the boy has to return to the nursery?"

When Homer reached for the boy's hand, Jaza pulled her son into her chest. "Good day, Homer." She lifted the child into her arms and turned toward the playground.

Dafnis froze, shuffling his attention from one to the other before dashing in pursuit of Jaza and his son.

Homer's dark humor wasn't aimed at Claudia. His intimidation depended on a vast imbalance of power, and, in his son's case, the perpetual naivety of Dafnis's brain damage. Whatever Homer was doing to grab his son's loyalty seemed to be working.

Homer watched them leave, turned on his heel, and *dammit* if suave Homer wasn't back. He'd changed channels once again. "I knew you'd get antsy for something to do," he said. "Two peas in a pod, aren't we?"

"I'll ask you to leave me out of your pod for now." She kept it affable. "What have you got against Jaza?"

Homer had a habit of ignoring questions he didn't like. "Come on, I'll show you a path to the beach which avoids the crematorium." He swung a carefree arm to catch her hand in his.

"What's this?" Try as she might, she couldn't resist playing along and said: "Are you inviting me to Ride the Horsey, too?" No doubt, he would have, but Claudia had no intention of jumping into bed with a man who would keep a loving mother and her child apart.

It was time for Homer to come clean.

———————◆———————

AS THE TWO OF THEM passed under the treehouse Claudia
peered sidelong for the hidden rope the midwife used instead of the
ladder. Had Claudia herself not seen Jaza loop it around an upper
branch and climb the rest of the way down, she would not have
believed it was there.

"This forest is quite unique," she said, figuring a dollop of false
friendliness might loosen his tongue. "I've never seen palms mixed
in with evergreens. What kind of tree is this one here?"

"The tall and bushy kind?" he joked. "I'm embarrassed to say I
don't really know, but it's the only one like it on the island."

Spontaneous humility couldn't be easy for someone as
calculating as Homer, but she noticed he gave it his best try around
her. Yet, she quickly withdrew the arm heading for the small of his
back—as tempting as the outcome might be. This hidden side of him
was like a virus she couldn't risk catching without knowing its source.

She scooted ahead with a backward glance. "Looks like Holm
Oak. A protected species back home also known as Holly Oak
because of these—" She pinched one of its waxy leaves from the
ground and wheeled around into his goofy grin. "What's so funny?"

"We are," Homer said. "I've never met anyone else who likes to
foist their knowledge onto others as much as I do."

"O—kay."

On the way down a steep switchback to the beach he grinned
over his shoulder. "Of course, it's also a way to control the
conversation and hide our insecurities."

In a few good strides she caught the loose end of his t-shirt. "*I'm*
not insecure."

Up ahead, a swagger seeped into Homer's pigeon-toed downhill
gait.

Just two memories of past insecurities came to Claudia's mind—the most vivid was a best friend she dumped because the girl scored higher on their arithmetic test. She was drilling deep into her motivations around the Johnson baby's implant when she stubbed her toes against something and landed on hands and knees in the sand.

Homer spun around. "That there," he said, offering his hand to Claudia and motioning toward the tarp and boat trailer she'd tripped over, "was what I used for transport before the hydrofoil."

Raised on a sheep farm at the shores of the English Channel, Claudia knew the eighteen-footer under the tarp was nowhere near seaworthy. "Good God. It's more than sixty miles to Malta, isn't it?"

"Well, yes. I had to keep an eye on the weather, of course. It hasn't been used in almost six months, but the outboard motor should still be under there somewhere. It's forty horsepower."

Claudia let fly a hoot. "I'll have to call you a liar, Homer. There's no way you took a forty-horsepower motor on the open seas for sixty clicks."

"Ah, but she's military grade. A rigid hulled inflatable built for navy seal units."

She watched him scoot over a section of jagged rock, an undeniable intimacy with this patch of his republic, and when she caught up with him asked, "Black market, I suppose?"

"Now don't you go passing judgment on this reliable little runabout. It was all Hocking and I had in the early days." Homer raised an eyebrow to an idea beyond the horizon and said, "I never intended for this to be anything more than a safe place to carry out my plague research. Dafnis was only thirteen when he pulled Jaza out of a leaky dinghy. The little ones were facedown at the center, drifting like flotsam in a harbor."

This was surely the stuff of nightmares for the sensitive boy, she thought.

"What happened to Jaza's family?"

Homer gave his head a weary shake. "We rescued the kids first and never did find the adults when we returned. She's alone, you see. Her four younger siblings all died of hypothermia.

"Back then, this place was nothing but a hollow stone garrison open to the wind. We didn't know about the abandoned leper colony, yet."

She saw her opening. "Why isn't Jaza over there with the others?"

"That girl—" Homer wagged his chin. "I'd never seen a young person so motivated to become a surrogate. An orphan, no less."

"What the hell? You impregnated an adolescent?"

From afar, someone might have thought Homer's animated arms were fending off an attack of killer bees. "It was her own idea. She wanted the money for nursing school on the mainland." His words tumbled out, faster and faster. "Then she miscarried and the next one was not right in the head, but would she give him up? No. So there she was, a fifteen-year-old with a disabled child and no family."

"You're doing it again," Claudia finally said. "You know as well as I that the boy is normal. Give her what she's owed and let her leave."

"Jaza can leave anytime she wants," he scoffed. "But the boy stays here."

"For God's sake, Homer, they've bonded. Purchasing someone's child is immoral."

A terrifyingly smug smile crossed his lips. "But not illegal in my republic."

She slumped, once again knocked down by Homer's secret motivations. "What's your excuse for entrapping Dafnis?"

Her words finally raised a frown on Homer's face. "I'm responsible for the boy and I intend to protect him as long as I can."

Claudia remembered a male wolf at her Romanian sanctuary who would go for your throat when you least expected it. It was a death sentence to release him into an area with an existing pack, but she did it anyway because it was the best solution for him—not her.

"Fair enough for a twelve-year-old," she said, "but Dafnis is an adult."

He was scrutinizing her as if trying to assess something. "Dafnis likes you. Maybe too much, so don't go putting any wild ideas into his head or I'll find a way to keep the two of you apart."

Whatever ghosts were hunting him, real or imaginary, they had him scared enough to use an unbelievably mean threat. Homer's fears were the kind that lodge in the bone and never leave.

As he strode ahead a few paces to stare at the open sea, Claudia closed her eyes. The same breeze that tore across the helipad now skipped across her cheek, caressing her into stillness. She needed this moment to herself.

Then she went after him.

"When the tide is out," he said, sensing her standing behind him, "one can get a bit of a jog going along the sand."

Homer turned, the corners of his mouth twitched upward, but Claudia remained gripped by their inability to move past the walled-off part of him. He must have been far more open and less ruthless within his marriage for it to be "bliss."

Despite the surface urge to escape both Homer and his island, Claudia had to admit he had touched her scientist's heart. He understood better than anyone the fire to create something which would change the world. For that, she respected him.

He took up the hand hanging limp by her side and when she tried to pull away, he tightened his grip around it while they stared into each other's frustration.

"The wind down here is like my personal oracle," Homer said.

"Not the bridge in the Japanese garden at the crack of dawn?" Her sarcasm broke the tension and he released her hand.

"I admit I haven't played that flute in years. A harmless extrapolation that served its purpose."

Too bad his disdain for the truth wasn't always so innocent. She was about to tell him this when he propped himself against a nearby boulder and said, "After all these years I still dream of my wife. My daughter, too. The last time I saw her alive was seven years ago, in Syria."

Finally, a crack in his wall.

"She disappeared the day the Arab Spring protests started." A vague smile, warmed by love, crept onto his face. "She was seven feet tall at fourteen-years-old and full of fight if anyone tried to bully her."

Claudia could not imagine this girl in the male-dominated Middle East. In more tolerant societies her height would be a curiosity—not a threat.

Homer shook his head. "If only she'd had an older brother to protect her."

"What about Dafnis?" she asked.

"Well, he . . . If I remember right he was away at a school sports competition."

If he remembered? Surely Homer had re-lived this traumatic day detail by detail.

"The first person I thought to call for help," he said, "was an old friend with a lot of power in Assad's government. He advised me to leave, but how was I supposed to abandon my patients and my research? The city of Homs was where I wanted to rest my soul for eternity.

"The last time I phoned he told me my missing daughter likely joined the rebels."

Claudia squatted in front of Homer's rock and studied his face. "No way. At fourteen?"

"I have no doubt that's precisely what she did," he said.

She wrapped her arms around Homer's torso, his body stiff with renewed grief. "You should go to Syria and find her," Claudia whispered.

Homer avoided her gaze and jumped to his feet. "I intend to but only when the fighting stops."

As much as she welcomed anything about his past, it crossed her mind later that she'd once again failed to find out why he was keeping Jaza's boy captive. If it wasn't for body parts, then what? At times like this Claudia had to remind herself she was living in an autocracy where secrets were not only tolerated, but the glue that held it all together.

Until she had proof, she'd best let it go for the sake of her research.

Chapter 17

A sky choked red with the wind-whipped sands of Africa was an appropriately depressing sendoff, perhaps, for the three waiting atop Homer's clinic. The *wop-wop* of the chopper's blades mixed in tandem with a dry-heave followed by Maya's soft sobs and her mother's words of comfort.

The unrelenting antibiotics were making the poor kid's life hell. It was like a dress rehearsal for a lifetime of anti-rejection medication after a transplant—if Maya made it that far.

Neither could the tarnished surgeon expect much from the dry, gutted life awaiting her in London. Problem was, no matter what she did, her surgical skills would soon atrophy while she waited for her medical license to be reinstated. Every time she thought of a good reason to go home and prostrate herself before the Thames' board members, Homer's lab idea reared up and choked the living daylights out of it. She might return only to find they'd hired a new surgeon—there was that clause about her being "incapacitated."

Of course, she expected the lads would soon sort them out and refuse to work with anybody but Claudia. Her team of scientists held all the knowledge and way more loyalty to Claudia and her creation than to the institute. It was so easy to imagine them settled in paid positions in Homer's republic.

She watched Benny hop from the chopper and rush to the side of his retching daughter. He'd be all over the lab idea if he thought it could save Maya. All she had to do was—lie.

"Ohhh . . ." Claudia groaned and slammed her eternally-stained backpack, glitter bag, and squashed briefcase onto the helipad's tarmac where the slowing rotors were laying down a dusting of red sand.

"Benny," she called out when he returned to the chopper. "I have something I want to ask you."

At the end of their chat a heavy hand grasped her shoulder from behind.

"Oh, Homer. Have I forgotten something?"

In his fist was a wind-tossed print-out of the kind which made Claudia's day—Parents of Dying Babies Cry Foul, the online news story blared. Underneath the headline was a photo of the greedy Johnsons surrounded by a crowd of irate people holding signs. One said, *Baby Killers!*

"Looks like there's trouble in London." Homer's face split with a rueful grin. "You better stay here until it blows over. Let your fans fight it out."

Claudia held the sheet at arm's length and examined the photo. "How do I know this isn't something you ordered from the black market?"

Her sarcasm made him smile.

"No one knows I'm here," she told Benny. "Keep it that way."

Homer looked from one to the other as he realized Claudia was staying put.

Once Homer had made up his mind, he didn't back down. The only way to change it was to give him something he craved even more. Like saving Maya's life in return for brain imaging on comatose patients. The day Homer went dancing higgledy-piggledy across the helipad, Claudia became the most powerful asylum seeker in the entire republic.

What Homer now craved was Claudia herself.

As he hauled Claudia's luggage off the helipad, Paula, who didn't yet know about her husband's pledge to fund a new lab, came up with a theory that was uncomfortably close to the bone. "Are you staying because of Homer?"

"Don't be daft." One emotional roller-coaster at a time, Claudia thought. She owed herself a bit of fun, but any romantic connection with Homer would have to wait until the new prototype was safely implanted into a test patient at his clinic.

For the past five years Claudia had slept, ate, and drank bionic hearts. What could be more sexy than bringing a new toy to the world which could save lives? The adrenaline rush felt like the wild unpredictability of new love. If Homer's attraction happened to wither in the meantime, nothing would be lost. She had her bases covered.

Paula's matchmaker grin remained even as she nudged her daughter forward.

"Thank you, auntie, for fixing me." Drawn with heartbreaking detail and the unsullied love of a child, the pencil creation showed the two of them hand in hand inside a heart.

"You're very welcome, sweetheart." A trace of regret seeped into Claudia's soul when Maya entwined her tiny fingers and pulled her down for a kiss—it was the same insistent tug she'd felt from the African boy during his final moments of life.

She was sure it was a tear Benny brushed away when it was his turn. "We love you, Claudia."

"We love you, Auntie Claudia," Maya jumped up and bellowed in a call-and-response style before tearing off toward her mother.

The love-in would soon end if Benny knew how he was being tricked into paying for a bionic heart that would never be able to save his daughter. "We can't get complacent," Claudia told him. "We're starting from scratch. In the meantime, I'm still going to do everything I can to get her to the top of the transplant lists."

A surprisingly faint twinge of sadness remained as the helicopter faded to nothing over the Mediterranean. Homer was her new go-to friend.

———◉———

CLAUDIA WAS WHITE-HOT busy again. The top-flight scrounger retired from beachcombing with nothing to show but a single rubber boot. Not even a pair. Nothing like her dumpster hauls back in London, was it?

Over the next few months, as much as she cautioned Homer to delay purchases until she'd consulted the entire team, each morning at his penthouse den she found another item ticked on her list. When her lead scientist arrived a week later he added to the frightening volume of equipment they would need, including the most important item of all—a 3D printer which would cast their heart layer upon layer from beakers of gelled alginate and collagen.

The lab was a dangerous infringement on the Thames's patent, yet the only team member to turn down Claudia's offer of work was a female scientist six months pregnant. Claudia wanted to laugh and tell her she wouldn't be the first or last pregnant resident at Daphne Technologies. She didn't dare, though. All the team needed to know about Homer's questionable set-up prior to arriving was that they were coming to a research facility that would put them back to work on their artificial heart.

His idea to house the men in the same dormitory as the young, female nurse recruits turned out to be an unparalleled success. Homer could piss her off more than anyone else, but the man knew how to keep his employees on the hook.

Once again, Dr. Hocking greeted each member of the team but did so from the dock at The Squats, where there were no worrisome guards with AK-47s. Otherwise, Hocking seemed to keep out of sight. Perhaps he'd had enough excitement for one lifetime and was content to be the guest services coordinator and babysit the frozen embryos stored on Level 1.

It was Homer's idea to build the lab on the top floor of the new hospital which sat at the very pinnacle of The Squats. A less controversial location would ensure the team's attention was on their prototype and not the organ trafficking transpiring around them.

Was it any wonder she found it a huge relief to leave it all behind and apply herself to the new lab at The Squats. Out of sight across thirty miles of water, the worst of Daphne Technologies was kicked to the fringes of her mind.

Getting rid of Homer wouldn't be nearly as easy.

Chapter 18

A s soon as the water in her cup of tea began to dance, Claudia's first thought was—rescue the used prototype from the lab's cold storage. Whether there was an earthquake or fire didn't matter; outside the hospital's ground floor staff room, bodies rushed past the open doorway. She stepped into the hallway and was instantly buffeted on all sides by a stream of construction workers and hospital staff surging toward the front exit.

At the familiar sound of a helicopter overhead, a man wearing paint-splattered overalls elbowed past her and shouted, "They're here."

Her mind swept the gamut of possibilities—the Pope? Angelina Jolie and the United Nations? Her money was on it being the latest bevvy of female nurse recruits. Outside the main entrance, islanders milled around the vast unfinished lot while the engine of an unseen chopper cut out followed by several moments of hushed chatter before the crowd burst into applause.

A chevron of human bodies parted as out strode Homer and Dafnis. The son branched off into a jeep likely bound for Jaza's clinic, but once Homer had made eye contact with Claudia he beelined for the door, all but ignoring those trying to shake his hand.

"Here's the fax paper you asked for." Homer, a man of fickle moods, seemed to have settled on devotion today. She half expected to see the sheets being borne on top of a red velvet cushion. Instead, a young man behind Homer handed over a paper shopping bag.

"I don't get over this way very often." Homer turned with a final grandiose wave before ducking inside the front entrance. Of course, he wanted to see the lab first. They climbed the stairs to the tight windowless office beside the lab where Claudia lived and finally had her own internet connection.

Homer stepped inside and stopped in his tracks. "Is this all we've given you?" His eyes swept across the cluttered desk and an unmatched conflagration of filing cabinets before honing in on what he likely saw as the real problem—a tumbledown rollaway cot and stacks of dirty dishes teetering atop a microwave station.

"I only slept in my dorm room for one week."

The bed's lumpy mattress and springs *zinged* shut as she shoved it aside. "But I still use their kitchen."

By the time she'd cleared two dirty mugs and a metal carafe from atop the lowest cabinet and hastily shoved them inside the microwave, Homer was settled into her office chair, a gift bottle of her favorite scotch perched on the desk in front. The sharp metal edge of the cabinet where she sat cut into her bony buttocks as she explained, "Even the dormitory next door is too far from the lab for my taste. Once I start building the heart, I'll be in here 24/7."

"Your team, too?"

"Hardly. They spend hours on-line with their families. The two single guys chat up the nurses, of course, but everyone will be happy to see the scotch. I won't touch it."

"You're *that* satisfied?" he said.

"*Pfft.* There isn't enough whiskey in Scotland to repay what you've done for me."

She tried to ignore those twinkling crystal studs under his thick brows. "You've come over here for something. So let's get to it."

He seemed amused at first before dropping into a forced gravitas. "You guys should be the ones to choose an implant recipient, not me."

"Isn't this a little premature? We're still waiting for parts and equipment."

Homer uncoiled his lanky frame against the full length of the office chair as if wanting to insert some space into what he was about to say. "And in the meantime how would you like to come with me on a business trip to the Middle East?" With nothing but confused silence from her, he continued. "They pay for everything."

This kind of manipulation never worked with Claudia, but Homer's attempts to get her alone were so transparently endearing. "Who are the *they* you're talking about?"

He wrinkled his nose, taken by surprise. "The Israeli government. They have a foundation which helps childless families find surrogates. We'd leave this weekend and be gone for just two or three days."

She looked around at her sad bunker. The thought of time away did appeal. "Okay."

"Really? But I spent most of last night working on my persuasion skills," Homer said. When he came to peck her on the cheek, she lurched up with a thought.

"*If* you do something for me."

He groaned and dragged himself back to the office chair. "Such as?"

Claudia quickly recalibrated her demand. "I want Dafnis to come with us—to Israel." Her original idea was the airport in Malta.

"As what?" Frame erect, a face of indignation, Homer jumped to his feet. "A chaperone? The company jester?"

"Don't be flippant," she said. "As your son, you idiot." Dafnis may be naive, but after Jaza's explanation Claudia didn't think of him as stupid.

"He could represent the lab," she said. "And answer any questions about how the embryos are stored and tested for mutant genes and diseases. He understands everything that goes on in there."

"That's only because he was immersed in it every night. Dafnis hasn't been in the lab in almost two months." Homer began pacing, his limbs swimming with agitation. "Take him away from this island and the boy could wander off. Forget where he's from."

"Your son's a man," Claudia corrected. "And by the way, he also thinks designer babies are a dangerous idea, so he's a lot wiser than Hocking on that front."

Homer captured her desk's wheeled office chair with his right hand and tossed himself into it. "There's no point arguing since Dafnis doesn't even have a passport."

"So get him one. He was born in Syria. Use that big shot friend of yours."

Homer shook his head; his nostrils flared. "A Syrian passport won't go over well in Israel. The two countries are at war. I'll be entering with my Greek citizenship. As long as the UK keeps sending them guns, you'll be fine, too. But Dafnis . . . " He wheeled himself up against the back wall and stared at the ceiling. "I don't know how to say this delicately, but—"

Claudia waited, hands on hips.

"You don't have all the facts to come to an intelligent conclusion. He's too easily manipulated *and* a security risk."

Claudia shrugged. "Then I guess this is Bon Voyage. I have lots of work waiting for me in the lab." At the door she threw him a final comment. "Be sure to bring Dafnis a souvenir."

Outside in the hall stood an eavesdropper. Dafnis jumped back as Claudia plowed through. He looked down and away, as if afraid of her, and a split second later she wrapped him in a bear hug.

"Come on," she said against his quivering body, "Let's get to hell out of here. I'll show you my lab."

THE OFFICIAL JEEP TAXI for The Squats pulled up to the hospital's double doors in the dark, and Claudia climbed in. A morning departure anywhere before ten would normally sink her into a foul mood, yet she was alert, contented, and more excited than she wanted to admit to be going on a trip with Homer and Dafnis.

The youth, trailed by Homer, marched from the dormitory where they'd slept in Claudia's vacant room. Dafnis handed the suitcases to their driver, and tucked in beside him in the front while Homer stumbled into the back beside Claudia.

Dafnis wore a perma-smile; the kid practically vibrated with the excitement of his first trip ever out of Homer's republic. Hyper-alert, it was obvious to her he hadn't slept a bit.

In the back seat Claudia snapped her fingers at Homer. "So, let's see it."

Bent over, fidgeting with the rubber band on his ponytail, he released one hand long enough to toss Dafnis's black market passport into her lap.

She opened it to the photo page. "Dafnis. Turn around . . . Remarkable," she said, holding it up for comparison. "You could be this Khalid guy's twin."

"He's a really nice guy. Smart, too," Dafnis said. "He came over from The Squats to set up all the electrical for the solar panels on top of the clinic. I had lunch with him almost every day and he told me lots about his life in Syria. So cool. I can probably answer anything I'm asked."

"No—You—Won't," Homer roared. "Play dumb."

"What—? You mean act stupid?"

"No." Homer pressed the heels of his palms to his temples. "Be smart for once and keep your mouth shut. Let me do all the talking."

His snarls sent Dafnis red-faced and quaking down into his seat until Claudia reached forward to pat his shoulder. "You'll be just fine.

"The guy didn't mind you using his passport?" she asked Homer.

"He doesn't know. I keep them all in my office."

Homer had a way of constantly reminding her he was a dictator.

"Anyway," Homer said, "It's only for identification. Israel agreed to issue Dafnis a diplomatic visa as my surrogacy expert."

"See how easy it is," she said with a patronizing squeeze to his closest hand, but Homer was in no mood for pre-dawn chatter.

"Pace yourself," he muttered. "We've got a long travel day ahead of us."

"Well then, why didn't we take the helicopter to Malta."

"No clearance."

"Then charter one," she said.

"They could be spies."

"What could spies want with a bunch of powerless refugees?" She jabbed a finger into his side. "You keep your dirty business out of The Squats, mate."

Had Homer himself not told her, *You'll see how the ends justify the means.* The Squats, a paradise of liberal ideals to her, was the *ends* he was talking about—and a line Homer had better not cross.

He raised his head and squinted, his anxiety reflected in the moon's glow. "Can we continue this later after I've had a snooze?"

Homer looked every bit his fifty-two years this morning, his untanned face lined deep as melted wax. He let his head sag onto her shoulder, closed his eyes, and a half-hour later he was passed out along one of the hydrofoil's padded benches as the sun began its climb over the Mediterranean.

South, across waves of gold—lay Africa. Such a duplicitous beauty for desperate souls crammed into boats. This might be the last sunrise of their lives. How many hundreds were out there right now, adrift, waiting for rescue?

The cabin filled with the sonorous seesaw and restless turns of an exhausted man carrying the weight of his state's secrets. Two months since this benevolent despot had entered her life, yet, she knew so little of his inner world. Was Homer the most complex soul she'd ever met, or, like the sea which surrounded them—another treacherous beauty?

This was her chance to see him outside his comfort zone and find out.

Chapter 19

I f anything, the three of them were in good hands for a freak high tide at Ben Gurion International Airport. Bedazzled with golden epaulets and embroidered anchors, a chauffeur in the crisp white uniform of a battleship commander greeted them. Not to be outdone, their hotel bellhop was in a tuxedo. Hardly Claudia's relaxed style, but it served to prepare her for what was ahead on the twenty-fifth floor of the Tel Aviv Grand Palace overlooking the city's sparkling white coastline.

Dafnis went straight to his room on the main floor of the penthouse and started channel surfing while she and Homer climbed a circular linking staircase and wandered through their separate ensuites.

Claudia ran a palm down one of the pillars surrounding the colossal marble jet tub inside her bathroom and looked up when Homer appeared in the doorway. "This can't be real gold plating."

"Twenty-four carats," was his reply. "I have a gold toilet seat, too."

Every corner evoked a different mood set around indoor and outdoor jacuzzis, pools, and waterfalls. The hotel obviously missed the news flash about Tel Aviv's freshwater crunch. The place was so monstrous, instead of following her suitcase into their personal elevator to the second level of the penthouse, she stood transfixed by the back-and-forth motion of tropical fish inside a wall-sized aquarium—their simple contained life soothing to her over-burdened senses.

"This penthouse is a cheaper version of the royal suite at Dubai's Burj Al Arab," Homer explained while doling out bills to the bellhop. He closed the door on the departing stainless steel dolly. "It goes for fifteen-thousand a night instead of twenty-five-thousand."

Her jaw dropped.

"Don't worry. We're not picking up the tab."

"Well, somebody is," she said. "Probably the taxpayers. I worry that some people on this earth have no clue what reality is for 99.9 percent of humanity."

A glimmer of a smile appeared on his lips. "And the mini-bar over there stocks your exclusive brand of scotch."

She grunted. "Point made."

"We'll order dinner in."

"Fine by me as long as it's not pizza."

"What's pit—za?" Dafnis said from behind them.

Claudia stared sidelong at Homer. "Let him try it."

Halfway through their meal they heard the telltale moans and cries of a sex act coming from Dafnis's room on the main level. The last they'd seen of him, Dafnis had a pizza box balanced on one hand, a liter bottle of beer in the other. One of the clinic's doctors must have smuggled some in at one point because the teen seemed to know what it was.

Homer scowled and left his seat, but Claudia jumped into action. "Get back here, you son-of-a-bitch and let him have his fun. I'm impressed he found the channel. That should be the takeaway from this."

Homer did as he was told.

At the end of the meal, which had been as far from fast food as gastronomically possible, Claudia pushed herself from the gleaming oak table and strolled to the closest jacuzzi. Outside the wall to wall window, the lights of Tel Aviv stretched to the horizon. "This looks tempting." She dipped her hand into the steaming water. "But after that meal I'd probably doze off and drown."

"There's one on the rooftop that's body temperature."

"Naw, I'm too tired to go out."

"It's on our own private rooftop above the bedrooms. We can stroll around up there and work off some of this food. How about it? Meet me outside your bedroom in ten minutes?" he asked.

Instead of taking their private lift, they climbed the circular staircase inside the spacious den which served as a hub between their bedrooms. Homer wandered off at the top, his hotel bathrobe flapping about his bare legs, but Claudia was once again mesmerized, hit by the intoxicating aroma of an entire rooftop of blooming cherry trees. The pink spectacle spread across a thick carpet of natural grass. Patches of simulated moonlight fell from mood lights hidden inside the trees.

"Homer?"

Up ahead he looked over his shoulder.

"These fruit trees." She did a theatrical twirl. "This is incredible, but how can they grow here in the heat?"

"Dry heat is what they need. They're from the Golan Heights, but it's chilly up here, too, before daybreak."

They arrived at a steaming hot tub, the earthy aroma from the heated cedar a balm to her conflicted mind as she untied her robe. "We must be the first—" The silky Egyptian cotton slipped from her grasp onto the wrought iron chair; Claudia couldn't have averted her eyes from the spectacle before her, had she wanted to.

Poised and smiling on the hot tub's top step stood a stark naked Homer. Tall and slender despite middle age, Homer had the chiseled torso of an athlete. He wouldn't have looked out of place at the starting blocks of an Olympic pool.

Oh, crap, she thought, *how did I not see this coming?*

From their first encounter in his office, it went without saying they would end up naked at some point, if only they could find a time and place which didn't reek of carbolic soap and dried blood. The zen guesthouse would have qualified except for Homer's comment about electronics being a security risk. Naturally, she assumed *sexual acts* would also endanger his empire.

She was flummoxed and what it came down to wasn't the threat of getting laid after innumerable years, or even her boss's genitalia in her face—but the fact she hadn't been consulted. If Claudia was going to reverse her aversion to geriatric sex, she would do it on her terms alone.

Loose about his shoulders, the curly blue ends of his hair framed his face in an almost ethereal glow. "Coming in, Dr. Vlakia?" Homer's front-facing body disappeared inch by inch into a swirl of steam.

It was his way of shaking his finger, or other parts, at her modesty. She thought of Dafnis suddenly appearing and followed Homer in.

His smirk persisted after she moved to the far end of the hot tub and suspended herself along outstretched arms. "Did my snowy thighs blind you?" she said. "I get my pale skin from my father. He was a sheep farmer in the gloomy English countryside. My mother, though, had the swarthy complexion of a Romanian gypsy. I used to joke that she was a runaway. In fact, her parents were the last count and countess of Vargas Castle in Transylvania. That was before the Soviets destroyed it."

Homer's eyes flew open. "Oooh. You mean I'm in a hot tub with a half-naked countess."

She snorted before immersing herself up to her neck. "Oh my. Between that dinner and this rooftop, this has to be better than sex."

"Your memory is still that sharp, is it?"

"Fun—ny. I bet you've got me beat by decades on the celibacy meter."

He went quiet and sank in up to his neck, too. "My wife was my only bed partner."

Good heavens. This man was not much more than a virgin. It was beyond her comprehension.

"Does that scare you, Claudia?"

"Umm . . . No. Well, maybe a little." *Shit.* Did he just manipulate her into agreeing to sex?

"It's hard for me to believe someone as fascinating as you never married nor had children," Homer said. "There must have been a lot of interest."

"I'm an expert at sabotaging relationships, you see."

Homer had his attentive and caring doctor face on.

Like anyone, she had her share of shameful secrets, but there was one which was ripe for someone like Homer to dig up. Only her dead mother knew the full story. It was as if Claudia had dropped the dark thing into the coffin that day, but salvaged all the regret.

"Was it an accident?" Claudia asked. "I mean—with your wife in Africa?"

"She caught the pneumonic plague."

In the modern age, death by plague was so shockingly rare.

"There we were, hundreds of microbiologists and virologists gathered together by chance in one city. I left the conference early to check on her at the hotel, expecting to see her up and about. Instead, I found her dead on the bathroom floor lying in a trail of bloody sputum.

"It happens," he said with an unconvincingly flat flick of the wrist. "Especially in Africa. She was gone within seventy-two hours of the first symptoms."

Modern plague cases weren't news, but the thought of losing someone so loved in such a cruel way rendered her speechless. When the restful silence ground on into edginess, she said the first thing that came to mind.

"I actually have . . . I mean—*had*—a daughter. I got pregnant during my first year of university in Bucharest."

Homer swiftly moved to her side. They weren't anywhere near skin-on-skin, but she found it intimidating to have his nakedness so close to her own after so many years of being alone.

"I put her up for adoption right at the hospital and when I was almost finished medical school, I went looking for her. By that time, I was more responsible and wanted to assure myself she was with a kind family. That's when I found out she went to an orphanage along with hundreds of thousands of others. Most born from a communist policy which punished families that had less than five children."

She looked over at Homer to see if he was still listening to her rambling tale. He was rapt. "I found the kids crammed into institutionalized squalor without adequate food or heat, not even toys to stimulate their minds. Emaciated zombies in rags heaped together on beds."

She paused because this was the hard part that she'd never spoken about to anyone except her mother. "My search for her ended at the very worst of these hellholes, the one for the disabled."

Flashes of the sights and smells of ragged children sitting in their own excrement hit her; she squeezed her eyes shut to block it out. "I didn't know it, but she was born with a heart murmur."

Homer grasped her hand in the watery space between them. "Was she still alive?"

Claudia silently shook her head.

"Her heart?" he asked.

Again, she shook her head. Their eyes met.

"She starved to death . . . Alone, Homer, with no one who loved her anywhere near."

After thirty-two years, Claudia couldn't hold back the tears any longer. "If I hadn't abandoned her—

"No. Dearest." Homer swished a palm into the water and dabbed at her tears. "You did what you thought was best." He pulled her head onto his shoulder and cupped her hand in the warmth between them. "Let it go, love."

Heaven help her, if only she could.

⎯⎯●⎯⎯

THE FIRST THING CLAUDIA saw the next morning was the fuchsia-colored silk swag hanging down from the ceiling above the bed. No Homer. Had he crept back to his own bed?

No, because this *was* his bed. Hers had the mirror on the ceiling which she remembered debating vehemently against. Her bathrobe was right where she'd left it the night before—tied securely around her body.

She wandered through the den they shared and took the stairs down to the main living room. No Dafnis, either, but he'd be fine with the long bedside note explaining where he was and how to order breakfast. What she did find was an orange sticky note on the coffee maker: *Good morning, my love. Off to my meeting. Wake Dafnis and order up breakfast. Enjoy the place. I'll be back at noon for lunch. Hugs. Homer.*

Love? She had a lover? Not only that, but it looked like she wouldn't be meeting the surrogate charity after all.

The heaviness of the previous night's swirl of sadness juxtaposed against the calm hum of the fish tank aerator. There was nothing like memories of tragically dead children and beloved dead wives to douse the flames of desire. Not since her mother's funeral had she felt so in need of human touch that she ended up inviting Homer to lay with her until she fell asleep.

Her antidote to lethargy was close at hand. She dressed, then jogged down twenty-two flights of stairs to the outdoor breakfast cafe on the ground level, and sat at one of the wooden tables encircling a hacienda-style courtyard. While she waited for her order, a heavily carved door opened on the far side of the courtyard and two men in immaculate suits emerged. The first, with a Jewish skullcap and tidy beard, she recognized from news items of the Israel-Palestine conflict circulating while she was monitoring her court case. The second, deep in animated chatter, she also recognized—Homer.

Their high-pitched laughter rang throughout the stone arcades and gurgling fountain before they embraced and parted ways—Homer into the lobby, his friend to a waiting limousine she could see parked on the street in front of the cafe.

Throughout breakfast her mind ran wild as to why Homer would be chumming around with a senior member of Israel's Defense ministry when he was supposed to be "making dreams come true" for childless couples. What kind of dreams might Israel's aggressive defense complex have?

She returned from breakfast to find Homer's shower running, the door to his bedroom open. Venturing through, she cracked the bathroom door. "Homer?"

"Yeah?" came a response from within the glittering gold-plated shower enclosure.

"I brought you a towel from the heated rack in my ensuite. It's here on the counter."

"Lovely."

"Who was that in the restaurant?"

The din of water ended abruptly. "What did you say?"

"I saw you talking to someone from the Israeli Defense ministry. Is he a friend of yours?" she said through the narrow gap.

The shower door creaked open, the towel disappeared from the counter, and suddenly a half-clad Homer was standing in the doorway, water pooling around his feet. "I can't keep up with these lies anymore," he said. "It's tiring."

"Then don't."

He backed up and slouched against the edge of the jet tub, and in plodding detail launched into what was no doubt one of the state secrets he kept referring to.

Once one heard Claudia's baby story it didn't take a lot of smarts to figure out her need to perfect an artificial heart for infants. What, she kept asking herself later that same day, could be behind Homer's interest in manufacturing armaments? A steadfast compassion for mankind one minute—hellbent on destroying it the next.

"I'm wasting my breath," she remembered him saying at one point before dismissing their argument with a wave of his hand. Homer had not only burst Claudia's bubble, but had almost done the same to her eardrum. How dare she call his stealth drones weapons of mass destruction. What the hell else would one call these high-speed killers capable of dropping cluster bombs on cities?

Oh, but according to Homer it was the fastest *this*, and the most efficient *that*. Something the world had never seen before. A keeper of the peace, in fact. Seventy years after Hiroshima, no one in their right mind would call nuclear warfare a keeper of the peace anymore. How were armed drones any different?

In so many ways, this latest revelation tore at her with greater vengeance than his immoral organ harvesting. "Are you planning to test these things over the heads of pregnant women already traumatized by war?"

"Of course not," he said. "The only place with enough air space is The Squats."

With that, he had crossed her line.

She tried in vain to check herself. "And who'll be running the arms factory? Your legless flute player?"

At least that memory remained sacred. His dark eyes launched disgust. "Dafnis is a natural with the controls."

Who better to entrust with the classified operation than Homer's very own forgetful son? Like all autocrats with many admirers but few confidantes, Homer needed to keep his right-hand man close by. The pieces finally fell into place—if Jaza and her son escaped, Dafnis would surely follow. Keeping them apart guaranteed nobody left.

Claudia jumped as he thrust out an accusing finger, seeming to read her thoughts. "Say anything to Jaza and your lab is gone."

Had they come to it, then? Homer finally had her under his thumb—seducing her with this repulsively opulent weekend, and if that didn't work, threatening her with the lab's closure.

In the end, he cinched in his bath towel and swept past her out the door. To his credit, it took courage to disclose as much as he did, wearing nothing more than a towel. Perhaps men didn't think of clothing as protective armor in the same way women did.

Late in the afternoon he appeared at the door of her ensuite to invite her to lunch. *Cut me loose*, she thought, not daring to make eye contact.

"You go ahead." She continued to toss toiletries from the vanity into her overnight bag. "I'll phone down for something." She could work off some nervous energy and get a head start on packing for their departure early the next morning.

They *were* leaving, he said, but not in the morning and not for home. "Masoud has informed me that his soldiers liberated my neighborhood last week. You're right. I should go find my daughter. We'll take an overnight flight to Syria."

Well played, Homer. Since it was her idea to begin with, Claudia couldn't very well refuse to go with him.

"I'm still mad, but . . ." Claudia reached up and grasped his hand. "I want you to find your daughter."

Apparently, so did his old Masoud friend. He'd put the last-minute security passes in place for all three of them. "Dafnis should see his homeland one final time," Homer said, "and of course visit his mother's grave."

Was the man's newfound compassion for Dafnis for real? How was she supposed to trust Homer when he kept pulling out wild cards that made her head spin? She watched his reflection bleed off the edge of the vanity mirror, and recalled how tight they'd been when they lived on separate islands and Claudia had no idea what this maniac was up to.

Piss on trying to save the world, she needed to stay focused on building her bionic heart. No more jumping into bed with Homer in any shape or form.

Chapter 20

Whether it was the somnolent white noise or her body surrendering to forced relaxation, air travel usually left Claudia clear-headed, the stress zapped from her system. As they entered Damascus airspace, however, sporadic flashes below reminded her they were about to land in a war zone. Isolated pockets glowed like lifeless constellations in the cold expanse of deep space. If they were over Syria's capital, where were all the city lights?

Claudia sent a sleepy yawn into the vacant middle seat, which she'd built up into a Berlin Wall of spongy airline pillows and blankets, plastic water bottles, magazines, jackets, and food wrappers. It was supposed to be Dafnis's place but, being a typical teen, he'd moved to a vacant seat to watch movies.

Homer reached up and switched on the light above their Berlin Wall. "We should give Dafnis your room and you can share mine."

Jumping back into the game of love was never easy for someone as headstrong and old as Homer. It must feel like a drunken zigzag through a mined No Man's Land; her rebuffs only seemed to excite him and sharpen his ardor.

"What do you think?"

She imagined a volatile night of political pillow talk. What Homer imagined likely didn't include talking over pillows or anywhere else. More time was what she needed, maybe an entire lifetime. She kept her voice down and offered up a crooked smile. "It's time to release me, Homer."

The brittle cord around Homer's ego snapped as he raked the pile of clutter onto the cabin floor, shoved himself into the cleared seat, and reached for her hand with tenderness, despite the urgency in his voice.

"I've decided to wind down our black market transplants. That's what this trip is for. And I'm building a new ward at The Squats for comatose refugees with signs of life."

"You're serious?"

He nodded, a touch mischievous. "I'm naming the ward after you—I don't *want* to release you. Ever. I'm pretty great already but with you—" Homer shook his head in mock overwhelm. "I feel like I can go farther than I ever thought possible."

Her lips were still parted in disbelief when he killed the overhead spotlight and came in for his first kiss. Her drought had gone on far too long. She waited for that delicious first second when a trembling hand lifts ice water to parched lips.

Ka-Bam. He handed her a popsicle, instead. His teeth made a hard landing on hers, bounced off, and accelerated into an emergency lift-off. Middle-aged Homer was one of those incomprehensibly bad kissers who only got worse with practice.

Oh, no. He was circling around—She immediately closed her airspace.

"My drones—"

Claudia groaned and turned away. Not the armaments again.

"Listen. I want them to be used for peaceful purposes. Search & Rescue. At worst, a bit of troop reconnaissance for resupply. I won't bullshit you, though. In the end I can't control whether the buyer arms them."

"See," she said. "If you want to do good, then get out of weapons mongering altogether."

"And make money how? Without my help The Squats will run out of food within months." Homer sat back and stared into her eyes. "I thought this would make you happy. We replace organ sales with respectable weapons manufacturing."

Unfortunately, he was right. The only distinction between these two deadly money-spinners was that selling weapons was legal the world over—selling body parts was not.

There was one other option which could generate a hefty and guaranteed return on such a tiny and remote island—cooking street drugs. Nothing else came to mind.

Homer, too, had his brows knit over something. "What do you think of this . . . If we cleared out the shipping containers on the flats, there would be enough land for both a drone factory and workers' dormitory next door. Those families in the camp have been waiting years to improve their lives. There's our instant workforce."

Claudia's wobbling attention attached itself to the laminated seat belt instructions in front of her. "Exhausted single mothers, old men and women, and the disabled don't sound that great."

"Well, no more freeloading on my goodwill."

"And the children?" she asked, even more deadpan, her voice dripping with sarcasm. "Would there be jobs for them, too?"

He chewed on his lip. "Naw, that won't work. Anyone under sixteen will have to live at the orphanage."

He was back at it, breaking up families, never mind the grotesque contradiction of forcing those fleeing war zones to manufacture weapons. "I won't be here," she said, "but good luck."

He gripped one of her wrists, his face so puckered with pain he could have been staked to a hill of red ants. "No matter who makes the weapons, war will always be with us," he said. "All we can do is mitigate it. That's why I want the Republic of Homer to play a part in the coming shadow wars—fought drone on drone."

She purged the words of this pro-war soliloquy from her mind until nothing remained to irritate her, and the captain announced their descent into Damascus.

Chapter 21

The arrivals hall at the well-worn Damascus International was deserted. A bored customs and immigration official, someone mopping floors, and no more than a dozen passengers from their flight was about it for traffic. Not surprising, considering the closed airspace and circuitous route one was forced to take via Dubai.

Claudia immediately pulled on her pea jacket as a frigid spring breeze tore through their limo stop and two military jeeps raced by to the clamor of helicopters and distant shelling. Claudia flashed Homer a pained look which said, *Sure you want to be here?*

It seemed the Deputy Minister of the Interior would spare no expense in helping Homer find his daughter, and sure enough a white limo pulled up with a driver in a dapper black uniform and the supersized gold-framed sunglasses double-agents preferred. He was all business while he transferred their luggage to the trunk, but as soon as he climbed into the driver's seat across from Homer, he whipped off the shades and his face split with a broad grin.

"Good heavens," Homer said, eye-to-eye with the driver. "Is it really you?" They leaned into an awkward hug, the *whap, whap* of back pats accelerating without pause. "I've often wondered what became of you, Faisal."

Homer twisted toward Claudia and Dafnis in the back. "Faisal was my security guard at the hospital's lab here for . . . It had to be at least twenty years, right?"

"The last time I saw Homer," Faisal told Claudia and Dafnis, "the entire hospital was burning. I found Homer trying to rescue his lab beagle."

Homer slapped his hand once more on the driver's shoulder. "You've managed to surprise me again, Faisal."

They shared a chuckle until Faisal said, "But sneaking up on people isn't my job anymore."

"Yet here you are—still in Syria."

"I'm just a tour guide. I work for the Assad government, but they pay me well."

From a view of him in the rear view mirror, Claudia watched a streak of red creep into Faisal's quickly fading cheer. Was it possible these old coworkers had shared a distaste for Syria's autocratic ruling family?

Seeming intent on sliding past the tension, Faisal studied Claudia, a hopeful gleam in his eye. "And . . .?"

"Oh, right. This is Claudia. A friend from my clinic. Beside her is my personal assistant, Khalid. He left Syria as a child and speaks only English. You heard I went to Malta, didn't you?"

"Got it straight from Masoud," Faisal said.

She couldn't imagine he intended to announce his new intimacy with Syria's most corrupt elements. What Syria knew of Homer's present life in Malta surely paled in comparison to the atrocities being approved through the Interior minister's office.

"We . . . We talk on occasion. And how is your daughter?"

Faisal's friendly question cranked up the tension as Homer twisted himself to examine a dozing Dafnis. Was it possible the youth didn't know he had a sister?

"That's what I'm here for. To find her," Homer said.

"I see." Tight, hushed words. "May God be with her. And what about your last beagle?"

"He survived. I named him Ten."

"Aha. Number ten is still alive. Are you famous now?"

"No. The vaccine had too many problems."

A quick nod as they pulled onto an airport motorway.

They rolled into the city's embassy district where Claudia was bracing for the same bombed out neighborhoods from the news instead of an ostentatious row of five-star hotels. Their own held a manicured garden and palatial pool sequestered behind high walls.

"The war never came to this district near the Defense ministry," Homer explained. "Reality will hit tomorrow when we go north to Homs."

———✦———

THE NEXT MORNING, HOMER wanted to start the search for his daughter at the family home in Homs. If his letter to her was gone it meant she was likely alive. In that case, Claudia and Dafnis would fly home while Homer stayed behind to continue the search.

The military's checkpoints for weapons and anyone without ID sprang up the minute they entered the freeway.

Homer scrutinized Faisal then whispered to Claudia, beside him. "The rebels have dug in north of Homs. When I fled in 2012, I expected it to soon end, but that was before Russia came in to help this murderous regime." Homer hung his head and sighed. "It was one of their barrel bombs that destroyed my hospital."

When she leaned in, a cautionary nod toward Faisal garnered a reassuring wink from Homer. "Does your friend, the deputy minister, know how you feel?" she asked.

"I hope not."

With Homs in sight, Homer told Faisal to turn off the main highway into the western suburb of Baba Amr where Homer's wife lay in a cemetery. Soldiers at the checkpoint into the ruined neighborhood weren't fooling around—Faisal's official government plates had no effect. A tense silence spread as they ordered everyone out while they checked inside and outside the vehicle.

"When I left five years ago," Homer whispered, "this area was the rebels' main stronghold." Claudia was more than happy to let Homer take up her hand, and soon an equally wary Dafnis nudged closer, too.

At the next checkpoint, a soldier replaced Dafnis in the front and focused on Faisal's every move.

Blackened streets emptied of people stretched across a dishwater-gray horizon where nothing lived. Like stage props waiting for the scene to start, stark silhouettes of bed frames, dusty couches, and children's highchairs rose up inside skeletal rooms. One kitchen table with the four chairs still in place waited for the family who would never have another meal there—children, husbands, and wives who now lay buried under a graveyard of pancaked apartments.

An occasional car or lone cyclist drifted by. A bent old woman with a shopping bag shuffled along, dwarfed and oblivious to the colossal ruin which surrounded her in every direction. Perhaps she imagined herself once more in the land of sun-drenched olive groves and bone-white colonial villas where neighbors relaxed in the shade of trees, passing around a metal straw stuck into a steaming glass of mate tea similar to the one she often saw Homer drinking from.

Claudia felt like an actor in an absurd playhouse. Backstage, a war raged while front and center the peaceful sights and sounds of daily life in a Middle East metropolis continued unabated.

"Where *is* everybody?" Claudia whispered after the guard hopped out at the next checkpoint and Dafnis moved to the front seat.

Homer thrust his thumb in the air while staring out his window. He turned to her with a face awash in mute tears and fury. "The Squats—or somewhere much worse." Like a man gliding through a time capsule of the civil war he'd escaped, each new street brought forth a low moan or gasp.

"What's become of the nine-hundred rebels who held out here?" he seemed to ask the mountains of broken rebar and concrete outside his window, rather than Faisal, who drove on mutely.

"I went through here every day on my way to the hospital, but I have no clue where we are. I'm depending on Faisal to find my house."

"You two were that close?"

Homer glanced once again at a dozing Dafnis. "His daughter and my Daphne were a women's badminton duo."

"Daphne and Dafnis," Claudia mused. "Didn't people get them confused?"

"It's what my wife wanted so . . ."

The concrete dust kicked up by their tires collected in ridges across their closed windows, the acidic odor blunted only by whiffs of moldy pockets in the ruins which hadn't seen the sun in years. Claudia pinched her nostrils as hard as possible, imagining the skeletal remains below.

"You know," Homer began, "when the fighting started I *could not* comprehend why my beautiful country was killing its own people. This was the place I wanted to live in and eventually lie for eternity in the ground beside my wife.

"I believed the rumors of brutality inside the jails. So why had a decent Greek man such as myself never given Masoud's ruthless side a second thought?" He was staring, not so much into her eyes, as beyond them.

At the cemetery, its iron gate hung askew from its hinges. Untended and weedy, the graveyard beyond appeared more intact than the gouged-out, charred ones they'd already passed.

A weary sigh escaped from Homer. "Let's go," he said, tapping Dafnis awake.

"Can you give me some time alone with her?" he asked when Claudia reached for the door handle.

She nodded.

An hour later, Dafnis was far ahead, pounding out a determined course back to the car, but when Homer appeared, Faisal jumped out to stop him at the gate.

Homer's eyes were puffy and lifeless, his hands and knees dirt-caked where he'd likely bowed down on all fours across the grave to pray. The two men looked down at something in Faisal's hands then pulled each other into a long, tight hug—their conversation meant only for each other.

Inside the car, Homer continued to stare at the photo from Faisal—and this time he didn't try to hide his tears nor stop Claudia from cradling his hand in her lap. In the shot, Faisal and Homer flanked two ecstatic young girls in shorts who were hoisting a trophy high overhead.

"Head to El Waer suburb, Faisal. I'm ready to see my home."

Whatever was left of it, Claudia thought.

———◉———

A WEEDY STRIP OF BLACKENED trees was the only remaining signpost of the former El Waer neighborhood. To each side, once solid structures lay pummeled senseless and formless like windswept hills of dusty confetti. She tried to picture the flats, offices, shops, parks, and houses of worship erected to celebrate man's goodness.

"I used to call this The Boulevard of Tears," Homer said. "Because that's all I ever did the entire way to and from my wife's grave. "I never imagined it would one day live up to its name for the entire neighborhood."

It wasn't until they turned a corner and passed the ruined innards of a villa that Homer straightened and shouted: "It's the striped curtains. I drove past these every single day to work. We're here."

Tattered remnants of mauve and white striped curtains still clung to a side wall. These fond companions of Homer's daily routine were the gaudiest things Claudia had ever seen. Missing a facade and roof and emptied of all furniture, the sprawling structure could have been mistaken for a lifesize dollhouse.

The limo rolled to a stop and Homer hopped out to silently brood over his own open-air wreck of a home. Windowless and doorless, some exterior walls still stood.

"Someone shot holes in the garage door, but otherwise nothing has changed since the day I drove off.

"I'll leave Claudia and Khalid in your capable hands, Faisal." This was the signal for their driver to station himself beside the limo.

"I want to check the underground garage first for anything Daphne might have left behind. Don't wander too far," he said to Dafnis before disappearing down concrete steps at the side of the house.

It was hardly a surprise when Dafnis turned to her in the back seat and asked in a guarded whisper: "Was Father talking about me?"

She dug the fingers of one hand into his closest shoulder as fiercely as she dared. "Come on, *Kha—lid*. Let's find Homer."

Instead of heading into the garage, Dafnis slammed the car's door on his way out and bounded up the front steps—Faisal on his tail.

Inside the garage below, Claudia found Homer tearing apart a utility cupboard, small tools like screwdrivers and oily rags scattered across the concrete floor. When his hand landed on a metal tool box, he hauled it out and flung open the lid.

"Homer?"

"It's gone." He had a death grip on the thing. "She's alive," he said, throwing the box aside and calling Faisal's name all the way to the street.

Claudia pointed at the ruined foyer of the split level. "They went inside."

"She's alive." His voice rose with each step to the second story. "Daphne's alive."

The two of them had almost reached the top step when Faisal appeared above on the landing. "Faisal. Daphne re—" The man pushed past Homer with such force that he spun Claudia off balance as well.

It was the first sign not all was as it seemed.

Chapter 22

Claudia headed for Dafnis, who stood transfixed in front of the corpse.

Human remains in camouflage gear dot war zones the world over. That was not what repulsed Claudia. Neither was it that this one happened to be in Homer's former living room. What twisted her guts was that this skeleton was in two pieces: The torso tied to a chair—its skull in a far corner, having rolled or been thrown there. The hollow room, including the skull's close-cropped black hair, lay under a netherworld-like veil of thick dust.

Claudia wanted to believe flying debris had dislodged the skull, but a red stain told otherwise; it stretched from the collar of the combat jacket, across the left shoulder, and down one leg of the chair to pool on the blue-patterned carpet beneath. This victim was very alive at the moment their head was severed.

Homer, a man of such a vivid presence, paled as he approached the skull. "What base madness has taken hold of the soldiers in this conflict?" he demanded from a phantom culprit. "The mismatched pants and jacket make me think it's one of the Free Syrian Army lads."

When Claudia pressed a comforting palm to Dafnis's shoulder, he turned, wild-eyed with shock before spiking into a swirl of lifeless dust. The movement brought Homer's gaze onto something in Dafnis's hand—a scrap of brown paper which Homer's limbs seemed useless to retrieve from his son's outstretched fist.

Now Claudia saw the fear in Homer's eyes.

"Check the pelvis. Male or female?" he said, as Dafnis stuffed the letter into Claudia's palm and barrelled from the room just as her mind latched onto what she might be looking at.

Claudia bent to the remains and ran her hands across the skeletal pelvic bone protruding inside the light cotton trousers. Her voice soft and low, Claudia said "It's a female."

Homer fell to his knees, cradled the skull between his palms, and immersed his face into the dirty, unkempt hair. Even from where she stood the hair reeked of sweat, soot, and dried blood. She waited patiently, but Homer seemed nailed to the spot, motionless on his knees, his body and mind shutting down molecule by molecule.

She raised the scrap of paper and read the words scrawled across both sides . . .

Jan. 25, 2012, Al Waer, Homs

My dear child Daphne,

I'm writing this in English for your eyes only.

Forgive me, but I have waited for you to return home as long as it is sensible. I fired up the kerosene burner tonight and dropped the last of my rice into a pot with some of my precious water, but I refused to start up the vehicle's heaters and waste gas I will need to escape.

When I leave Syria in the morning, the only thing I will take from my former life is a briefcase full of ideas. All that awaits me here is starvation and the loss of my research. My hospital is long gone. I emerged from the underground garage of our house today for the first time in almost a month and set eyes on the decimation to the horizon in all directions. In the smoldering rubble nothing moves, not even a bird crosses the sky. There is no longer water nor electricity and our own house is open to the rain and cold.

For a time, I convinced myself you would return when one side won over another. I scavenged what I could and hunkered down underground inside the ambulance—yes, of course, you don't know—I salvaged it from the hospital's ER bay the day I fled from the lab.

Normally, I would say an adolescent such as yourself is too young to understand war but perhaps the destruction of our beautiful Syria has made you a woman, a revolutionary. As for myself, three days ago when a military vehicle tracked me down to serve at the only functioning hospital, I gladly went, embarrassed to be hiding while others died.

At first I hoped you might be brought into the military hospital but then I prayed you would not. The place is a house of torture for the injured Free Syrian soldiers who are chained to the beds naked, whipped, and electrocuted. My job is to revive them each time so the interrogations can continue. I too was serving under threat of torture.

But today, hearing some neighborhoods will soon be bombed into submission, I was allowed to come home to retrieve what I could and check my dog. Yes! I finally have a puppy for you. I'm snuggled into my usual bed on top of one gurney, the blanket at my feet vibrating with the swish of the beagle's tail. Bonded for the moment, I know he'll forget me and be skittish as ever in the morning. How I would love to tell you that in the months since your disappearance I've found a cure for the plague which killed your mother, but one of the side effects of my vaccine is memory loss so it's back to the beginning when I get into a lab somewhere.

My opening has arrived to make a run for the Lebanese border. From the rumblings of passing military tanks, I know the government has routed the rebels from our street. Not that I feel partisan to any side. I've had an abundance of hours to contemplate my place in this war. The government's bombing of my hospital catapulted me out of my complacency. You remember Masoud from our Greek Orthodox church? I still carry his personal cell number, have memorized it, in fact, and won't hesitate to call him if I think it can save me.

As for the rebel side, doubt is the one thing we now share in common. Our mutual doubt is stronger by far than the faith I shared with Masoud. But it is still not enough to send me into their ranks.

My life will always be dedicated to saving lives no matter what side they're on.

I won't dare drive the M-1 for the border. Who knows whether the checkpoints will be government soldiers or rebels or even ISIS. On the backroads I can bargain with the ambulance fuel and drugs but the best I can hope for is to arrive at the Lebanese border with my life.

My hope is that someday you will return to find this letter and, God willing, I will lay eyes on your beloved face once again. Until that day, whatever you've heard about me, forget that now and know the focus of my research has always been to save lives.

With so much love, your papa.

. . . Claudia handed the wrinkled paper down to Homer who folded it into itself, taking pains to follow the original creases before slipping the tiny scrap into his jeans' pocket.

"What should we do?" she whispered.

He murmured, "Nothing. I'm not going to leave Daphne now that I've found her." He did get to his feet, though, and with the skull still in his hands, his face a shattered ruin, he seemed bewildered by what to do next.

"Should I send Faisal for a shovel?" she asked.

"No," Homer snapped. "He knew what we would find here. ISIS never entered the city. That means Assad's men did this."

He poured over every inch of the room, not with the despair one would expect but a bright yearning. "Let's pray this house entombs Daphne in the place of her happiest days."

She watched him plod to the corpse, churning with the dread he might place the skull in his daughter's lap. Instead, he lowered it to his feet where he came to stand before his daughter's bound hands. In the meticulously loving movements of a mother braiding her child's hair, he loosened the knots one by one. This, his final fatherly duty playing itself out in hideous fashion.

"She was so upset with me when I wouldn't let her wear a woman's hijab. She wouldn't let it go. 'Papa, please. My friends think I look like a man.' His eyes shone oddly above a faint smile. "I feared covering her head would only bring more eyes on her."

Homer frowned and flung the first binding aside, indignant fingers tugging at the rest. "These were the impossible choices before her—alienate herself at school or draw the rancor of men who would see her as a freak. So what was I to do? I gave in and told her never to walk the streets alone. And she didn't—until that day a missile struck near her school and they let them out early."

A puff of concrete dust billowed up as the final binding fell away. "Masoud," Homer grunted. "That was my first shock." The skeletal arms now free, he guided them into his daughter's lap, then dropped to his knees and lay his head there, his life force seeming to evaporate in sharp watery pants.

When she crouched and wrapped her arms around his waist, he moaned. A gift of human touch in a hellhole of butchery. If there was any way to keep Homer in this embrace all day and night until they were safely out of Syria, she would have gladly done it.

Her arms fell away as he stirred, the two of them now on their knees face to face. "Strange how I've traded places with Faisal. I used to be the one who made everyone watch what they were saying."

As they got to their feet, Homer crunched across the shattered remains of his picture window—some of the largest shards capable of piercing any ribcage, but it was only memories he was after.

"I sat right here all night," he said, "when she suddenly showed up at the checkpoint over there." He scowled at a phantom enemy on the street below. "She must have hid herself all night because her skirt and white hijab were stained. When she ignored the soldiers, one of them stepped forward and shoved her off-balance.

"Quick as lightning, she hoisted him off the ground and tossed him into a tangled heap against the other soldier, then took off running. I watched one of them limp forward and fire, but he missed."

Homer's chest heaved as if he too was dodging the bullets. "She could have easily pummeled both of them into unconsciousness and climbed the stairs to this room, but my child was a gazelle, not a hardened criminal."

"She got away," Claudia murmured.

"That time," he said. Homer's bottom lip trembled—reality was crowding in and his tears wouldn't be so easy to turn off. He dug out the folded letter. "We should burn this so no one else reads it."

Claudia snatched it up and slipped it into her bra. "I'll keep it safe."

He took in his daughter one final time, ruination in his eyes. "We can't bury my baby without causing suspicion. We'll have to pretend everything's fine."

Halfway down, Claudia halted on the stair in front of him and turned. Her voice thick, she drew his icy fingers to her cheek. "How in the world are you going to get through this? I'm about ready to scream myself."

A blank, bloodless expression greeted her. That's how he was going to get through it. "Can you talk to Dafnis for me?" Homer said. "Find out if Faisal read the letter."

Faisal was outside the limo, intent on the figure of Dafnis far down the street, staring at his feet.

"Your father wants me to talk to you," Claudia said when she caught up.

"That—thing—is my sister, isn't it?"

"Yes. I don't know why he didn't tell you about her, but I'm sure he will eventually. He's really hurting so let's be nice to him until he does."

"Even when he's not nice to me?" Dafnis scowled. "He wrote about this girl and our dog. It's like I don't exist."

"It is strange, isn't it? Dafnis, it's important. . . . Did Faisal read the letter?"

When he nodded, Claudia's chin fell to her chest as she cupped her palm to his shoulder. "Dear, try to remember that you're Homer's employee, not his son."

"When I woke up this morning, I couldn't remember Homer was my father. Now that I do, I still screw it up." Dafnis slouched with utter defeat. "I'm such a loser, aren't I?"

The liquid despair in his eyes beseeched her to love him anyway. "It's not because I want to be."

His sadness ripped to her core. "The brain is still a mystery," she said. "You may wake up one day and find everything is back to normal."

"Do you really think so?"

The white lie had him smiling, at least. Dafnis was another version of the hapless beating-heart cadavers in his father's clinic, but unlike those victims, he would have to forbear every relentless, confusing minute to his final breath.

"I know you've seen a lot of death, but a skeleton is so much worse," Claudia said.

"Did it scare you, too?" he asked.

"Not this time, but my first time I almost fainted." Her second lie also raised a smile. If there was ever a time Dafnis deserved a hug from her . . . she thought about it but gave it a pass.

"I don't worry about the dead," he said. "They're not suffering anymore. It's the living I cry about." He scanned both sides of the demolished street. "I don't know what happened here, but a lot of people suffered. Do you think Homer wants me to stay on the island so I only see nice things?"

"I guess so."

With his head cocked, Dafnis rocked on his heels before asking, "Do you love Homer?"

"Sometimes. How about you?"

"He's my father. I probably have to, right?"

No, you don't. Before she could tell him this, they turned in tandem to Faisal waving them back to the car.

Inside, with Homer in shock and Dafnis drifting in a cracking deep daze, Claudia grabbed the seat behind Faisal to pump him for info. "Have you never seen that before, Faisal?"

"Oh yes. It's horrible to think I will never again doubt the darkness of the human soul."

How could a man so decent, and one audition away from the Shakespearean stage, be serving a ruthless dictator. "And yet, you don't worry about aligning yourself with Assad?" she said.

"Believe me," Faisal said, countering her harsh accusation with his own bright future. "I didn't hesitate one second when I was offered this chauffeur job. My wife needed cancer treatment. Masoud got her to the head of the line."

Claudia glared as if he'd lost his mind, when Homer suddenly spoke up beside her. "It makes perfect sense to me."

"Please don't feel you have to defend me, Homer. We all make choices we have to live with. I, for one, don't see this war as very complex. I'm Shi'a Muslim, you're Christian, and my neighbor is Sunni. Religion isn't the main issue. The Assad family figured out long ago the more they turn the wealthy against the poor, the more power they hold onto.

"I look at your wealth, my friend. Money I don't have. If I want some of it, I can fight and die, or I can support the Assads and live. I made my choice. But they can't stay in power forever and when they're gone we must try to live side by side in harmony. I pray to Allah for that day."

A pensive Homer seemed to be taking this to heart. While admirable, the driver's confession didn't mean they were safe, especially if forced to choose his family's safety over surrendering Homer to the secret police. Syrian jails were filled with refugees tricked into believing Assad's amnesty, only to be tortured into a confession and imprisoned.

Homer's request came at the end of a long silence. "Faisal?" His old friend checked the rearview mirror. "Can I ask you to make another stop at my Orthodox church in Old Town before we leave Homs?"

"I'm very sorry, but it's nothing but rubble. I could stop at Umayyad Mosque in Damascus if you like."

When they reached the arched entrance to the mammoth house of worship, Faisal urged Claudia and Dafnis to also enter. "It's a mosque but this is also a place revered by many religions. Christians believe the head of John the Baptist lies here from when it was a Byzantine church."

Inside its vast shining courtyard, picnicking families were packing up their baskets and leaving—the kind of tranquil setting they all needed.

Homer wandered into the mosque's interior while Claudia found Dafnis circling impatiently around the outside courtyard. She sat with legs crossed just inside the arched entrance to let the cavernous stillness slow her racing heart, but soon felt a hand on her shoulder. She looked up into the face of Faisal.

"My sincere apology, ma'am, but Masoud is waiting for us at the hotel. Can you fetch the men?"

The echo of their pounding heels on the marble mirrored her unease at this sudden meeting with a man as busy as the deputy minister. With all of them out of earshot, Faisal had the perfect chance to set up an interrogation of Homer.

Homer's tight features told her he thought so, too. "This might be a trap," he said while still in the mosque's courtyard. "Here's what we should do. I'll go straight into the lobby. You two wait outside until Faisal has left. Hail another cab to Old Town and remember the name of the restaurant Le Jardinier. Find the owner. He's a trusted Greek friend on the right side of this war. Wait for me there.

"I hope you guys have your passports with you instead of in the room."

They did.

"Remember. Le Jardinier restaurant."

His escape plan seemed solid except for an odd but major last minute request. Masoud wanted Dafnis at the meeting.

Chapter 23

Claudia pulled Homer's hand into hers, each lost to their own thoughts until the limo pulled up to their hotel where he cemented the ongoing deception with a request Faisal take them to the airport early the next morning. About seven would be fine.

As soon as Faisal's taxi disappeared Homer spun to face Dafnis. "You need to go with Claudia."

"But . . . Why? You think I'll embarrass you, right?"

"Dammit. Don't argue."

"But I want to record the meeting. Isn't that what secretaries do?"

"He's right," Claudia said before Homer could utter another word. "As Khalid, he has no connection to your letter."

Homer's nostrils flared in the direction of the lobby's glass door. "All right, but if you haven't heard from us within an hour, take a cab to the border of Lebanon. Cross on foot and get another cab to Beirut airport."

Teeth clenched, she shook her head. "I can't just abandon you guys."

"Something goes wrong," Homer said, "there's no embassy here to help you. Take these and do what I say." He fished out a wad of American hundred dollar bills which he discreetly forced into her palm.

It was when Homer glanced over his shoulder one final time, his eyes swimming with a regret she'd never seen before, that the woman in Claudia finally broke. The edges of her downturned lips trembled with the realization Homer had gifted her the most fulfilling days of her life inside The Squats lab. Her chances of meeting another man as brutally compatible as Homer were nil.

Dafnis turned at the lobby door with a tight shy wave, perhaps ignorant of the possible danger ahead.

Would she ever see him or his father again?

Claudia now needed a delay tactic less conspicuous than fiddling with her phone. She pulled a tube of lipgloss from her pocket and in the second she raised it to her lips a man jumped out of a cab so fast he bumped her elbow. She swore and swung around to find him laughing at her red mustache. On any other day, she would have slapped the guy. Instead, she slid into the back seat of the taxi he'd exited.

Click. Click.

She was locked in and not only that—a dark-skinned, gaunt face with weedy, invasive brows eyed her from the front passenger seat.

"Oh. Sorry. I didn't know this taxi was taken," she said, giving the door handle a futile tug. "Could you please—" A glance from the taxi driver plunged her into a sickening deja vu moment because this time Faisal was anything but friendly.

"Relax," he said. "You're not in danger. I'm here as a translator."

That did nothing to quell the panic that something very fucking awful was about to happen.

The other guy gave Faisal an offhand wave of his thumb which she took to mean *go ahead.*

"It seems," Faisal began, "that your secretary Khalid Khazim is wanted by the Military Intelligence Directorate for terrorist activities two years ago."

His words ricocheted inside her brain like a dozen shiny pachinko balls. He might not be a government tour guide at all but an agent of the secret police who had played them from the beginning. Instead of a wail, all her frozen vocal cords could manage was a nervous chuckle which garnered a fierce look from the guy whose face needed a good mowing.

"Dafnis—that's his real name—is Homer's son, not his employee," Claudia told him. "We needed a last minute passport and Dafnis has a remarkable resemblance to the real Khalid. In fact, if you want the real Khalid I'm sure Homer—" Her mouth had gone rubbery and more gummed up than a dog toy. She was rambling and not at all sure Homer would allow the extradition of his asylum seeker.

"I won't translate that because I know it's a lie."

Her resolve was running on nothing but fumes.

"I happen to know Homer doesn't have a son," he added.

Co-workers often mixed up the details of each other's children, but there was a lie that would sound even more believable. It would have to do. "He isn't the brightest boy," she said. "Did you notice?"

Faisal nodded.

It was working. "Homer is so concerned with image he keeps his dull-witted son as hidden as possible." It was a nasty lie, of course, since inside the fertility lab Dafnis was the picture of intelligence.

On cue, the other agent seemed to hit Faisal up for a translation.

"Okay. Okay," she said, breaking in on this back and forth. "The point is—Dafnis isn't Khalid. He doesn't even speak Arabic. Or did you think that was an act, too?"

"No," Faisal admitted. "He looks genuinely ignorant . . . And far too stupid to have infiltrated the presidential palace and set off a car bomb that killed seventeen of the staff. It doesn't matter what *I* think, though. No one is interested in the opinion of a driver."

Another long exchange with the other guy.

"He says the truth will come out in the interrogation. Their methods get results."

"What! No." The thought of Dafnis being tortured kicked her rage into overdrive. She wailed on the car door, then Faisal, then the door again until both Faisal and the underfed agent entered the back seat from outside and, with great difficulty, got plastic ties around her wrists.

Before returning to their front seats, they gagged Claudia and let her bash herself against the doors and seats for a while. Panting, she made one final thrust against the door. *Pop.* Her shoulder exploded with pain; a muffled scream from deep within her gut filled the taxi.

From his driver's seat Faisal reached back and pressed the heel of his hand onto her intact shoulder. "I advise you not to get involved. Leave the country as soon as possible. Our argument is with Khalid, and when Masoud comes out that will be the signal for agents to go in and arrest him."

Claudia trained her gaze on the hotel's double glass doors.

"Gather your things. It would be my pleasure to drive you both to the airport."

His pleasure? Her pleas hadn't made one speck of difference to the only person who would possibly care whether Dafnis *was* Homer's son. Claudia sat, too spent to move; her body throbbed, her face was a welt of angry tears.

Oh, Dafnis. Sweetheart. My poor Dafnis. Claudia was no quitter. Her body was on the outs, but her mind was hyper-charged on adrenaline.

There had to be something she could do for her boy.

Chapter 24

Dafnis's journey out of Homs and back to their hotel lobby was a blur, but a good kind, tumbling with the idea that Homer kept him on their island, not as a punishment, but for his own protection. It meant his father cared. Maybe even loved him.

The morning started good enough with lots of strange cars and buildings like in the last city but a lot more banged up and dirty. The people were identical to the ones at home so that was one big snooze, but thanks to Claudia's strong fingers not the deep kind that made him an instant idiot. His favorite doctor was such a pain in the butt!

It was about halfway through the day when everything got dull—we're talking dormitory quarry dull—mountains of rock and no people, either. Even the place called a cemetery was crap. All the trees and grass were dead and, can you believe they put people in holes instead of burning them? Hopefully Homer didn't get any ideas from that because guess who'd be digging the holes?

Good grief but adventures off-island could be stressful. How come Jaza never told him about that part? There were people here who made Homer look like a pretty nice guy. The vibes coming off these guys shaking his hand inside their hotel lobby were not only phony, but scary phony.

Ahead, one guy was standing at the center of about six bigger guys all scrunched together and looking like some kind of team with identical black and white uniforms, buffed up and pressed out.

When the little guy spotted Homer, he shot Dafnis a rotten eyeball and waved them over. "Ah, here's the other man we've been waiting on." He hugged Homer with a round of back thumps. "So good to see you again, my friend."

If this was his father's buddy, Masoud—*Oops,* his *boss's* buddy—then the guy was a real rude bastard. He ignored Dafnis until Homer introduced him as, "Khalid, my secretary." No hug (of course), but shaking this man's hand was like trying to cozy up to a wet dishrag. So much for old friends.

"Mr. Lukin." Masoud turned to another shifty-eyed geezer. "This is my dear friend Homer. He has a devil of a Greek name. Just call him Papa K."

When the hand pumping and naming stopped, everyone except Masoud went to a circle of spongy seats. "Homer, these gentlemen have come all the way from Russia to speak with you. I can't stay but Mr. Lukin speaks fluent English and will be the interpreter."

So they were from Russia, were they? That's why Homer had his "eat shit" face going. His father was always fighting with the Russian surgeons about the drinking rules. The red-faced guy beside him looked like he could kill for a drink right now.

Before Mousey Masoud left, he grasped Homer's hands a final time. "May Allah protect you, my friend."

That didn't sound good. Dafnis knew this Allah guy as a great friend to everyone but someone you only called up as a last resort. Even Homer squirmed. Was that not a chuckle that Masoud made as he walked away? He was chatting on the phone by then so maybe it was for something else.

His father took the vacant seat right next to Lukin. Dafnis took the other one across from him, and oh boy was Homer taking a long look at the line of slippery smiles. It seemed this gang already knew more about the two of them than Homer would like.

"I must warn you, gentlemen—" The metal legs of his father's chair squealed across the floor as he butt-scooted his seat away from Lukin. "—that I don't have a lot of time before my next appointment."

"Neither do we." Lukin reached into a briefcase between his feet and sent a single sheet of plastic-covered paper spinning across the glass tabletop in front of them. Homer took a look then crossed the circle and handed it to Dafnis.

It was getting to be early evening, a time when Dafnis's brain easily mined for memories and knowledge from his past. One glance at the strange characters, triggered an explosion of chemical formulas deep within his subconscious. The words: *Gram-negative—Non-motile—Non-spore-forming coccobacillus*—flashed on his internal white board. Within seconds, he'd matched these words to the symbols within the rambling formulas on the page. After that, the memories flowed in like an unstoppable waterfall.

Behind Dafnis came a wheezing breath. He looked over his shoulder at a huge, blubbery man. The guy was all stiff with attention, his legs spread just like their guards on the island.

"So, how can I help you Mr. Lukin?" his father asked back at his seat.

Dafnis got out his notepad and started recording—not the conversation, but the chemical formulas on the page he held.

"You can give us the redacted lines to the formula I handed you," Lukin told Homer.

One of the other men yelled at Lukin in a strange language, maybe pissed off at being left out of the conversation. "Don't you want to know how we stole your information?" Lukin asked Homer.

"I'm not interested in your pathetic past victories," his father said. "Are you here to do business with me or not?"

It was only when Lukin jumped up and shook his fist that Dafnis caught the sarcasm he always found so confusing. Homer crossed his arms and waited. "I suppose you hacked into the hospital servers at my lab here in Syria. Of course, that was before *your* country's bombs blew the entire complex to bits."

"Stop," Lukin said, and blabbed some more to his group.

"I have to wonder," Homer said, his jaw out of joint—a sure sign he was getting ready to screw with someone—"Why are you so interested in my vaccine formula for pneumonic plague?"

Dafnis stared at the paper in his hands—a conversation with Homer from long ago replaying, line for line, in his subconscious. Dafnis remembered that as a vaccine the Yersinia Pestis bacteria had been a big fat failure. It screwed up a person's mind.

"Is Russia planning to release an aerosol form of the pneumonic plague somewhere?" Homer said.

Dafnis understood every word in the sentence, and this time caught his father's sarcastic tone—Lukin's eyes looked like they were getting ready to shoot poison darts.

"I am impressed," Homer continued, "that you saw my cure for the plague as a potential bioweapon long before I did myself. At the time it seemed all I had was an imperfect cure for the disease—not a history-altering weapon. Tell me, was it Syria's paranoid government that sent you on a search for unauthorized bioweapons? It must have felt like you hit the jackpot when you found mine."

Lukin's translation got the goons smiling, but not for long.

"But," Homer said, "You didn't figure in me being shrewd enough to leave out crucial steps when I uploaded it to the servers, did you?"

Lukin whipped out a notepad and pen from the inside of his suit jacket and crossed to Homer. "You will give us the missing parts." He thrust the pen in Homer's face. "Now."

Dafnis understood enough of this meeting to know these jerks would slit Homer's throat unless they got what they wanted. If it was the bioweapon formula, then his father was in big trouble.

Homer lowered his voice. "What you have there is enough to create the modified bacterium in a lab. Unfortunately—" His father looked almost giddy by now. "The missing steps hold the key to weaponizing it."

Dafnis finished copying the page of formulas and returned his notepad to its home in the inside pocket of his leather jacket.

"To begin with," Homer said. "If you're going to be manufacturing this as an aerosol, how will you keep the compound stable while stored? Secondly, you'll want it to be resistant to antibiotics.

"And surely you know the most effective bioweapon is one that can't be detected and replicated. The North Koreans seem to have mastered this with the recent return of a brain-dead American journalist."

Homer pulled a rubber-necker around Lukin's frame. "There was a time when I was just as enthused as all you gentlemen, *and* foolish enough to believe my vaccine could become an even greater weapon of war than the A-bomb.

"Unfortunately, today is the first time I've seen any of it in six years. My mind was sharper back then, but now . . ." Homer shook his head. "I doubt I could remember the redacted parts," he said.

Lukin clenched his fists before he turned his back and started speaking to the group.

"Neither is there a record," Homer said. For some reason his father seemed to be having fun. "The briefcase with the formula was confiscated by rebel forces during my escape out of Syria. When they saw there was no money, only papers inside, they dumped the contents into the trash and forced me to drive on."

Oh, crap. Was Homer ever digging himself into a hole. Did he just tell these guys he lost whatever it is they want? Dafnis didn't think this scowly crew could get any angrier. Wrong. A Russian circus of flying arms and shouting broke out.

Why they would want to hurt people with a bioweapon, Dafnis couldn't imagine, but he had a feeling they weren't anywhere near done. Neither was Homer.

His father held up his hand. "Your attention, please. There is one other problem with the formula for the bioweapon. A daunting one.

"I myself carried a swab of the live bacterium all the way from Africa," Homer said. "To create the bio-weapon, you will need a culture from a West African strain. Good luck tracking down an outbreak." Homer shrugged and examined his wristwatch. "This is the best I can do for you, but I should go since my wife is waiting for me upstairs. You know how impatient wives can be."

This time Lukin dragged his entire chair in front of Homer and sat down. "Papa K, don't fuck with us because we do know where to find you."

Homer hesitated no more than a few seconds. "Dafnis, can you bring the formula over here so I can have another look to see what I might recall."

He did so while Lukin translated and everything went quiet while Homer stared at the paper.

"All right." Homer lay the formula facedown on the glass. "If one of you could bring this incomplete formula to my island, I will let you remain while I fill in the missing steps and test the aerosol to verify the formula is accurate."

This had to be a Homer story. Did he really want these jerks on their island?

Lukin shoved his chair back in place. He didn't get far with the translation when most of his gang charged out of their seats and roared like the lions Dafnis watched on the Animal Kingdom program in Israel.

Dafnis was just about the only person behaving himself, but that didn't stop Lukin from eyeing him. He cringed as the man left his chair and sent his stinky breath up Dafnis's nose. "Little turd. *You* will give us the formula, then." The man's hand flew up and Dafnis's cheek exploded in pain.

Nabi had slapped Dafnis in the past, but this time he wouldn't make the same mistake of doing nothing. Lukin's stomach was right there in line with his fist. He wound up and pasted him straight in the gut.

The wheezing guy behind Dafnis's chair appeared a lot faster than he could have imagined. He twisted Lukin's arms behind his back and said, "The kid's ours, you scum. Move and I'll cut your balls off and shove them down your throat."

Dafnis glanced down at his own crotch, relieved to be on this ball-stuffer's good side. When he glanced up everybody else was out of their seats, following Lukin's flailing heels to the lobby's main exit where the big guy tossed him into the street like a cigarette butt. Masoud continued to chat on his cell phone in a corner, his back to all the yelling, slapping, slugging, tossing, and possible stuffing.

"Dafnis, hurry."

He looked over his shoulder at Homer, yards away, holding the elevator doors open. Dafnis dashed inside to see the buttons of all five floors lit up. "Aren't we going to our room?" he asked.

"We need to get out of here," Homer said as the elevator lifted. "Follow me and stay quiet." At the next floor up they brushed past a housekeeper and trolley outside the elevator and pounded toward the neon exit sign at the far end of the hall.

"Shit. They'll know where we went now," Homer cursed inside the stairwell. "We're fucked if there's an agent in the alley."

The only people outside were two men in dirty yellow jumpsuits about four cars away, flinging a steaming pile of rotten trash into the back of an idling truck that Dafnis could smell from where he stood. They ducked down and looked at each other before making a run for it.

NO MORE THAN FIFTEEN minutes after being bound and gagged inside the taxi, Claudia thrashed like a hooked fish at the sight of the hotel's glass doors being flung wide, but instead of Dafnis, it was the same guy who had bumped into her. The giant holding him tossed her former tormentor to the sidewalk and waited while the guy limped to a vehicle across the street and drove away.

Minutes later, the same agent burst from the lobby once more and yelled to the one inside their car.

Faisal immediately turned to her. "It seems Homer and Khalid are both missing." As he said this, three unmarked black suburbans, one after the other, screeched to a ragged halt and disgorged teams in riot gear. Another fifteen minutes passed before the original scrawny agent stomped out, spoke to Faisal at length, and went back in.

"He thinks they got away," Faisel said. "Intelligence has checked almost every room in the building."

Without knowing what went on with Masoud she couldn't speculate how they escaped—but they did. What would Faisal do with her now? She instantly got an answer to her unspoken fear.

"We have to let you go. Turn around so I can release the gag and ties. Please don't hit me anymore."

She lunged for the door handle as soon as her hands were freed but found the door still locked. "Let me out, you bastard."

"I will, but there is something you need to know. They want me to follow you. I'm not going to because after my time with Khalid—or, whoever he really is—only a fool would believe he's a terrorist. The guy should know Arabic and . . . I did hear him call Homer 'father' at least once."

Claudia clutched her injured shoulder and squinted at Faisal, not totally convinced it wasn't another trap.

"Get in that taxi ahead of us and go straight to the airport. I'll get out and raise the hood as if this car wouldn't start." He rubbed the heel of his hand against his forehead. "I truly wish this reunion with Homer had turned out better for both of us. But I guess we're on different sides now so . . ." He shrugged, his sad smile reviving the gentle soul she first met.

Click. Click. The door locks released. Free once more, she paused. "You're still on the good guys side." Before she climbed out Claudia reached into the inside pocket of her jacket and pulled out the wad of cash she estimated to be as much as five-thousand in hundred-dollar bills. She split it, returned one half to her coat and set the other discreetly on the back seat in case anyone was watching them. "Look after your family, Faisal."

He sat wide-eyed, then held out his hand. "God be with all of you," he said as they shook hands.

Chapter 25

The cramped space at Le Gardinier restaurant was what you'd expect of a commercial linen closet. Lit by an obligatory forty-watt bulb at the end of a frayed cord and dirty pull-string, the room reeked of chlorine bleach and swirled dust every time Claudia rubbed against the stacks of cardboard boxes. She sat on a stool jammed between a hill of stained tablecloths and a plaster wall chipped and cracked enough to have been lathed on by the very sects of Syrian Christians who'd sheltered Christ's apostles.

She checked her watch.

Dammit. Stop looking at the clock every minute. If Homer and Dafnis don't turn up, just do what he told you and head for the border in a taxi . . . That's right, leave them behind and forever wonder what happened to the poor bastards.

Not that Homer's friend was any less anxious. The man kept poking his head in to refill her wineglass and ask if Homer had sent a message to her phone.

Finally, she could say *yes*. He'd sent three words—*On my way.* Shouldn't it be *our* way? she thought and drained her wine goblet.

Ignoring the owner's pleas to stay hidden, Claudia left the second floor closet and stood with eyes transfixed on the main entrance into the restaurant's courtyard below. Ten excruciating minutes later she dashed to the stairwell and squeezed the hell out of Dafnis.

Homer stood aside with an unpracticed smirk. "Seems like this boy can look after the both of us. He punched that Russian bastard but good."

"What Russian?" she said. About to plant a kiss on Dafnis's forehead she held him at arm's length. "And what the hell is that putrid smell about you?"

The owner showed up. "Please." He motioned to Claudia. "Hide yourselves."

In the lead, Claudia looked over her shoulder. "Did Masoud send a Russian to interrogate you?"

Between her hug and a rare compliment from his father, Dafnis wriggled with uncontained delight. "We escaped on a garbage truck. And it was awful. There were about six of those guys," he said. "They wanted—"

Homer hopped in front of his son just before they entered the linen closet. "I'll tell the story."

Dafnis rolled his eyes, seeming amused for once with his father's overarching self-absorption.

Homer pulled up one of the many boxes inside and sat down. "The meeting wasn't with Masoud's men at all. They were Russian agents trying to steal the classified technology for my drones. I wasn't willing to disclose it so one of them went after Dafnis. *That's* when Masoud's security threw the agent out of the lobby into the street."

"I know . . . I saw it happen."

The men's grins turned to confusion.

"That's right," she said. "I didn't get far. Faisal had me tied up and gagged in a taxi during your entire time in the lobby."

"What?"

"Why?"

"You don't even know, do you?" She looked from one to the other as they shook their heads. Claudia moaned into the incredible realization that these two had no idea of the danger waiting at the sidelines for Dafnis, yet had escaped. "Before Khalid Khazim escaped Syria he detonated a bomb at the presidential palace that killed people. They want him caught—badly."

Long, very long, minutes passed until Dafnis turned to his father. "I guess that's why the big guy said, 'He's ours,' right after he grabbed Lukin."

"What? I didn't hear that."

"You were probably thinking about our escape into the elevator."

Thud. Thud. Homer drove his fist into a paper box packed solid with some kind of linen.

Dafnis merely frowned, looking more confused than worried.

Claudia studied him in earnest. "The Syrian government will execute you if they find you. But first they'll torture you for the names of others fighting for your cause."

"What's a . . . cause?" Dafnis asked. "I don't have one of those, do I?" He pulled out his notepad, opened it to a page, and brought it to Homer. "Can you spell *cause* for me? Here's a pen."

Claudia cringed, expecting Homer to shove the notepad into his son's face, or worse, but instead he raised it to his eyes and gawked at the page. "You have the entire formula?"

Still in the act of nodding, Dafnis staggered as Homer grasped the boy's shoulders. "You're an absolute genius." He slapped his thigh and swooned. "I can't believe you actually remember it."

"I'm pretty sure that's it."

Claudia had no idea what they were talking about and didn't much care while Homer and Dafnis were getting on so well, but it was at this point that Homer's story took an astonishing turn.

"I told Hocking you'd remember everything someday. The thought he might have some competition again sure had him worried."

Had Dafnis's accident snatched a scientific savant from the world? Claudia wondered.

"How you could understand the complexities of manipulating the human genome as an adolescent, I don't know, but it was something to behold." Homer cupped his son's face in mute wonder before sadness overtook him. "I'm so sorry you had to lose that beautiful mind of yours."

Dafnis tried to dislodge his father's hands and said, "But it wasn't *your* fault. I'm the one who built the treehouse and I'm the one who fell out of it. I don't remember the accident, but that's what I was probably doing up there—building a treehouse to get away from you."

The final revelation killed what was left of their celebration as Homer's arms fell to his sides in stunned silence.

"So don't feel bad for me anymore, Father."

Claudia was about to comfort Homer when he abruptly slipped out into the corridor and pressed the door shut behind him.

She was entertained for the next twenty minutes by Dafnis's breathless version of their get-away on the garbage truck and escape at the first traffic light. She recalled how Masoud's man waited until the Russian drove away before returning to the lobby. Perhaps that gave them their head start.

"Room service," Homer said when he finally returned laden with dishes of food. There was cheese and fruit, roast pork tender as butter, fluffy spanakopita, three kinds of salad, baklava, and a bottle of vintage red wine which she was sure Homer had specially requested.

The owner refused payment, but at the end of a lengthy back and forth, he agreed to take a five-hundred-dollar tip. Obviously, the man wasn't intimate enough to be privy to Homer's grief, and if not for Dafnis's teenage appetite most of the food would have gone to waste. For the moment, Homer's only focus was the fatherly affection he owed Dafnis. The two men huddled together, reliving the day and filling each other's wineglasses, no longer father and son, but comrades.

Hip to boney hip, Claudia shunted herself onto the same linen box as Homer. "We're not out of danger quite yet so maybe go easy on the wine." She was serious, but both Homer and Dafnis responded by filling each others' glasses to the very top.

"I wondered when we'd get another chance to be this close," Homer said, handing a smaller shot to Claudia. "Not a rooftop hot tub," he whispered, "but that's okay, isn't it?"

How Homer could be so upbeat after finding his daughter's corpse was not only testament to his ability to survive under stress, but his eternal optimism that good could spring from the worst of circumstances. He linked his arm around her waist and was moving in for a kiss when the closet door banged aside.

"A car is on the way," the owner said. "He's a reliable man I see almost every weekend for off-roading in our jeeps. He'll be able to avoid the checkpoints and get you to the border safely."

Fortunate not to have luggage, their story, if stopped, was to pose as a group of stupid tourists lost on the backroads with their guide. Outsmarting the checkpoints with snarly guards would be no small feat. If not the military police, then the Russians might track them down.

Night's dark veil obscured anything upbeat. The four occupants inside the jeep were already wrapped in the gloom of sundown when they rolled past the decrepit stone buildings of Old Town Damascus. Their route passed through a major roundabout which then exited onto a main highway—the divided thoroughfare surprisingly quiet as it climbed from the Damascus plateau into arid farm terraces. No one spoke except for a comment from Homer that the snow-capped range ahead separated Syria and Lebanon.

But the longer they drove, the more agitated he became, constantly twisting to gaze back at the teeming patch of humanity they'd left. Was he rethinking the decision not to bury his daughter's remains, or was he simply grieving the final curtain on his life in Homs. Mile after mile, sinew by sinew, Homer was losing a part of himself.

After an hour, they exited onto an unpaved road through a rural village and climbed through a mountain pass. It was here the jeep bounced into a gully and emerged on what was no more than a goat trail winding between scrub-covered cliffs of tan soil.

There wasn't a building in sight but she noticed the driver hadn't turned on his headlights even though the path disappeared whenever clouds rolled across the only light from a half-moon.

The vehicle rocked side to side over the rough terrain; the front wheels becoming airborne at times.

"It's okay," Homer said as she reached out to clutch his knee. "Our driver knows this road well."

Ten minutes later, the moon pierced through clouds, illuminating the trail's route up a low rise. "Lebanon is on the other side of this hill," Homer said at the end of a long monologue from the driver. "There's a gas station he's used in the past and a paved road that leads to a place called Yata." The Canadian-Lebanese station owner would help them hire a car bound for Beirut, no more than an hour away.

"Come on, we're here," Homer said. The jeep had halted. The driver was out. Homer turned to her. "Those dollars I gave you. I want to give them to our friend."

But the driver refused the money. The reason: The two thousand dollars was more than he made in two years.

Claudia grabbed Homer's arm as the guy started to climb into the vehicle to leave. "Tell him he needs to deliver it to your friend at the restaurant. That'll work." Homer's eyebrows shot up. The white lie did work and the money remained with those whose only stake in helping them was goodwill.

"Go ahead," Homer said to both of them as they began the climb, "I need to pee before we reach the main road."

About to crest the hill, she turned for a last glimpse of Syria. With the onset of night, a ghoulish canopy of blood-red flashes illuminated the sky over Damascus's northern fringe. People—children—were dying down there, Claudia thought.

Below, outlined against the twilight was a solitary figure lost in mute fascination, not facing Damascus, but staring northward where the ruins of his former life lay. Head bowed, hands pressed to his knees, Homer's body suddenly quaked. One arm rose in the direction of Homs, as if trying to reach into his past and pull all that he cherished to a safer place and time.

How could any human being ever recover from such a tsunami of loss—his family, career, home, friends, city, country. All that remained was Dafnis.

She tramped to the bottom and waited until Homer came alongside and all three of them marched out of Syria, together, in silence.

The linen closet, Faisal, and their bouncy jeep ride to safety were the precious memories Claudia took with her. The same could not be said of Homer. Over the following weeks he aged before her eyes; the last image of his decapitated daughter seemed to be devouring him from the inside out.

Chapter 26

Faced with multiple problems, one should solve the easiest first. Wasn't that what the wise always said? Or did Claudia get that off an old *Gomer Pyle* rerun on the BBC?

Nevertheless, it was a practical credo, close to her own heart. *If you don't want bitter exes—don't get married. If you don't want ungrateful children—don't have kids.* By and large, Claudia was so generous with her wisdom it sometimes led to a dearth of friends.

If you don't want to be bored, stay busy.

A fellow university student once asked Claudia to go with her to a singles all-inclusive resort for a week. "Why would I pay to get drunk and get laid when I can do it here for free," was her reply. "I'd die of boredom in a place like that." Boredom was stalking her again—persistent as a vulture circling a bloated carcass. Her body heavy, her mind dull, as far as she was concerned this thing called *relaxation* was overrated.

The inactivity started soon after the Syria trip with an unexpected catastrophe. Her lead scientist lurched in from the lab one afternoon and announced, "We're short one tube."

"Are you effing kidding me?" she shrieked.

This phrase was the same one uttered by a subset of modern consumers trying to construct a prefab bed frame short one bolt from the factory. But instead of a missing bolt, her lab was in lack of one polytetrafluoroethylene tube critical to their 3D printer.

"To put it simply," Claudia told Homer over the phone later, "the tubing delivers the alginate used to form our heart from the print head." She stood inside her lab, the sweat dripping from her chin—a no-no inside a sterile lab. "The damn air-conditioner over here is buggered, too."

"The AC is a quick fix but the tubing could take weeks to be delivered," he said. "The team would be better off with their families in London, don't you think?"

"You won't catch *me* back there, yet."

"Then go to the beach in Malta. I know the perfect—" he tried before she cut in.

"I'm not one to sit around on a beach. I'm still expunging the Tel Aviv Grand Palace from my system, but I'm happy *you're* feeling better."

She was ready and willing to be a shoulder for Homer's grief, if only he would use it. In fact, Claudia found herself thinking about the man several times a day. Was she worried about him? In love? Or simply bored? Since boredom was the easiest to tackle, she phoned Homer then took the hydrofoil to Homer's office to volunteer for the dark side—work on one of his black market transplants.

As she entered his outer office, she could hear Hocking on the other side of the smoked glass door arguing with Homer. When Claudia lived at the Daphne clinic, the flighty little man reminded her of a pesky insect that silently reappears from dark corners. She'd never imagined he had a volatile side to him, but of course, everyone did.

"I never understood why you destroyed it in the first place," she heard him say, "You've been wanting a permanent solution to these terrorists since we arrived here. We should seize on the opportunity that Dafnis has given us. Take it as a sign."

There was a long pause before Homer replied: "If you can track down the bacterium, I'll think about it, but you need to get out of here because Claudia is on her way over."

This sounded like a good time to duck back into the hall and pretend to run into Hocking. As she did so, the man broke out into his usual slimy smile—then winked.

What the fuck was that supposed to mean?

"Have you been telling Hocking tales of hot tubs?" she asked Homer at his desk.

"Hardly," Homer said while scrolling through his schedule of urgent cases. "He knows about my business with Israel and my daughter in Syria, but I'd rather not speculate on whatever fantasies may be in that head of his." He stopped and backtracked a screen. "How about this one? It's so basic you could do it blindfolded. A girl of five needs a kidney." He raised his focus from the monitor. "She has a rare AB blood type, but we've already—"

She grabbed his wrist. "If you're sourcing through the black market, then count me out. Adults, fine, but children are too vulnerable."

"Actually, the girl and the donor both live in The Squats. Her kidney will come from a relative with the same blood type, so the entire transplant will be free for the family. I'm hoping you'll settle for a small stipend."

"Don't worry about it, Homer. You must be so proud of what you've done for the families at The Squats."

One would expect him to be waltzing around the room, high on helping the most vulnerable in his republic, yet the corners of Homer's mouth did little more than twitch. Since Syria, he'd become almost morose. Was he finally seeing how repugnant it was to manufacture arms in the midst of his traumatized refugees?

Claudia would gladly take the cantankerous crusader who kissed her on the plane over this empty version of Homer.

———●———

CLAUDIA'S FIRST UP-close visit to The Squats' shipping container camp was to evaluate the family's kidney donor, who thankfully was not this frail, worn down nub of a man at the door of his allotted metal cubicle.

In fact, the head of the family looked far too old to have a five-year-old daughter, but that was before Claudia learned what might have aged Pastor John Yen on his two-thousand-mile odyssey by land and sea out of Africa. This, after his church and home were confiscated by Sudan's Islamic government.

From what she could glean from his broken English, despite paying huge sums to human smugglers the extended family still had money when they boarded their first transport truck in Khartoum. One month later, theft and extortion had taken the rest, and out of the eight who started, only five remained alive. One of those was the five-year-old daughter who needed the kidney transplant.

Biking from Jaza's clinic put Claudia's boots closer to the ground than the helicopter had and knocked the stuffing out of any fantasies she had about how quaint life could be in a settlement of tiny homes. The rectangular containers were just that—a metal box with a door and window punched at each end. She already knew there was only one communal kitchen and shower block for about a dozen families. Despite the tidy gravel pathways and an impressive playground, this was the Republic's version of an overcrowded slum.

She stepped inside the gloomy building and concluded all five family members lived in the one compact room. A wardrobe, two sets of bunks, and a wooden desk took up most of the space. A bony finger emerged from a painfully hunched torso, and pointed her toward a beaten down easy chair dead center of the sparse room.

The pastor collapsed onto the bottom bunk, his supine body soon reduced to a still-life portrait of two lean tibias draped over the edge of a sagging mattress. Hard to know the last time the man had managed to stand tall or get himself to the shops. With nothing but bicycles for transport, the uphill footslog to the main square she'd visited with Benny would still take at least a half-hour from this camp.

When her eyes finally adjusted to the unlit space, Claudia noted two things: wayward cushion springs were invading her private parts, and the Yen family at least had their own stainless steel sink and toilet. The computer tower and chunky monitor atop the desk stood out as from a bygone era. Hopefully the wifi connection was more up-to-date.

Right about the time the bone-weary pastor began lapsing more and more into his local Sudanese dialect instead of broken English, a round-faced African girl of about two years peeked in from outside. When Claudia smiled and waved, she crept forward and climbed onto the saggy couch, stuck a thumb into her mouth, and drifted to sleep in the surgeon's lap, lulled by the sound of the adults' chatter.

"My—my . . ." The pastor pointed at the child, then wobbled to his feet. Locked in a stiff-kneed gait, he headed to the open door with the energy of a shackled prisoner nudged to the precipice of a grave he'd been forced to dig for himself.

Leaning on the doorframe like a crutch, he managed a raspy caw. Only then did it dawn on her: this emaciated soul might have tuberculosis in his joints. Was that what finished off his young daughter's kidneys? What was wrong with the clinic that they couldn't see this? For all Homer's bluster about "no fuck-ups," it seemed the Republic's benevolence had so far failed the Yen family.

An adolescent boy soon appeared and joined the pastor on the lower bunk.

"Papa wants me to answer your questions."

Claudia made a mental note to give this adolescent the instructions for getting his father TB screening.

"Today is my younger cousin's turn to tend the store so I have lots of free time."

"Younger? How old are you?"

"Fifteen."

Since the Yens spoke no Arabic, like most Africans in Homer's republic this boy must have had a steady diet of English and it had paid off. "That girl is my cousin."

Claudia felt the child stir and tuck her chubby legs into an even more compact ball.

"But she lives with us now," the boy said.

"My wife worked surrogate," Pastor John chimed in.

For long seconds Claudia tried to organize the pieces of this defeated man's life. He was not only operating a corner store, but was the sole caregiver of four children—two not even his own. "Did she die during childbirth?"

"He means my *aunt* is a surrogate," the boy said. "She's been living on the other island for two years. In a ladies dormitory, I think. But she gets to visit us one weekend a month. *My* mother died of cancer a long time ago."

Apparently, six years, at most, qualified as a long time for a teenager. The woman couldn't have died before her five-year-old daughter was born. Claudia shook her jowls against a long-winded sigh. "So—let me get this straight. While your aunt works as one of our surrogates, your father is responsible for you and your ill sister, his niece here in my lap, and nephew at the store."

The teen nodded.

"Has someone talked to you about what will happen during your sister's transplant?"

Another nod.

Everything was in order, except for the poor aunt pumping out surrogate babies to pull the Yen clan out of their cubed existence.

Nevertheless, Claudia had what she came for. The family donor was not only healthy but short for his age which meant the kidney he was donating would be a better fit for his young sister.

Since he was only a child when they were violently forced from their home in Sudan, it was his emotional health that was more of a concern. Could he handle more disruption? At fifteen, he wouldn't have reached the age of consent in many countries, but if he was mature enough to tend a store alone, he was capable of knowing whether he wanted to donate one of his kidneys.

The boy smiled politely while she sized him up. "And what has happened to your uncle, dear?"

Beside him, the mattress came to life with the jerky movements of an ambulatory skeleton. "My brother works slaves at a Libya farm," the pastor said while propped on one elbow.

She hoped not. Claudia was sure the Sudanese father meant *employees* when he used the word *slaves*. Once more, she looked to the pastor's son. "My uncle and my other cousin are slaves on an olive plantation."

Back to his recumbent posture, the pastor spoke in his African dialect and the teen translated. "The Libyan police took all of us to jail and we had to pay them to feed us."

He listened to his father's next installment, but Claudia suspected he didn't need to. The boy was steam-rolling through his father's phrases as if by rote. "Well, maybe they just looked like police. When the money was gone, my brother and I had no one to phone for more so they beat us every day with batons."

More input from the pastor. "My eighteen-year-old nephew, too," the teen translated into English. "They took us to an olive plantation. We lived with the chickens and they fed us only after we filled our baskets. I couldn't stand so I didn't eat for two days. Then they put me in a truck. I thought they were going to shoot me."

The boy paused his translation and looked to his father but got nothing but a weak wave of the hand to continue. "But they took me to a boat with hundreds of people inside and gave me a phone. If I didn't answer their call in one week, they said they would kill my brother and his son. I found my family in the boat and my brother's wife said everything will be fine. She—"

The boy stopped, as if expecting a signal from his father. Seeing none, he whispered. "She will sell herself in the big city."

The pastor grunted and came alive. "Homer saved us. Everyone happy now."

The boy gave her a sheepish shrug. "I don't think my uncle and cousin are happy. They're still in Libya. We send the slave traders money every month when they call."

———◉———

THE DAY OF THE TRANSPLANT, the donor kidney was there for her in a stainless steel basin when she entered. Everything fell into place but only because she'd watched the same team at work earlier in the day. As basic as a kidney transplant was, at forty-seven, her visual recall needed all the help it could get. Of course, she didn't want that to get out.

After the transplant, she sat in the empty staff lounge, visualizing, her hands moving to the steps needed for a successful implant of her bionic heart. She went through it over and over, but always got stuck at the same point. Eventually, like a missing puzzle piece she worked around the gap, and finished the imaginary procedure. Then she tried to work the puzzle in reverse but still couldn't recall the missing step.

A pitched squealing ripped through her. She gasped and turned to see a cleaner vacuuming between the round laminate tables—the plastic chairs already upended onto the tabletops. Somehow she'd missed that symphony of clatter. The wall clock was at ten after eight. She'd been trying to recall the bionic implant procedure for over two hours and her head pulsed as if someone was spiking a volleyball off her temple.

Another day in Homer's Republic had ended, one of the best so far, yet, a sense of urgency thrummed in the background, the clock on her career running out. Here she sat totally dependent on a nefarious facility and megalomaniac to bring her bionic heart to the world.

Was she destined to be the worst kind of ordinary? A bitter researcher who never managed even a pinch of what she'd hoped. She remembered how her mother, too, complained about the uncontrolled passage of time, but for an entirely different reason. The old woman wanted a quick exit ramp.

Claudia used to drive to the family farm from her hospital job in Bucharest only to find her mother sitting in her dark kitchen, moaning.

"What's the matter?" Claudia would then ask. "Where does it hurt?"

Suffering from nothing but old age, her mother always said, "Oh, everywhere, I guess. When is it all going to end?"

When Countess Vlakia's pain finally ceased, so did Claudia's temporary connection with Romania. She picked up and transferred to a London hospital where she could build her artificial heart theory into a working prototype with the latest 3D advances.

Until the bio-printer's missing tube came in, her cutting edge research was at a standstill. Perhaps it *was* time to go in search of a transplant recipient in London. Go home and check the mail at her apartment overlooking the Hackney race track. Sit on the balcony with a steaming coffee, and soak up the comforting smells of ripe horse manure floating on a morning breeze.

Inside the staff lounge Claudia realized she was famished, but since the choppers didn't fly after dark she'd have to crash in Homer's penthouse again. However, it would save her having to fly back to check on her patient.

She headed to the round-the-clock take-out at the cafeteria and found two surrogates drinking tea inside the darkened kitchen. One spoke enough English for Claudia to order— "Whatever you've got"—but regretted the open-ended statement later when there seemed no end to the stream of dishes brought to her table.

Between the banging pots, loud chatter, and spit and sizzle of fried foods she wondered if they'd brought in reinforcements. At the end, just as Claudia put down her fork and shoved the empty plate to the side, at least six women crept out of the kitchen. They eyed each other as if one of them was carrying a cake with sparklers. No cake, thank goodness, or she might have burst a gut with one more bite.

The group parted to one side and a cook with passable English said, "This is Mrs. Yen."

For a second, Claudia wondered if the pastor's "long-dead" wife was in fact still alive and it was another failure of translation. The woman who stepped into the spotlight turned out to be someone Claudia already knew as Saania, the spirited woman who had choked the living daylights out of Homer that day at lunch.

Saania and the aunt which The Squats boy had spoken of were one in the same. Claudia may have saved Saania's niece, but what was that compared to this stout-hearted woman's struggle to keep the entire Yen clan and her enslaved husband and son alive with endless surrogate pregnancies.

Saania wrapped Claudia in a bear hug, and one after another the other women did likewise, riding the same river of joy. Dour-faced Claudia always had to psyche herself up prior to the inevitable outpouring of euphoria in the family room after a successful transplant.

This time it came out of nowhere. Claudia had many years of practice with *hugus interruptus*, but these young women were more tenacious than they looked. When it finally concluded, or seemed to, the gratitude circle stuck with her all the way to the elevator, bawling without restraint as the doors closed and Claudia fell into the silence of the elevator's cold steel siding.

Homer was asleep when she crept in and found the blankets in a closet right where she'd left them months earlier. These days, she had more than enough access to the internet in her office.

She lay in the dark with the faint seesaw of waves far below. It wasn't a particularly windy night so perhaps this calming sound had always been there for her to relish—if only she had listened.

Unloved and unclaimed by any nation, the postcard had said, yet it wasn't nearly as unloved as she'd first thought, nor unclaimed. The Republic of Homer and its thirty-thousand inhabitants were more than happy to make a life here. After all, Homer's creation, while no Xanadu, was saving far more lives than it was taking. Had she judged his republic of tough love too harshly?

You've given him space to grieve his daughter, now go and ask what else he needs. Isn't that what friends do? She wasn't entirely sure. Homer might just be her first true friend of the opposite sex. He cared not that she'd lost her medical license and reputation. Her medical expertise was valued here rain or shine. It was more than she'd got out of Bags.

Gratitude and discretion in return was all Homer wanted. If weapons production was the quickest and most legal way to turn a profit, what right did she have to foist her liberal ideals on him? How could she deny him his dream of a better future for the refugees when he had so selflessly promoted hers?

She drifted off swiftly, held in the palm of exhaustion, but it was the best kind of tiredness possible: created from knowing one had saved the life of a child.

———◆———

HOMER WAS CLOSING THE door to the Yen girl's ICU room when Claudia snuck up behind him and slipped an arm around his waist the next morning. When he turned, not uncomfortable, but seeming a touch surprised by her intimacy, an impish grin emerged.

"Did I just break protocol or something?" she asked.

"Not as far as I'm concerned. I didn't expect you back until this afternoon."

"I never left. Slept on your couch."

His gaze migrated downward. "I can see that."

Claudia surveyed the linen shirt and pants she'd worn from The Squats the day before. Subjected to a sweaty night of tossing on Homer's couch it now resembled a laundry basket of crumpled clothing in need of an intervention by an iron.

Homer got on his haunches in front of a nearby laundry cart and thumbed through a stack of scrubs. He rose with an armful, pinched a blue muslin overcoat off the top, and motioned to the Yen's room. "Wear this in there, then change into some scrubs for the transport home. There's both medium and large here."

"Okee dokie, boss." After he helped her into the jacket, she tried to jam the two sets of scrubs into her briefcase but found it wouldn't close.

"No. No. That won't do," he said. "At the very end of this hall is a shower room for patients. I'll leave them on a bench inside. And you might as well take a shower, too."

"What?" She lifted her armpit to her nose. "I smell?"

"Well . . . Not really."

"Which is it? I either smell or I don't."

"Okay. You smell."

She reeled back. "It's that damn leather couch. It doesn't breathe."

"Claudia. Don't worry about it. It happens. We all sweat."

It was something she might have said herself. What *was* she worried about, anyway? That Homer might find her too stinky to sleep with?

She handed him the scrubs and motioned toward the ICU room. "Everything fine?"

Homer nodded. "Her father's in there. Listen, before you catch the helicopter back why not have an early lunch with me?"

From the way he was pinching his bottom lip and suppressing a smile, she instantly knew why. "The tube. It's finally here, isn't it?"

"You'll have to have lunch with me if you want an answer."

"Homer, come on. Tell me."

"I'll be in my office." He patted her shoulder.

"Damn," she said under her breath. "Okay. See you in a bit."

She watched him scoot around a series of yellow caution cones halfway to the shower room then stop and joke with the cleaner swiping a mop across the tiles.

They all loved him—the clients, the guards, the patients, the refugees, even the cleaning staff. Not once had Claudia even acknowledged the existence of her London hospital's housekeeping staff.

Homer—a universally despised thief of body parts. What might those sanctimonious types think had they shadowed her the past twenty-four hours and heard the Yen family's story of survival? Seen the gratitude in the eyes of the surrogates? Or watched Homer's regard for every person in his republic no matter how insignificant?

Pastor John was the only visitor in the room when she entered. His daughter was sitting up and smiling. She'd met Claudia only once during a pre-surgical evaluation but the girl had been dizzy and nauseous at the time. No wonder she thought Claudia was another nurse coming to check her vitals.

"They just did me."

"Great. And now the doctor is going to do you, too. How do you feel, sweetie?" The question seemed redundant since the child was too busy scarfing down a mouthful of chocolate cake to answer.

Claudia tried a wink in her father's direction but found the pastor with the same vacant stare as before. "How is your son, pastor? Has he come by yet?" It was such a simple question, yet the man's eyes flew open.

The girl stopped chewing. "My brother didn't visit me. He's at home now."

"Oh. Well, that sounds good enough. You seem like a very resilient family."

The entire time she did her follow-up examination the girl chatted non-stop about her friends at school and what she was going to do with them when she returned—so full of life after being on the brink. Children were amazing survivors and that's why Claudia wanted to spend as much time as possible with them while she still walked the earth.

Inside the shower later, with the hot water cascading over her back, she remembered the pastor's odd silence. The poor guy had a lot on his mind, but how defeated did a man have to be not to rejoice in the saving of his child's life?

The shower room was spotless—the guards who did double duty as cleaners may not be able to cook but they did a bang-up job on the housekeeping and she told Homer so during their lunch in his office later. It was right after he revealed that the part she'd been waiting on was indeed on-board The Squats hydrofoil.

"I would love to give the men at The Squats the cleaning work here but it's safer to keep traffic between the two islands at a minimum."

"What do you mean by *safer*?" There was a rap at the door which turned out to be their lunch. Homer rose from his desk and raised a finger to his lips before letting the guard in with the trays. With the guard gone and the two of them facing each other across his desk, Homer peeled the lid off a steaming container of roast potatoes. "I'm going to tell you something which only Dafnis and Dr. Hocking are privy to."

What in the world had she done to earn this? Homer now trusted her as much as his own son.

"We have a special key which sends the elevator down to the dungeons," he said.

The veal cutlet at the end of her fork froze mid-air.

"It's okay," he said. "I like to oil people's imaginations, but the only thing down there these days are our drones." He took in Claudia. "You don't seem upset."

"I don't live at the clinic anymore, do I?" she said. "Anyway, I figure since it was armaments which drove the asylum seekers from their homes, there's a case that it should be the same thing which gives them a new one."

Homer's palm sent up a thunder clap. "Aha. I knew it." He began doling out the potatoes with more gusto than a soup kitchen volunteer. "Eventually, we'll open a factory at The Squats, but in the meantime I don't want the technology stolen. Not even the guards can access the dungeon labs."

"That must be some outsized underground which can test a drone."

"Hardly. Dafnis flies them along that stretch of beach we went to. It's remote enough that nobody ever goes there."

After their lunch, while she wound her way to the elevator against a stream of waddling surrogates it was as if this moment in time was where she'd been headed all along—not just since that first day in Homer's Republic—but her entire life. She had her own lab independent of any financial constraints or outside influence. And she had a trusted and valuable friend in Homer. It felt like they'd been orbiting each other from the start, spinning in their separate voids, closer by the hour, until finally, today, Homer's vision pulled her smack into his world.

The elevator doors parted and before Claudia could resist, a hand emerged to yank her in.

"How lucky is this to run into you?" The male nurse was someone she recognized from the Yen family transplant. "We need someone to sign the Yen girl's death certificate before we can send her body to The Squats. The helicopter's waiting."

Claudia couldn't have been more mystified by all the moving parts to this statement had she been peering into the jet engine of a space shuttle.

"What? I saw the girl just—" She checked her watch. "This morning. She was fine."

"Sepsis." He punched the Level 3 button. "Wasn't much we could do to save her once it took hold."

Okay, sepsis *was* a nightmare of an infection which could kill within twelve hours of a surgery, but . . . Shit . . . the child's vitals had been so strong. This nurse must be confused, especially since . . . death certificate? Homer didn't do death certificates.

The nurse exited into the ICU hallway one level up, forcing Claudia to trot alongside. "Who wants a death certificate?"

"Homer. He said the family will need it on the continent."

"What continent?"

"They're all moving to Europe." He slowed and flung a door open for her. It was a different room from where she'd done her examination of the girl only hours earlier. "You didn't know that?"

Claudia stopped in her tracks, her heart pounding at the sight of a sheet draped over a small body. The nurse brushed past and flipped the shroud from the figure's face.

Claudia took one wobbly surreal step forward. *How could it possibly be?* It was all she could do to stop from crying out. Claudia cupped a trembling hand against the cold, gray cheek—not of the five-year-old but the same toddler who had snuggled into her lap inside the Yen's container home.

"Doctor?"

She took the stethoscope in the nurse's hand and with automaton efficiency her mind landed on the raw silence inside the tiny figure. Claudia scribbled her name across the death certificate, knowing exactly where she was headed next.

———◦———

SHE FOUND HOMER ON a bar stool inside his penthouse, thumbing through documents.

"Claudia. Stop." He tried to corral her thrashing arms. "Settle down."

"I don't want to settle down."

He wasn't on the phone, but it wouldn't have made any difference to her when she burst in.

"What in the hell is going on?" he said, staggering back from the stool.

"How could you harvest an organ from a healthy infant? It's not ethical."

"Why did you go ahead with it, then? You saw her donor report."

"No, I did not. I visited the family instead. I assumed it had to be the older boy's kidney."

In Homer's lawless republic, Claudia had become sloppy, and now an innocent child was needlessly dead. She paused. "Look at you." She knew her accusatory finger reflected in the bar mirror behind him could just as easily have been aimed at the pathetic ball of rosy delusions she'd been spinning since Syria.

Of all the ups and downs of their journey to the Middle East the image which kept coming up was the humility on Homer's face inside the linen closet when he realized how expendable he was to Dafnis. He lost a daughter that day, but gained a son. The grief gave her a kinder Homer—so she thought.

The cathartic shift she imagined in Homer's soul was merely a revised business plan to generate GDP from bombs rather than organ harvesting.

Claudia's hands went to her hips. "You just killed the Yen baby and it's business as usual, isn't it?"

"For God's sake. I *did not* kill her. It was sepsis. Living donors do die sometimes. As sad as it is, the girl became a statistic."

She bent double. "What of the girl's poor mother. You—" She thrust her finger at him again. "You will be the one to march down to that dormitory and tell Saania. Not me."

"Of course I will. I would never dream of shirking my duty to this facility."

"How could you sit through lunch with me and not say a word?"

"She wasn't your patient."

"Then why did I sign her death certificate?"

Homer slumped against one of the bar stools. "I'll have a word with the procurement team. That shouldn't have happened."

"Oh hell. I don't care about that." Claudia was now sitting at the bar, eyes squeezed shut, a thumb and forefinger pressed deeply into the bridge of her nose.

She heard him move behind the bar and lift a bottle from the shelf. A gurgling of liquid followed. *Clunk.* Cool glass brushed against her fingers: the intoxicating aroma of her favorite scotch wafted upward. She opened her eyes just long enough to lash out and send the glass scuttling along the countertop, not intending for it to slide off and smash as it did.

Homer simply grunted.

She glared while he poured a tumbler for himself. "I suppose this was the pastor's idea," she said. "The mother doesn't even know."

He downed the drink, skirted the counter and slid onto a seat, leaving a buffer of one stool between them. "The toddler's mother was the one who asked for the blood tests on her child. She wanted a way out of surrogacy. I made sure the compensation would be enough for all of them to move anywhere in the world they wanted."

Claudia whipped around. "But you said—"

"I said the procedure was free. I decided to compensate the donor family, which is my right as the owner of this clinic."

He held up his hand as Claudia tried to cut in. "Yes, we could have left her on dialysis instead of endangering another child's life, but think about what I was up against. Everyone was set to benefit and there was a miniscule amount of risk."

"And you explained that risk?"

"Yes. To both the pastor and Sannia. I gave them all the possible outcomes, verbally and in written form. But in the end Saania only had her eye on the money.

"I came so close to rescinding the payment, but then I imagined how I would feel every time I saw Sannia waddling around the garden with a big belly. . . . You knew about her husband and son enslaved in Libya, didn't you?"

Claudia nodded and pushed herself off the stool. "If that's what this was all about, surely one of your black market thugs could have arranged an exchange."

"Believe me, we tried offering money. Those bastards in Libya know a bottomless money stream when they see it. And they know how to consume your patience."

"The Libyan government must know about the human trafficking," she said.

Homer threw his head back and let out a wheezing belly laugh. "It's anarchy. Why, oh, why did NATO ever get rid of Gaddafi?"

"He was a dictator."

"So? *I'm* a dictator. Does that mean I should be strung up? Gaddafi's downfall was underestimating the fury of his enemies—especially the foreign oil companies he kicked out. If he had succeeded in uniting Africa, what with all the oil they have?" Homer shook his head at the very idea of it.

As political as Claudia was, she had never given a thought to this portrayal of Western bullying.

Homer sank onto the closest stool. "Not all strongmen are on the wrong side of history, Claudia. It's the wealthy who want you to think that."

With his republic perched at the intersection between the West and Africa, it made sense he would feel the refugees who floundered off-shore were still in the grip of the West's slavery. As were the two men sold to a Libyan plantation.

For the longest time, neither of them spoke, until Claudia rose. "Filling my time with your transplants was a bad idea. The team will have the prototype printed and programmed to the power pack in a matter of days. I'm going to London to start preparing for my first recipient." She left without so much as a glance in Homer's direction.

Chapter 27

S hut that rattling window, or you won't get any sleep. Claudia shook off her grogginess and reached for the cord on her bedside lamp, almost tumbling to the floor. There wasn't any lamp to turn on, nor any window to shut because she was in her windowless office, not Homer's guesthouse.

She swung her legs over the side of the cot and checked the digital display on her watch. Two in the morning. *Oh shit.* She had to be up and at the hydrofoil dock in just four hours. Since she'd forgotten to arrange a ride from The Squats' only taxi, she'd also have to hoof it down to the dock with her suitcase for fifteen minutes.

Rattle, bang, rattle. Was someone trying to break in, unaware she was inside sleeping? Good thing she'd reprogrammed the door fob. It couldn't be security, because other than her bionic heart lab the second floor was still blissfully bare of activity. With no elevator nor operating rooms yet, all the in-patients stayed on the first floor.

Two more leaden raps. She crept to the door in the dim glow of a nightlight inside the bathroom. Best to first scare the hell out of whoever it was, then page security.

"Who's there?" she demanded.

Instead of shocked silence, the break-in artist said: "Homer."

She flung the door open to find him drenched from head to toe; standing in a pool of water which trailed all the way to the stairwell.

"What in hell are you doing here?" she said, squinting while the room's overhead fluorescent sputtered to life.

He staggered in, water gushing over the lip of his runners with each step.

"No. Not there," she said when he lay a hand on her cot. "Jesus. You're drunk, aren't you? Don't move until I get a towel. How did you even get here at this hour?" She shoved a towel from her shower into his hands and draped another one over the desk chair. "There must be one hell of a storm going on outside." She wheeled the chair over and pushed him into it. "Take off those soaked shoes."

He tugged one off and poured its contents onto the lino flooring. "No storm," he said through quivering pale lips. "The boat filled with water." He flicked strings of dripping hair from his eyes and thrust an arm in a shaky arc which she assumed meant waves.

"What boat?" She paused to imagine a drunk but determined Homer staggering down the steep trail to the rigid inflatable before somehow hauling its trailer to the water's edge and launching it into the waves. "Are you nuts? You got here with that hokey motor? In the dark? During a rainstorm? You could have died if the outboard gave out."

He tugged at the other runner; the momentum sent him tumbling to the floor. "It's not raining." His butt on solid ground, he upended his second shoe. A dash of water hit the floor.

"Right. I can see we're going to need more towels." She whipped some scrubs from a coat hook on the bathroom door and placed them in his lap. They were the ones he'd handed to her the previous morning at his clinic. "Put these on. I'm getting more towels."

She jabbed a finger in his direction. "Don't go anywhere." That qualified as possibly the most ridiculous thing she'd said all year. By now, almost flat on his back, Homer resembled road kill splatter.

Minutes later, she swept in carrying a stack of dry towels. Homer was minus the wet clothes all right and back sitting in the office chair, clutching nothing but a wool blanket off her cot, his hairy legs shaking and bluish.

He struggled to his feet and planted a steadying foothold, the pointed ends of the blanket playing peek-a-boo with his genitalia.

"Are you leaving me?" Sounding like a child with two front teeth missing, his plea whistled through chattering teeth.

"I thought I told you to put the scrubs on." She plunked the towels onto her cot, and whipped up the now pancaked scrubs he'd been sitting on. "Here." Down Homer went into the office chair, the scrubs in his lap once more. "I don't want to have to say it again."

With that, she hit the light switch and flopped onto her cot, fingertips to eyelids. Not to give him privacy. No. They were far beyond that common courtesy. Her bloodshot eyeballs were burning like a son-of-a-bitch.

Whoosh. Plop. "Are you leaving?" he repeated.

Thud. Bang. He was finally getting into something dry.

"Yes." She continued to massage her eyes. "The hydrofoil is coming at six."

A cold trembling hand pawed her arm. "Please don't leave me. I love you."

She opened one eye to find him on his knees beside the cot. "Wha—?" Bare-chested in the glow from the tiny nightlight, the scrub bottoms more or less over his butt, she dragged him up to lie face to face beside her.

"I didn't want her to die. Such a beautiful child." Propped on one elbow, his alcohol-soaked regret tumbled out. "I'm sorry Claudia."

The man wasn't talking about his daughter at all.

"What kind of bastard lets that happen?"

"The kind that doesn't do her job properly," Claudia moaned. "I should have checked the donor report. Although, I'm not sure I could have resisted that poor woman's pleas much more than you."

He lay back, sniffed and dragged a knuckle across each cheek. "This thing I've started has gone to hell. A thief. A con man. That's what my staff call me behind my back. Fuck 'em. Ungrateful freeloaders."

There was nothing Claudia needed to say because Homer was doing it for her.

"All I've ever wanted was to help people. Not kill them."

She freed one arm and snugged it under his neck, then lay back to let the silence still their aching hearts.

"I'm so tired," he murmured. "I want to go home to my own bed. Take my wife out to dinner. Pick up Daphne from school and go to the zoo. She really loved the elephants. But I guess they're probably dead now, too ..." His chest heaved once again, his voice a halting mess. "Oh, child. Why didn't you wait for me at the school like I told you?"

Eventually, Homer's body and his grief stilled. She reached down and pulled one of the laundered towels across his shoulders. Three hours of restful slumber. Surely she owed Homer that much.

Claudia drifted, roused by the occasional cry from the depths of Homer's nightmares. Dull and aimless since he found his daughter's body, Homer needed a good poke with a sharp stick. Drain, patch, and pump new life into the guy. He might be self-righteous, but he wasn't a particularly *bad* man, afterall. Thanks to Claudia, had he not promised to end his predatory organ trafficking?

He burrowed like a cold kitten into the space between her warm body and outstretched arm, the fight knocked out of him. "Poor Homer." She stroked his cheek with the back of her hand, only because he likely wouldn't remember. "I'm coming back as soon as I find my recipient. You don't think I'd leave my team and the lab behind, do you?"

What was she supposed to do with this gutful of tenderness for Homer when the battle to bring her bionic heart to market ruled her life? Neither was there room for him inside her race for a Nobel Prize. A mere human, Homer had stiff competition. If by some cataclysm Claudia could no longer work and got a notion to lie like this with just one man—Homer would be it.

The deep lines on his face came into focus. Here was a man of convictions and dreams, certain humanity could be compassionate if only people would get out of his way. Strange how easily she'd come to admire Homer the strongman.

How easy, too, it had become to turn her back on the immoral trade-offs she now found herself in.

CLAUDIA WOKE TO THE click of a door, and reached to cancel the final ten minutes left on her phone's alarm. With both Homer and his pile of wet clothes gone, she figured it was possible he'd taken them to the hospital dryers, intending to return. To keep the hospital staff ignorant of her lab, she posted a generic goodbye note on the door saying they could expect her return in two weeks or less.

At the dock she paced up and down for want of a seat. It was while she stared at the dark foamy waves rolling in and out that the sun's first rays lit up what looked like a half-submerged inner tube but which was, in fact, Homer's navy seal inflatable and motor all but underwater. She was still chuckling when a voice behind asked, "What's so funny?"

Claudia turned to see a properly dressed Homer in dry jeans and a t-shirt. He followed her gaze to the swamped inflatable and grimaced.

"Are you waiting for the hydrofoil or just stalking me?" she said.

Homer held up a satellite phone she recognized from the hospital's reception. At least he'd been lucid enough the night before to leave his own behind. "Benny's on the phone. He's calling from their chalet in Romania."

Had she missed his call while showering an hour ago? She grabbed the phone. "Benny? What's wrong?"

"Nothing. I can't thank you enough for suggesting we take Maya home to Citadel Island. She loves the wolf sanctuary, of course, and everything is so fresh and clean here. I'd forgotten how beautiful the mountains are in—"

"Benny. Bad timing. I'm heading to London."

From the corner of her eye she noticed Homer edge closer.

"If it's for recipients for your bionic heart trials, why not let Homer find them while you finish the prototype," Benny said.

She had this vision of Homer scheming with Benny before casting off in his leaky tin can. She wandered out of earshot. "Did Homer call you yesterday or is this a coincidence?"

Benny chuckled. "Homer loves you. At your age, how many more offers of this caliber do you think you will get? Do not bugger it up."

She sighed. *Offers of this caliber* was it? Was Benny intimating her love life was an estate sale of ancient old crap nobody wanted.

"We love you, Claudia. More every day," Benny said. In the background, Maya chimed in at the top of her voice: "We love you, Auntie Claudia."

"Tell Maya I love her more than the sky is wide."

"Take care until we meet again," he said and ended the call.

The hydrofoil had docked while she was on the phone. She sauntered toward it and wordlessly returned the phone to Homer, who was struggling to head her off with a spirited backward skip.

"What did Benny say?"

She ignored him, a touch irritated he'd brought one of her friends into their bizarre relationship.

Claudia halted and glanced down the dock at the ferry. "He said you love me and I better not bugger it up."

Homer's eyes widened until she cracked a smile and he grasped her hands and raised them to his lips. "He's still flying in, though, isn't he?" Homer said.

"I sure as hell hope not. I don't want him knowing we're starting the implants." Claudia tried to slap a hand over her stupid blunder, but it was too late.

His eyes narrowed. "What are you talking about? You promised Maya the first implant."

"Yes, but I didn't really think . . . I mean, I was expecting Maya would be offered a heart on the transplant list by now." She was babbling as if Homer wasn't there. "I was counting on it."

"Maya *was* offered a heart last week," he said, "but they turned it down so she could get your implant instead. I promised to phone when the tubing came in and that's what I did."

She grabbed his shoulders, her voice shaking. "You didn't." Stay cool, Claudia told herself. The secret was out, but there was still a chance Maya was eligible for a donor heart.

"Homer. This is important. What did they tell the registry?"

"That they could take Maya off the list. They found a heart out of country."

Arms clutching her midriff, Claudia turned from Homer to rock back and forth in disbelief: "She's done then."

"What does it matter?" he said. "She has your prototype."

"No." Claudia said, shaking her head, her words now riding a wave of panic. "I can't implant the bionic heart into Maya because it's only for infants. A bionic heart can't grow in the same way one would from a real baby."

An expression of gaping, twisted confusion came over Homer. "You knew this all along?"

She lowered her head in silence.

"You would risk your goddaughter's life to build a measly lab?" As the ferry captain approached, Homer stomped off to the edge of the dock.

"I'm leaving soon," the captain told Claudia.

"Thank you for stopping, but I won't be going today," she said.

"And you, sir? Can I take you to your clinic?"

Stiff with rage, Homer raised a finger. "I'll be there shortly," he said over his shoulder.

"It's not a measly lab," Claudia said to Homer's back when they were alone. "It's going to save hundreds, thousands of sick babies. How many young lives did you snuff out by lying that they weren't worth saving?"

That got him turned around. "We're giving Maya her new heart before anything else, so don't even think about sneaking off to London." Homer started toward the ferry. "And if that gang of yours abandons you in the meantime, so be it."

Chapter 28

D*ammit.* Claudia tossed her satellite phone into the crumpled sheets of her cot and tiptoed across the chilled lino of her office. Four minutes later, coffee in hand, she refreshed the messages. Day eight and still no word from Homer on a donor for Maya, which meant her scientists were also going snakey with boredom.

"Stop phoning me every day," Homer told her on day two. "You'll be the first one to know when I find a donor."

Most mornings the hallway outside her office would have been humming with her team's chatter and the constant click of the lab's door as they arrived. But with prototype number one finished, she imagined them languishing in boredom at their dormitory where Jeremy was likely cuing up his morning check-in.

She had such a variety of lies going it was hard to keep the details straight: Homer was always *hours away* from firming up a recipient for her team's prototype, or, when it concerned Paula and Benny, the team was *working their tails off* to get Maya's implant ready. The old lie to Bags was the least troublesome since they were both avoiding each other for completely different reasons. The story for him was that team members were away, "picking up lab work around the EU."

Minutes later, the chat app in her satellite phone beeped. "Nothing new, guys," she said, not even bothering with a *hello.*

"Claudia, is that you?" It was Homer.

"It's me." She put him on *speaker* and gulped a mouthful of coffee.

"I sympathize with your restless scientists," he said, "but Maya is still my priority. It's taking longer than usual. The black market

238

is a bit of a deadzone for children." (Homer wasn't one for word nuance).

"That's why I've always sourced from the locals." (Again, calling a coma patient a local was a stretch.) "You may not know, but we've stopped all the hydrofoil rescues, too. The Squats is at capacity."

"You can't take the chopper up for a look?"

"You mean pick some children from the sea and abandon the rest?"

She did, but actually voicing the concept made it sound a lot harsher. "I guess not."

"Good, because I would never allow that. There are two comatose youths over there in long term care, though. Their EEGs are showing better than average for full or partial recovery. The boy's family has refused, but you could harvest the girl's heart. She has no family."

"But I thought . . ." she started to say.

"That I had some kind of epiphany?" he asked. "No. I agreed to contain my harvesting to the brain-dead, only because it made you happy. Do you want the girl's heart or not?"

Yes would be the wrong answer, Claudia thought, but so would *No*. "I'll think about it," she said.

"Fine. By the way, Maya has asked me to deliver a message. She wants everyone to call her 'the bionic woman' now. The kid is over the moon to be the first person in the world to have a bionic heart. She's drawing pictures of herself as a superhero and posting them on the walls of the garden guesthouse."

A rare heaviness lodged in Claudia's chest. She was going to have to break Maya's heart.

"As research trials go," he continued, "you couldn't have asked for a more willing participant than her. Or Paula and Benny. They're just as excited."

Now he was breaking her own heart, too.

"I hate to say it, but you're going to need one more story as to why we can't implant the bionic heart into Maya. . . . Claudia? Are you still there?"

"Yes," she croaked, followed by a long silence. *Damn. Now he knows I'm crying.*

"Claudia, dearest, I understand how exhausting these deceptions are. It took me years to accept that when it comes to human progress, there are always going to be hard choices. My advice is to keep your eye on the goal, and when you're sad, think about the kids you're saving."

None of this was easy. Gutted, she dressed and headed into the heartwood of her lab for inspiration.

Inner Sanctum: Purify Yourself Before Entering! On the day they pulled their first complete heart out of their tabletop sterilizer, the giddiest among them had scribbled the words onto a wrinkled surgical drape and tacked it above the door to their inventory. It was, her research team joked, a flawless biotech invention from a less-than-flawless heart surgeon.

After her rogue implant into the Johnson kid, they'd nicknamed her The English Pointer. Prey-driven and determined, their rebel leader wasn't one to run with the pack, you see, she took shortcuts through bogs. Fair enough, considering what she'd put them through to get ahead of the competition.

How neurotic she must look to these young lads, virtually unpummeled by life and still certain it would grant their every wish. It wouldn't cross their minds that the alginate and collagen prototype flowing from their 3D printer was her last chance to leave a mark on biotech history.

And now that they'd landed here, who was she to ruin their fun in a place so morbidly unhinged even the dead didn't know if they were coming or going. Claudia eked out a grin for the team, swiped her fob, and entered.

At eye level was the sterile aluminum container which held her team's bionic creation. Below it, encased in a vacuum-sealed bag of alcohol, was the used prototype from the Johnson baby. The team may have dreamed of a steel shelving unit brimming with tiny bionic hearts, instead of the two solitary items so far.

What they all needed—an infant dying of heart failure—was proving difficult to come by in Homer's republic.

⎯⎯⎯◉⎯⎯⎯

WHEN CLAUDIA LOGGED into her email the next morning the sight of an unopened message from Bags had her twisting her beaded bracelet up and down her forearm. The three months since the team started their illegal prototype was long enough for something to have slipped out.

No denying it, this sudden distance between them hurt. Until now, their business partnership was the kind legends were made of, cemented under the smug knowledge they weren't creating something as mundane as engine parts or designer clothing, but saving tiny human beings.

She clicked.

I've got news. Why aren't you answering my calls or texts?

Because the team and I are having the time of our lives building an illegal prototype, she thought. If the institute was inviting them back to the lab, the timing couldn't be worse. No way would she abandon the completed prototype.

Best to put Bags off.

Sorry you couldn't get through. I'm on a remote island on the Mediterranean. It doesn't have cell coverage. Great to hear from you, though. What's up?

Her finger froze above *Send*. Shouldn't she include at least a veneer of excitement? *Have those Johnson clowns finally settled out of court? Sure as hell hope so,* she typed. Within seconds, her chat app rang. She answered but kept the camera off. Bags didn't have his on, either, and she would soon realize why.

"Well. It's happened," he said. "Remember that Thames board member I know? He invited me to go sailing yesterday, but we never left the dock. Rumor is that someone has put in a bid to buy our patents and the institute is considering it."

"I don't believe that one second," she said.

"Can you blame them?" he went on. "Without you, we have no way to start the human implant trials. Our competitors are coming in for the kill. We'd do the same thing, given the chance."

"What's the board's problem?" she asked. "The Johnsons get their money. I get my license back, and we start the trials in a few months."

"The fat arses at the hospital are refusing to settle out of court," he said. "This could drag on for years."

At precisely the moment Claudia felt the foundations of her world shift, a cue stick at Bags's end cracked apart a rack of fifteen tightly packed balls.

"Are you in a bar?" she asked, knowing Bags had three years of grinding sobriety.

A slight pause, then, "Yeah."

"What's going on?" She meant with Bags, but instead he said, "I can see why they would try to recoup some of their investment while they have the chance. The Thames institute is out a fortune if our competition gets their artificial heart to market first. "

She guffawed and said, "How the hell are they going to do that when we're years ahead of them?"

"By paying one of the team for info."

A pitched shriek and crazed cackle from somewhere in the bar filled the gap where Claudia's would have been, had her vocal chords not frozen up. The pregnant scientist who'd stayed behind came to mind.

This was what Bags had tried to warn her against the night she saved the Johnson baby—*You're not invincible. The institute could sell your research off and there's nothing you can do. Think about it.*" She had, but couldn't come up with a reason why they would want to give up on their precious research.

Now she knew.

"There might be something I can do," Bags said.

Of course there was. The man lived to problem-solve.

"My sailboat guy also sits on the hospital foundation. By threatening to cut off millions of his own donations, he might be able to force the chief of surgery to back you and get your medical license reinstated. I reminded him it would qualify as extortion, but he wants to try it anyway."

"Sounds good to me," she said, trying to boost Bags from the sinkhole he seemed to be in.

"Yeah, well . . . I guess he's got a lot of pull because one of his projects is the sick kids' cancer treatment center. Remember the big ground-breaking ceremony? Without his money that whole thing dies."

Her fingers raked her skull. "Piss on them. I don't owe Hackney hospital anything."

"What about the kids, though?"

"None of them are patients of mine," she snorted.

"I suppose not."

"Hey, Bags. Lay off the bottle," Claudia said before signing off. "And let's not get the team's hopes up until my license is reinstated. Okay?"

If her scientists knew the London lab was open to them they'd leave her in the lurch with no way to troubleshoot the heart's electricals and external battery pack. Screw Homer and his outsized loyalty to Maya. She needed to get to London and find a clandestine implant recipient from within her former patients.

Claudia put in her request to see Homer and by the time she was dressed he'd responded in the chat app.

As it turns out, I had planned to contact you today regarding the unborn baby of a brain-dead woman. We suspect problems with the infant's aorta. I'm wondering if you can take a look at the scans and if the defects are severe enough I may want you in the room for the cesarean.

Claudia's brain began spinning faster than an H.G. Wellian time machine. *On my way as soon as I can reach the hydrofoil captain*, she wrote.

Chapter 29

The infant's imaging showed the fetus would likely die soon after birth unless she performed open-heart surgery to widen the aortic valve. "There also appears to be a minor dilation of the left ventricle," she told Homer. "The problem often resolves itself once the aorta is repaired."

When Claudia realized the mother had birthed other children she shuddered to think where they might be—rolling in and out with the tide on a corpse-strewn Libyan beach? Or being tossed into the incinerator under the gondola? They may not be looking for bodies anymore, but they still turned up on runs between islands.

"I'd like to perform a C-section right away and take a second scan of the newborn." Claudia could fix anyone's heart, but it was the neonatal ones she was drawn to.

Except for the purplish hue of the body, the newborn she lifted from the woman's womb the next day was perfectly formed. Alone in the world, the critically ill newborn pumped her pudgy fists against anyone who might try to harm her in the short distance from the womb to the transport incubator.

Taking care with the tubes, lines, and hoses, Claudia wheeled the exhausted newborn as close as possible to the motionless woman on the operating table who would never feel the tug of curious fingers or the tiny heart beating against her own. With one palm extended into the incubator, the other resting on the new mother's belly, she made a pledge. "We can't help you," she whispered, "but I'm not going to let your child die. I promise."

Mother and child went their separate ways outside the OR—the newborn on a journey to the new echocardiography machine in a vacant utility closet of a hallway vibrating with the past misery of Jaza's tasering, vats of pillaged embryos, and stacks of pitifully tiny body bags. To Homer's credit, the cadavers were down to a trickle.

She plodded behind the incubator with an old but persistent regret. *I won't let you suffer the way she did.*

The aorta would be an easy repair, and barring an infection survival was assured. It was the left ventricle that might suddenly fail mere months from now. Why wait for that to happen when she had an artificial heart ready to implant at this very moment? She could save the child's life and save some of her research all at the same time. It was a win—for the newborn, her team, the future of heart transplants, the families of dying babies, science . . .

She was still adding to this list when the technician raised the hand-held transducer to scan the newborn's heart. "I'll take that off your hands." Claudia offered her open palm. "I'm sure you need a break."

As soon as she was alone, Claudia pushed the knobby tool across the infant's chest and turned her head to the monitor. Everything appeared the same except for—she leaned into the monitor. *Damn*—the left chamber of the infant's heart had returned to normal size. Not the outcome she expected—nor wanted.

If this newborn became their first human trial, Claudia could start saving critically ill babies right here in Homer's republic, within weeks instead of years. She was fighting for the survival of her life's work and for once there was no rulebook standing in the way.

She pressed her bowed frame flat against the utility room's closed door as a bulwark against what she knew was wrong—but it didn't work. Like a flawed benediction, the surgeon decided to let the power of science guide her instead of her conscience. The world needed her artificial heart more than it needed the human heart of one infant.

Back to the ICU she went, pushing the incubator and this new notion before her. After she slipped the newborn's scans into a patient file at the nurses' station there was still time to stop herself from doing the unthinkable to a defenseless baby. Instead, she entered Homer's office and said, "The ventricle has deteriorated to the point only a transplant will save her. This is an opportunity to implant the bionic prototype."

She expected him to be suspicious of this seemingly fortuitous outcome, but he simply wrapped Claudia in a bear hug. "I'm so happy this is working out for you."

Her body seized up.

"This will give us more time to find the next patient," he added.

Afterwards, instead of going for lunch in the cafeteria as she told him, Claudia wandered in circles and found herself back in the ICU room of the newborn, staring into the child's gaping mouth. The poor thing was too exhausted to hold it closed.

I'm about to trash a perfectly fixable heart. Was this not a secret far worse than any of Homer's?

This newborn didn't deserve to have the heart she was born with cut out and replaced with a lump of gel. She needed to track down Homer and come clean on her lie about the echocardiogram results.

Why was she in such a hurry, anyway? When her medical license was restored in two or three months' time, she could begin the clinical trials at a new hospital. Or could she? Bags himself had said it would take years. Indeed, why leave The Squats' hospital where she had complete control? Better to let most of the team go home while she stayed behind to build bionic hearts in Homer's republic.

Home . . . Claudia lay her palms on top of the incubator and studied the infant's deep slumber. Go home and sleep on it.

At the elevator, she scanned her fob and hit the lobby button, but the doors parted onto two armed guards in Hazmat overalls and respirators. "Sorry, this elevator is out of service at the moment," a muffled voice said. He raised the metal box in his hands as if to explain. Written on a label was the international biohazard symbol and the words *Infectious Substance (Xenopsylla Cheopis/Y. Pestis).*

"We'll send it back up from the underground level," he said as the doors closed.

In a Dafnis-like move she took a scrap of paper from her briefcase and quickly scribbled down the two words she didn't recognize before she forgot them. Y. Pestis was the plague bacterium from Homer's past research. This was strange enough, but why would they be taking it to the dungeon level rather than the lab behind the lobby?

While Claudia puzzled over this label, the elevator suddenly returned and inside was one of their own guards. "Homer wants to see you in his suite."

She could imagine Homer at a slow boil after pulling the newborn's heart scans from the file and figuring out she'd lied. The choice Homer was about to force on her was the right one. Like anyone else, she'd bent the rules and got caught. She wasn't so special after all.

"Tell him I'll be there shortly," Claudia said, gazing at the deserted nursing station. She logged into a browser and typed: *what is Xenopsylla Cheopis?* According to a medical site, it was the scientific name for the Oriental rat flea—widely known as the host carrier for the pneumonic plague bacterium Yersinia Pestis, which in turn was the causative agent of plague and a Tier 1 agent of bioterrorism and a future pandemic.

Why in hell would Homer be bringing plague-infected fleas into his precious clinic?

———◈———

SHE STEPPED OUT OF the elevator and into a penthouse humming with animated voices and a roomful of radiant faces.

"Here she is. Raise a glass to Claudia," Homer said when he saw her. "This is a new dawn for the transplant world and a new era for The Republic of Homer." Her entire team of scientists crowded around. "To Claudia. To Claudia. To—"

She stood unmoving at the center of Homer's surprise. Toast the transplant world, but don't toast me, she wanted to shout.

Her skin crawled every time someone hugged her. Her mouth ached from the plastered-on smile. At the first lull in the commotion, she edged to the fringes and fled into Homer's shower room where she slid to the tiles and closed her eyes.

A knuckle-tap sounded at the door. "Claudia? Are you okay?"

Her head sank between her legs. Homer *would* have to come looking for her. He meant well but . . . Claudia struggled to her feet and stared into the mirror above the vanity. There was no way she would let him, or anyone else, see her like this.

"You know how I don't like being in the spotlight."

No response. He wasn't buying it. "It's making me think of my dead mother. How proud she'd be. Would it be okay to name the infant Eliza after her?"

"Of course, love. Can I come in?"

She leaned across the broad vanity to stare at a reflection of her hands. She would soon slice into a delicate chest and discard a healthy heart for something experimental that would only be able to keep up for two years tops, if deadly sepsis didn't set in first.

Homer squeezed by the minute she unlocked the door. She hid her face from his furrowed brow. There was no turning back.

"Oh dear," he said. "You're much too special and beautiful to be this upset."

He smiled at Claudia's shock. "I saw the newborn's file," he said, "but I understand why you would want to propagate a lie. Go ahead and use this newborn's heart to save Maya and your friendship—and move up your bionic trials at the same time. There's no reason why you shouldn't. This is one of those hard choices I talked about."

Maya? Claudia thought. Her goddaughter's life had never crossed her mind when she hatched this plan. It was her bionic heart that was in immediate danger—not Maya. In Dr. Vlakia's world, the life of one girl would never trump the hundreds saved by her bionic heart. That used to be Homer's mantra, too—before the old man went soft on her over Maya.

"Don't worry. Your team won't suspect a thing," he said. "I'll get my nurses to whisk the infant's heart away the minute it's out."

Homer pulled her rigid body into his chest while his palm strummed against her back like the beating of a war drum.

TO MEDICAL TYPES, THE deep silence which hung over Claudia's OR might have sounded foreign. Not even the beep of a heart monitor or pulsing *whoosh* of an external compressor could be heard doing the heart's job. None of these were needed today. The baby Eliza's heart no longer *beat*—it *clicked* with the opening and closing of the two collagen valves.

Claudia placed her stethoscope onto her patient's chest, barely visible in the swarm of nurses, surgeons, and scientists. The bionic heart was implanted and functioning as expected.

"Pressures?" she asked, removing the stethoscope from her ears and looking at her lead scientist.

"Both systolic and diastolic are operating as presets," Jeremy said. He stepped back from the table. "We've done it again, team."

Smiling eyes all round, except for Claudia. Her mood, always guarded at the end of a transplant, was especially grave today. As she passed the stethoscope to a nurse, Claudia's attention wandered to the shining basin which held the infant's duplicitous heart. Like a callous wink between two cohorts, the blue surgical light sent a blinding flash careening off the steel and into her eyes.

She peeled away her blood-splattered gloves and gown and passed through a gamut of throbbing chatter and boisterous back pats, her team's ghastly grins nothing but a mockery of everything they were trying to accomplish.

A cart holding the stainless steel basin passed her and disappeared around a bend in the hallway.

"It's packed and on ice," a low voice behind her said. It was Homer. "Maya's on her way down. You've got a thirty-minute break. OR number four. See you there."

Until today, it had been easy to believe in her own moral superiority over Homer's lies and wrongdoings. It now occurred to her that his actions, at least, were always aimed directly at helping the refugees. How was turning an innocent newborn into a scientific experiment benefiting anyone but herself?

In the blind ambition category, Claudia was killing it.

Chapter 30

U tterly alone with her guilt, she kept busy and found, like the mounds of trash she used to root through outside her London flat, her crime was easily buried and forgotten under life's relentless garbage.

Until then, what played with the mind was not knowing who to blame—behind every ruined life on Inquisitor's Island was a good intention. All scientific research had its collateral damage. How could it advance, otherwise? She'd done it for all the newborns in her future who would enter the world one day and leave it the next if not for her bionic heart.

Even Homer, a man with his own trail of dead children, had encouraged her to ruin the newborn's life for Maya's sake. Crikey, but people could be so intransigent when it came to their progeny. Let that be a lesson to those who would allow love to pull them around by the nose.

It was this kind of reasoning that got Claudia out of her dismal office and over to the newborn's ICU room each day for the next week. Was it any wonder she entered the lab one morning wrapped in an overwhelming sense of satisfaction with what she'd accomplished in Homer's republic. Human trials on her bionic heart had started, albeit not the official ones. If Eliza was still clicking away two years from now, Claudia could declare herself a success.

With the infant Eliza stable and out of the incubator it was time for her team to head home for a break—all except Jeremy and another single lad who had volunteered to live at The Squats for the next year and start building heart number three.

Other than checking in on Eliza's progress, she said, these two shouldn't expect to see her until Claudia had found their next recipient. She checked her email morning and night for the reinstatement of her license, gleefully gloating on the thought of Sailboat Guy forcing a dose of extortion down the throat of Barb—Hackney's stooge lawyer.

Days later, she gave her scientists a final sendoff salute at The Squats' helipad where Nabi also turned up to squeeze in the strafed Russian. What was Homer thinking to risk putting this casualty of his bioweapon in with her team of "innocents?"

"Have a nice life, sucker," Nabi told the dull-witted man, who stumbled up the ladder in a daze. Someone from London's Russian embassy was apparently at the other end.

With the chopper gone, Claudia slogged down to their vacant dorm rooms to check for anything that might help the Thames institute incriminate them in patent infringement. Since The Squats was now in the hands of its town council, Claudia feared they might be naive enough to let a team of investigators in.

Almost finished her sweep, she exited one of the rooms to the *ding* of a notification from Bags. *Call me! Johnsons finally settled out of court but T not onboard.* Bags knew she had told her team to gather in London for possible news on their bionic research. Had someone handed in their resignation? she wondered.

Claudia ran through every scientists' first and last name, but not a single T in the bunch until it dawned on her that "T" was the Thames lab and the unthinkable had happened—she'd been cut from her own bionic research.

"There you are," Claudia heard someone behind her shout. She turned to see Jaza wandering down the hall with a preschool girl in tow.

"Is that where you're staying now?" Jaza pointed to the door beside Claudia.

Despite living only minutes from each other, in the excitement around the lab, Claudia hadn't seen Jaza in more than three months.

"Uh. . . . No. Sorry. I sleep at the lab's office. My team of scientists stayed here."

"They're the guys from England, right? Dafnis won't tell me anything else."

A wave of relief swept Claudia. "He's just doing his job."

Jaza bristled in a way Claudia recognized from her own former suspicions that Homer was conducting a cover-up of illegal activity.

"And who is this little lady?" Claudia shoved the annihilation of her life's work aside for the time being and peered down on a girl with olive skin and light brown hair.

"Her name is Lena. She arrived a few days ago and speaks Syrian Arabic."

Claudia squatted to get a closer look at a palm-sized bruise on the girl's face. Three slender marks were already turning yellow; this was no playground accident. At some point in her journey to safety, someone had slapped this precious child.

"She's the reason I was looking for you. Can we talk somewhere private?" Jaza picked up the girl and they headed down the dormitory stairs, which, like the hospital, still lacked an elevator. The nurses' dining hall on the ground floor teemed with hospital staff eating lunch.

Jaza set the girl down. "How about your office?"

Not a chance, Claudia thought. The less traffic past the lab, the better. "Let's talk inside the hospital's lobby. It'll be quiet there. Ambulatory care is the only part open so far." Best to leave out Maya's in-patient room.

While they crossed the dusty expanse between the two buildings Jaza said, "Believe it or not, this will be my first time inside the new hospital. I never get a day off anymore."

Claudia cut in front, but instead of tears Jaza was the picture of contentment. How striking she was when animated, a hint of the exotic Silk Road in her oval eyes and aquiline nose.

"But how will you see your son?"

"That's a long story."

A happy one, apparently.

The minute the double glass doors of the hospital parted, the girl broke free of Jaza's hand. "Mama. Mama." Lena tore down the length of the lobby to the admitting desk where a burka-clad woman sat across from a clerk. As soon as the woman caressed the child's cheek and said something, Lena collapsed into sobs.

Jaza plodded to the sad scene to scoop the girl from the floor and lay her within a corner of padded benches.

"She's been doing that since she arrived about four days ago," Jaza said after Claudia pulled over a plastic chair.

With soft words and rhythmic strokes to the child's hair, her whimpers tailed off.

"Every time she sees a woman in a burka she thinks it's her missing mama. She told me her mother was asleep when they took her off the rescue boat."

"You mean unconscious."

"Of course. I guess their dinghy flipped over and dumped everyone into the water. She said her mother managed to lift her onto the boat's overturned bottom and that's where she stayed for hours before rescue. We have a morgue at the clinic and a holding area now for comatose victims. I took her through both." Jaza shook her head. "Nothing."

"Having to put a child so young through that. And the father?" Claudia asked.

"I tried. If he were here we would have found him by now."

Claudia stared at the dark shadow of exhaustion ringing the girl's sleepy eyes. Who knows what she'd gone through.

"I want you to help me find out if Homer has her mother," Jaza finally said.

Four days was a long time to be in a coma at Homer's clinic. "If the mother is truly brain dead," Claudia said, "her body is likely gone already."

Jaza wagged her chin. "I doubt it. A lot has changed. Homer won't take anyone's organs until he's sure there's no family."

"Blimey. He's kept his promise, has he?"

Jaza shrugged, minus the relief one would expect. "I used to get so angry when The Squats sent us their comatose patients because I knew the only way they were leaving was in a metal box of ashes dumped into the sea." Jaza's eyes grew wide. "But now that I'm here at The Squats clinic myself I see that we don't have enough workers for coma patients."

Jaza, one of the most compassionate souls Claudia had ever met, was admitting to sending refugees to their deaths at Daphne Technologies. Was Homer's sinister actions due to a simple lack of staff? An unavoidable triage.

"I hear Homer's making a ward for them inside the hospital. Something called long-term care." An unbelievably warm smile spread across the face of Homer's greatest hater.

"Are you two friends now?"

Jaza grunted. "We talk sometimes. That's all."

"About . . . ?" Claudia prodded.

Jaza's jumpy shrug put the boots to her curiosity. Strange that Homer hadn't mentioned this breakthrough, either.

Claudia pulled her satellite phone from her pocket. "If I'm going to bring you and the girl to the wards, I'll need Homer's permission."

"There's a new orphan at The Squats searching for her mother," she told him when he answered. "Do I have your permission to take her into the ICU ward?"

"Yes, of course. I want families reunited. If the mother has been declared brain-dead, she'll be here, but check the new long-term care at The Squats' hospital first."

From the lobby, it took the three of them only minutes to reach the treatment room where six comatose patients lay—none of them adult women. The young girl didn't seem fazed by the feeding tubes, catheter lines, and intubation. Ever hopeful, at the end of the line of beds, she turned and spoke to Jaza.

"She wants to look again." Jaza flashed Claudia a weary toss of the head.

"Tell her we're going on a boat to another hospital."

The words were no sooner translated than the child grabbed Jaza's hand and pulled her to the hospital's exit.

At The Squats dock, Lena yelled something when she saw the hydrofoil, then bounded up the gangway. They found her sitting on the tiled floor of the lower deck's lounge in a corner Claudia knew was used for triage during rescues. The three of them were the only passengers.

Claudia snugged herself in beside the orphan and caught Jaza's eye on the opposite side. "She's so well-behaved, isn't she?" Claudia said. "Most children would be running around up and down the decks."

"Probably afraid of the water." Jaza patted the deck. "And this might be where she last saw her mother being treated by the paramedics."

———◉———

AT THE CLINIC, HOMER seemed to have kept his word as they passed guard after guard without a single delay. "Go ahead," Claudia said to Jaza and motioned down the ICU hallway. "There's a patient in this room that I need to check on."

The patient in a room across from the nurses' station was Claudia's artificial heart recipient, snoozing to the clicks of her bionic heart. The week following the implant, Claudia had slept in the newborn's room. Not because she didn't trust the nurses—they were competent and just as discreet as the island's guards—Claudia now thought of herself as the baby's guardian.

She picked up the bedside chart, crossed out "Jane Doe" and wrote in "Eliza." This was the best Syrian version of her late mother's name, Lisbet. Before she could cross the hall to speak with the head ICU nurse, she heard Jaza calling her name a few doors down and nodding toward something inside a room.

Had the girl actually found her mother?

Claudia arrived to find a patient hooked-up to life support, Lena chatting non-stop to the unresponsive woman. For a lonely child, this mother-daughter reunion was a blissfully bittersweet moment.

For Claudia, though, it was a tragedy.

The comatose woman was even gaunter than the surgeon remembered from the day she lifted her sickly newborn into an incubator.

She turned to find Jaza watching her guarded reaction.

"I'll let the nurses know about transferring her to The Squats hospital," Claudia said, already out the door.

Finally alone in one of the wheelchair bathrooms, Claudia pressed her cheek to the wall's cool tile. She thought of Lena's baby sister lying just yards away from the sad scene—perfectly healthy until Claudia seized the infant for her own purposes. Would the baby die before the two sisters got to know each other?

The cold water she splashed onto her flushed face calmed her enough to arrange the transfer to The Squats. She hadn't planned to see Jaza again, but there she was exiting the comatose mother's room, mouthing soothing sounds to the bawling girl in her arms.

Claudia ducked into the nurses' station and watched as Jaza paused at the open doorway of her heart recipient, looked around, then entered, emerging minutes later.

"Oh. I thought you left to talk to Homer," Jaza said when she saw Claudia standing at the elevator.

"The nurses are going to phone him." It was best to avoid Homer while this sudden attack of guilt still tossed her inside out. From Jaza's chilly expression, Homer wasn't the only one Claudia would need to avoid.

The two women tramped out, silent and tense, until they had passed the main gate where Jaza lifted Lena onto the gravel path. "Go for a little walk, honey, but not too far."

"You trust her around the electric fence?"

"*Pfft*. I've known for years it's phony. Have you forgotten how expert I am at spotting lies?" The young woman's eyes drilled into Claudia. "When were you going to tell Lena that she has a baby sister?"

"What?" Not only was Claudia a piss-poor liar, but this attempt to cover up was pathetic.

"I saw the newborn's chart. As a midwife I hear about all the pregnant women brought off the rescue boats. When Lena told me her mother was having a baby, I realized she must be the one here in a coma." Jaza turned as if to satisfy herself the girl was safe, then came at Claudia with a vengeance. "Did you sell that infant's heart to a client and replace it with a faulty one?"

Jaza seemed to have missed her true calling as a criminal trial lawyer. Up until now, Claudia knew her only as a passive victim who constantly needed help.

"Well?"

"God, no. The newborn's heart was diseased." Claudia had left the bionic implant off the charting to make it look like a transplant.

The midwife wasn't falling for it. "There's no way Homer would buy an organ for the baby of a brain-dead refugee. I'd like to see the heart scans."

Shit. The ones she sent to the incinerator? By now, Jaza was almost nose-to-nose with Claudia. "Patient imaging is confidential and what I do in my surgery is none of your business. The child is lucky to have one of my artificial hearts."

"Is that what you've been working on in your lab?"

"Yes. And don't you go telling anyone at The Squats. Not unless you want to face Homer's ire."

Jaza smiled and shook her head. "Threatening me with Homer won't work."

Jaza drew her brows tight, letting her gaze roam from one end of Claudia to another. "You're probably the smartest woman I've ever met, and yet, you've fallen for Homer's trap. Let me ask you this, Claudia—What would you like written on your gravestone?"

What the hell was this girl on about? Gravestones were filled with mindless pap. After her mother's death, she gave the undertaker full reign and wouldn't you know he chose, *A Beloved Wife and Dedicated Mother.* Her mother was neither. The countess, however, *had* made the best of a loveless arranged marriage and one arranged child to carry on the bloodline.

"Come on," Jaza pressed. "What do you want people to say about you when you're dead?"

"Good grief, child. You're already planning your own funeral?"

Jaza pulled her shoulders rigid and glowered, not that Claudia expected anything less from this suddenly pensive teen.

"I really don't give a shit what's on mine," Claudia said.

The corners of the midwife's lips curled. "Oh, but I think you do. *A Blameless Life*, that's how I want people to remember me, and Dafnis, too. For most people it's the best they can hope for. People think Dafnis can do no harm because he's simple. No. It's because he's a good man."

The midwife paused as a bout of melancholy crept into her eyes. "I thought you were my friend." Jaza turned and marched to where her young charge sat in the dirt, talking to a handful of stones. Lena in tow, she hustled toward the gondola.

How quickly it could happen. In a matter of minutes Jaza had gone from trusted friend—to foe. Would her betrayal of the Thames institute leak out and make Bags her next instant enemy?

No answer at his number.

Chapter 31

From the top of the gondola, Claudia looked out to sea, the sting of her argument with Jaza still fresh.

It was the height of summer in Homer's republic, the forest never greener or more alive with delicate pastel-hued flowers. Why ruin such a gorgeous day with things out of her control. She had nothing to be ashamed of. All Claudia had ever wanted was to help the dying, and in doing so help herself.

She watched Jaza and the girl until they boarded the hydrofoil. In the desolation of a lost girl's world, a few moments cheek to cheek with her unresponsive mother was better than none at all. One day, she would also walk hand in hand with her baby sister. Claudia intended to make it happen. It was her responsibility alone to give the newborn what she had taken—a long, healthy life.

At the first squeal of the hydrofoil's water wings below, Claudia beat a path to the treehouse where she stretched out amongst the birdsong and filled her lungs with the salt air and leafy aroma of late spring.

She drifted into the watery space between dreams and wakefulness, washing in and out. As the next wave broke it deposited the wet, chalky corpses of the African boy and the Sudanese toddler. The newborn, too, reached for her with the blazing red eyes of an albino lab rat.

The helicopter's blades whirred high above on the helipad. One after another, out stepped the beating heart cadavers, their veined hearts pulsing and roiling on the outside of their chests. An endless stream of fathers and sons, mothers and daughters of every nation and age tried in vain to duck from the blades, but the spinning rotors sent their heads rolling across the tarmac. Onward the headless cadavers strode one by one across the arched bridge in the garden and into the elevator. Soon, they were wading through the carpet of severed heads in their determination to get down to the operating rooms.

"Ohhh . . ." she gasped, wide awake. A wind whistling through gaps in the treehouse mingled with a high-pitched buzzing from down on the beach.

She stood to peer through the foliage for a better view and caught sight of an airborne drone zipping above the hard-packed sand at the shore. A man she didn't recognize ran ahead of it, constantly peering skyward as to its position. As it dove low over his head he stumbled and fell face first into the wet sand. The drone banked out to sea and disappeared.

Claudia waited for him to get to his feet but he didn't move, not even when a wave splashed against his legs. She might have concluded he'd hit his head on a rock, had there been any.

He must be having a heart attack or stroke. She unhooked the hemp rope and slid down fireman style before cutting corners down the switchbacked path. One side of the man's face was caked with sand as she flipped and dragged him away from the water. He had a pulse and his chest rose and fell. Suddenly, he moaned then tried to push himself onto an elbow.

"Take it easy," she advised. "Don't try to stand until you're steady."

His fingers explored the caked sand on his cheek before he scrubbed it off with the heel of his hand. They exchanged startled stares because it dawned on her she knew this man. Here was the rude Russian who had bumped into her outside the hotel in Damascus, sending lip gloss up her nose.

"You're the man from Syria, aren't you?"

"What's Syria?"

Nonsense talk like that could also point to a stroke. The man was sitting up now, squinting at something behind her. She turned to see Homer, Dafnis, and Nabi trotting down the beach from the direction of the dock.

"Claudia. Get away from him." As Homer broke to run, Dafnis tried to grab his shirt tail. He was red in the face, practically hyper-ventilating when he reached her and tried to pull her away from the man. "Are you all right?"

"I'm fine," she said, then pointed. "Do you remember this guy?"

Homer pressed her head into his chest. "Thank goodness you're okay," he said while Nabi twisted the stranger's hands behind his back and snapped on handcuffs.

"Hey." Claudia reached for Nabi. "What are you doing? He may have had a massive stroke."

"He was trying to escape onto the hydrofoil," Homer said. "He's an intruder. A Russian spy."

It made no difference to her what the man was to deserve such rough treatment while vulnerable. She glanced at Nabi and thought twice before saying anything else. Was he in on their Syrian misadventure, or not? Claudia could keep a secret, but this new tendency to paranoia wasn't how she wanted to live. Soon, she wouldn't have to.

Homer stood in front of the Russian and demanded, "What's your name? Do you know where you are?"

This was precisely what Claudia would be asking if the man were her patient.

He was trembling as he scanned each person in the group. "I—I don't."

"Keep an eye on him." Homer motioned to Dafnis. "See what else he may know. I'll join you guys later."

The two men turned toward the dock, Nabi prodding the man forward where he could see him. The captive stumbled up the beach twisting his torso in every direction. "Where are you taking me?"

The scene germinated an unsettling knot inside her. Claudia would have expected the Syrian police, not a Russian spy, to be tracking down Homer or Dafnis.

With the trio gone Homer eyed her. "You should go and take a shower."

Her feet slid around in the sand while Homer tugged one way, then another.

"Wash your hair and your clothes, too."

She gazed down at her clothing, then yanked her arm from his hands. "You're scaring me, Homer. What in the blazes is going on?"

"You could be contaminated. We strafed that Russian with an experimental drug. The airborne particles should be harmless within ten minutes of being released, but . . .Were you directly under the drone when it made the drop?"

This had to top even the most outrageous of Homer's lies. "You can't be serious? You're dropping biotoxins on visitors?"

"He's a combatant."

"Excuse me for not knowing we're standing in a war zone. What is this stuff, anyway?"

He took one wary step closer and his voice all but disappeared. "It's an aerosol form of my vaccine. The one for the pneumonic plague. One of the side effects is permanent loss of memory. Short-term *and* long-term."

Everything the Russian had done and said made sense to her. But why unleash such a horror on a fellow human being? If what Homer said was true then this man would have nothing but the present moment from now on. "What has he done to you to deserve it?"

Homer cocked his eyebrows, a weird gleam in his eyes. "He came here of his own free will to steal information. We decided to use him as a guinea pig for our formula."

"Homer. No." She closed the gap between them; his panting breath, hot and humid, washed over her. This went far beyond what she thought him capable of. "This guy's life will be meaningless going forward," she said. "No capacity to form relationships or learn anything."

He squared his jaw, his eyes fierce. "And no capacity for evil, either."

Homer stepped forward and jabbed his finger into her chest. "I didn't come here six years ago intending to weaponize my vaccine, but Hocking is the one who changed all that. He showed me how to develop it into an aerosol. Someone will pay for what they did to Daphne. The shadow war I'm fighting now is for her."

"You've been churning out this poison all along," Claudia asked. "Inside the fertility clinic?"

Homer paused and frowned. "Absolutely not. We had a lab accident our first year. After that, I destroyed every trace of the aerosol. Helping the refugees became my life's focus."

So that's what happened to Hocking, Claudia thought. Genius no more. "I don't understand—if you destroyed the aerosol, then what did you use on this Russian?"

He paused, so much so she braced for another privacy tirade.

"I've been manufacturing it since Syria. Remember? Dafnis reconstructed the formula."

When he tried to take her hands she shoved them into her pockets.

"Please don't let this come between us." He gripped her elbows. "Let's go home. You can take a shower and I'll fix your favorite drink."

Never taking her eyes off his, she let her windbreaker slide from her shoulders onto the sand. Inside was her phone, wallet and fob keys for both islands. He may have assumed she was marching to the water's edge, but her automaton pace didn't slow until she was far enough in to ease down and float on her back.

The cool silence of the sea's water flooded her ear canals. Homer's yells faded. Her brain released and all that remained in the profound stillness was a blameless blue sky. Clouds stretched in every direction. Another immaculate day on the azure sea if not for the two defilements at its shore—the one who would trade an infant's life for a Nobel Prize, and the one who would hijack the human mind for vengeance.

You and I are more alike than you think. For all her self-righteous BS, Homer knew this fact long ago. It was time to end the most hellish day of her life.

Homer was wet to his knees as she waded ashore and scooped her jacket. "Don't need a shower now. Goodbye, Homer."

Ten paces away, she turned on her heels to find him on a log, pulling off his wet runners. She bellowed, "Jaza wants the brain-dead Syrian mother reunited with her daughter in The Squats. If I hear you've dumped her ashes out there—I'll kill you."

Claudia slogged across the sand in the direction of the hydrofoil dock. It was going to be a brief but soggy ride back to The Squats.

Chapter 32

What does it mean when someone instant messages that your life as you know it is over—then doesn't return calls. In the case of Bags, it likely meant he crossed a lane while well-sozzled, got nailed by a bus, and was in hospital at this very moment with no memory of what happened or who he was. Lucky bastard.

At the moment, Claudia had other kites in the air that needed her attention. Clipboard in hand, she shuffled around her lab for an inventory of what she might be able to smuggle out. "I can't leave baby Eliza behind," she muttered to herself. "But neither can I take her with me." Just her luck she implanted her experimental heart into an infant living on a remote rock with nothing but a vegetative mother and four-year-old as supports.

Days since the argument on the beach and the complexity of cutting all ties with Homer's republic was sinking in. How was she going to care for her young implant recipient from London? When Homer realizes he can no longer control her every move, he might prevent her from checking on the child. Neither could she assume he would let her take a single thing from the lab Benny had paid for.

She walked to the 3D printer her team built piece by piece, and ran her hands over the shining base where the bionic heart had materialized before their eyes. Her most valued piece of equipment, but not so easy to smuggle off the island. Unless, . . .What had become of the box and packing material for the staff room's microwave? That might work.

It was telling that Homer hadn't shown up. Claudia had set aside an entire day to be alone and mourn the man, but still couldn't get him out of her system. Like the night of his drunken visit, an apparition of a benevolent Homer kept staggering into her room to lie with her on the narrow cot, triggering even more confusion.

But that was yesterday.

People as intelligent as Homer did change their minds, she thought while doing her inventory. Guilt was such a powerful motivator. If it forced Homer to abandon his bioweapon years ago, why not again? Dr. Hocking, the victim of the lab accident, might be able to play on Homer's guilt.

Time to pay Hocking a visit inside his lab.

———◆———

THE FIRST THING SHE noticed was a sign on a trolley at the door that demanded visitors don a lab coat, surgical cap, and shoe covers. Ridiculous precautions since she knew the so-called fertility lab functioned as little more than a storage locker for embryos. A shining countertop along one wall certainly held the trappings of DNA sequencing—a computer monitor and keyboard, microscopes and test tubes, centrifuges and incubators—but not a soul was using any of it.

She donned the works and strode to where Hocking sat immersing long test tubes of the latest batch of frozen embryos into a tank swirling with liquid nitrogen. *Which country had these been pilfered from?*

The mystery of how this genius could be content to deliver frozen zygotes into the surrogates' embryo implantation rooms—was solved. Similar to head-injured Dafnis, since Hocking's accident with the aerosol, duties had to be repetitive and straightforward.

"Good afternoon, Claudia. Is that you behind the mask?" Hocking slammed the lid on the tank closed and locked the padlock with a key around his neck. "I do believe this is your inaugural visit."

"Right you are." The level of condescension she was aiming for was gag-worthy, but why in hell had she never learned the man's first name? "It's you I've come to talk to. Somewhere private, if possible."

He glanced at the surveillance camera in a corner above them. "Such a beautiful day. Shall we sit outside?"

Homer had always claimed the purpose of his surveillance wasn't to spy on staff. Hocking's subtle glance got her rethinking that.

He tore off his face mask and shoe covers on his way out and grabbed a door wedge for the side exit. In the yard, Hocking set out two folding chairs with the exactitude of a procedure manual then turned decisively to clobber her with his marionette grin.

What to lead with, she thought, while pulling off her own wooden smile? "You've no doubt heard I could be leaving soon and I, well, you know, we never did get to know each other very well, did we? Sorry about that."

The man said nothing. Did nothing. The picture of grinning creepiness.

"The other thing, or main thing, I guess, is . . . I've just found out Homer is manufacturing a bioweapon on site."

He nodded, no more disturbed had she been reading a list for the grocer. He either knew and approved, or his faulty brain couldn't comprehend the danger.

"Dr. Hocking, you used to be a brilliant scientist before the lab accident involving this biotoxin. Do you remember?"

"Oh yes. I remember the accident, but I wasn't in the lab at the time." He winked at her. "I'm still brilliant, by the way. I think you mean Dafnis. Unfortunately, the seal on the canister was faulty and he couldn't see the aerosol escaping. We've colored it red since then."

Claudia's mind slammed into overload. "But—I thought Dafnis fell out of a tree."

He raised his eyebrows. "Nothing but a story. I tried to tell Homer the boy was too young to be around a compound so risky. It's a shame because Dafnis used to have a real gift for biochemistry."

Claudia rose from her chair and stared down at Hocking. "I can't believe Homer would lie about this to his own son."

Hocking shrugged with an affected air of exasperation. "The poor man is afflicted with loneliness. He doesn't want to lose his only child."

Claudia shivered to think how painful loneliness must be for people like Homer who craved company at any cost.

"He's too proud to admit an error in judgment which cost Dafnis a normal life," Hocking added.

No wonder Homer had vowed to protect Dafnis until his dying day. The boy was a captive of his father's guilt.

It was Dafnis she needed to recruit.

Hocking looked over his shoulder at a half-dozen guards exiting their bunkhouse near the gate. "I think my guests are here early." He jumped up and pointed to their chairs. "Please. Can you take them in? I must go," he said, then dashed inside.

She sat there, astounded how Homer had made them all believe Dafnis had nobody but himself to blame for his brain damage. He'd given her a play-by-play of finding him unconscious under a tree at thirteen. And there was Syria, too. The bastard had stood silent inside the linen closet while Dafnis absolved him of all blame. Even whip-smart Jaza, who always started her stories with, "According to Homer," fell for the man's selfish lie.

Stunned and seething, Claudia removed the door stopper, dumped the chairs somewhere along the hallway, and plodded to the elevator. While she stood pondering where Dafnis might be, the elevator doors parted on her side to a jam-up of men and women in lab coats and surgical caps, identical to the ones she still wore.

A guard poked his head in from the lobby side, a key in his hand. "Come on, then, squeeze in," someone said as an arm shot out of the crowd to yank her inside.

Thud. The doors closed; the elevator descended. Just like that, was she about to set foot inside Homer's off-limits bioweapon lab?

Chapter 33

The lift deposited Claudia and the others into a claustrophobically narrow passageway where it was easy to imagine the long-silent sobs and clanking leg irons of four-hundred years earlier. She tailed the group all the way to where a modern steel staircase gave a view of a grand limestone cavern—the width and height of an airplane hangar.

Blinding yard lights ringed the space. Perfect. She dug out her sunglasses, expecting to run into Hocking at any moment.

Before her was a typical factory floor of industrial steel vats, counters of laboratory equipment and computer screens, and robotic arms attached to an assembly line. All of it idle at the moment. Different from any other factory floor she'd ever seen were the hundreds of missiles the shape and size of a milk bottle, piled five-foot deep on pallets. Two dozen guests milled around rows of folding chairs.

Claudia slid by and sat in the back row.

As expected, Homer appeared on a raised dais at the front. "Welcome to Daphne Technologies. Please take a seat, and make use of the translation headphones on your chair." He waited for silence. "You've been invited here today because you're pillars of peace within your chosen fields. You share my vision for the future. But before getting to the crux of my presentation, allow me to show you one of our stealth drones."

Hocking appeared, pushing a wheeled table containing a drone like the one used on the Russian on the beach. He lifted its control console from the table and the drone began to hum.

"Obviously, it's not armed for this demonstration," Homer said.

The drone lifted off. "This is the smallest stealth drone in the world capable of being weaponized. It can track a target for over a hundred kilometers and return home automatically after dropping its payload."

The crowd stared at the drone as it flew by overhead.

"What makes it special is the ability to evade both high and low frequency detection due to its fiberglass construction and slow speed.

"Our drones are for sale to anyone with the money, however, what I am about to show you is *not* for sale. The real star today is what the drone will be carrying. The world's newest bioweapon destroys nothing—kills no one.

"To be clear." Homer held up his hand against the din of voices. "I'm not the first to think about the benefits of a benign biological weapon. You might remember the military experiments to weaponize hallucinogens during the Vietnam war. The US military concluded that taking someone's mind was somehow worse than taking their life.

"Here at Daphne Technologies we aim to show there is nothing more precious than life itself. That's why the only thing our aerosol takes is a combatant's memory."

Homer clicked a remote which dimmed the lights and illuminated a theatre-sized projection. "I've prepared a reenactment."

The video began with a bird's eye view of the drone's radar locking on a target running along a beach. It swooped and sprayed a swathe of red aerosol onto the man. The figure continued running, looked skyward, then collapsed. The face was blurred, but Claudia knew from the clothing it was the same Russian she found on their beach.

The cavern sizzled with tension even before a written plug proclaimed, *Whether it's regime change or a hostage extraction, no job is too small or too large for Daphne Technologies' intelligence unit.*

"We conducted the test under the most difficult conditions," Homer said after bringing up the lights. "On a windy beach with a running subject—a volunteer and dummy aerosol—but had this been a real attack the aerosol's bacterium would cause the brain to instantly swell, thereby destroying the lobe which controls memory—both long-term and short-term. That would be the extent of his injuries."

Homer pointed to an upheld hand. "I'm here on behalf of the Institute for Non-proliferation of Nuclear Weapons. Why hide the volunteer's face?"

"For the same reason any special agent would want their identity hidden. Let me disclose that there is no antidote to the aerosol, no way to reverse the damage. Nor do I see why we would want to."

"The victim's family might," someone said. "You would use this on children?"

Homer searched the crowd for the voice then said, "Like anyone, I want a world where all children are safe from war, but in the case of the terrorist cells, yes, children might become collateral damage."

Claudia gasped.

"Today," Homer continued. "The greatest terrorist threat facing the world is awakening at prisons and refugee camps in northern Syria. What shall we do with these war-hardened men and women of ISIS? Fifty-seven thousand alone at the al-Hol refugee camp. They're a cancer that needs to be contained. As we sit here, those in charge have allowed my special forces to release the aerosol onto the occupants. Think of it as a test."

Murmurs rolled through the crowd.

Oh, Homer. What has happened to you? She shut her eyes. True, ISIS was universally hated and an easy target, but they had nothing to do with his daughter's death. What was he trying to accomplish?

"These are citizens of your countries," Homer said. "And now they can be safely repatriated back to you. Ask yourself—Does my bioweapon make the world a safer place today than yesterday?"

There it was. Somewhere inside Homer's scrambled brain was the belief his bioweapon could annihilate war itself. Unfortunately, the leading lights of peacekeeping seemed to have decided the thing was dead on arrival.

A voice at the back asked, "What's stopping someone from analyzing the aerosol and creating it?"

"If it was somehow stolen the bacterium itself is only viable for ten minutes after release. It can't replicate. That should comfort you."

"Not really," someone called out. "There isn't a single member of the UN Security Council who'll be comfortable with this bioweapon." It was the non-proliferation rep again. "Release this on a NATO member and you'll have them in here shutting down your lab."

"My operation is impregnable against the conventional bombs we all loathe."

"Still," the man said. "You're on the Mediterranean, not the moon."

Claudia had had enough. She headed up the staircase along with a few others bailing out early, careful not to make eye contact with the guard operating the lift. From the work roster in the lobby she knew Dafnis was on his day off and likely at The Squats, but no way was she going to join the maelstrom of outraged guests at the helipad. Would Homer's bioweapon reveal party go down as the worst advertising campaign ever, or was it genius—the Bad-News-Travels-Fast principle in play?

AT THE TOP OF THE GONDOLA, Claudia raised her fob to the signal box; a faint clang and purr from below kicked in as the car crept up the rails. There was a good chance she was wasting her time—even if Dafnis remembered who she was this early in the afternoon, one had to wonder if Homer was too obsessed with his bioweapon to care about his son anymore.

Her satellite phone rang as it often did at the edge of the escarpment where the signal was strongest. Finally, Bags. "What the hell, Bags. Do you know how many messages I've left? Has the institute sold off our bionic heart?"

"No. We've still got it."

"Then, what's going on?"

"The signal is cutting in and out. I'm convening a meeting with the entire team tonight by video conference. Does eight work for you?"

"Yes. But—"

"I'll email the video link. Talk later."

Her confusion hung in the air as the gondola cleared the lip of the ridge. Inside was Dafnis.

"What have I done wrong, now?" he said, and brushed past her onto the pathway.

"Nothing at all." Claudia trotted to keep up. "Homer unveiled his drones and bioweapon to potential clients today. They weren't impressed."

Dafnis halted and gaped.

"I've known about the biotoxin since that day on the beach," Claudia explained.

"Of course, but—I can't believe he did that without me."

"Hocking was there to help."

"He's only an assistant." Dafnis's broad feet pounded down the trail.

This sounded like another convenient lie to keep Dafnis from leaving. She caught up and pulled him aside. "Why are you supporting the use of this toxic bacterium?"

"Homer said it can't kill anyone."

"It can't, but—you're a victim of it. How does that feel?"

He frowned and slowed to a standstill.

"You didn't fall from a tree. Hocking told me you were only thirteen when the yersinia gas escaped from a canister in the lab."

Dafnis kicked at a fallen palm frond. "Hocking's an idiot if he thinks I could work in a lab at thirteen."

"You were gifted at biochemistry. Homer said the same thing in Syria. Don't you remember?"

Dafnis shook his head. "I only remember the plane."

"What about your sister?"

His face lit up. "I have a sister?"

"Not anymore."

"Why not?"

"Jeez. I see what Homer's up against." Claudia snapped her fingers in his face. "Focus, Dafnis. You read the letter. Same as me."

He shrank from her with the face of a lost child, his eyes glassy.

"Look how this biotoxin has ruined your mind. And he's already dropped it on hundreds of other children, too."

"Father wouldn't lie about something like this," he said.

What was she thinking? The only children Dafnis cared about were his own. "Jaza's not happy, either," Claudia lied. "She's threatening to leave unless Homer stops."

He stared in terror at the gravel path, licking at the tears on his lips."I can't help you." he said and fled down the trail she knew led to the treehouse.

So much for that effort. She punched in Homer's number and when he answered the chopper's rotors were cutting in on his voice. "We need to talk," she said. He suggested the rooftop garden, probably thinking she wanted to reconcile after their fight on the beach.

———●———

BESET WITH THE UNCONSCIOUS twitching which usually telegraphed one of his grand ideas, Homer was a more vulnerable version of the drone reveal tyrant. He offered up a soft smile and raised his hand to help her down to the same spot where they'd played their flute duet. She took his help, careful to open a space between them that said all was not right.

"Do you know why I love you?" Homer asked.

The beta brain wave Claudia was surfing started to short-circuit.

Love? As in the way she loved a dram of Tobermory, and Homer loved his conch-encrusted flute and crippled African? To give him his due, they'd had moments of genuine tenderness. She got Homer as well as any human could. Had even tried out his principle of sacrificing the few for the greater good, but taking the minds of children went too far.

If not for that, they might have made it work in the way two dark visionaries meet and see themselves reflected in the eyes of the other. The world was woefully short of their kind—the vast majority only available for conjugal visits inside jails.

There would be no more Homers in her future. And yet, had listening been one of Claudia's strengths she might have taken what came next to heart.

"No one has ever challenged my beliefs as much as you," he said, taking up her hand. "I need that in my life."

"Look at what this has done to your own son. You've been lying to Dafnis. An accident with the yersinia aerosol damaged his brain, didn't it?"

By the time the rancor in her voice registered, it was too late to hide his torment. Still holding her hand, he looked down and away into the cascading water. "Dafnis isn't my—" he said, but stopped.

"I thought you, at least, would appreciate the lives I'm saving. Did you know Churchill was prepared to use mustard gas to end the Second World War sooner?"

"Stop spouting the works of great men and try to be one yourself," she said. "You're not saving anyone. Memories are what bind us to each other. Without memory we can't learn or feel."

When he refused to look up, Claudia shot to her feet and growled, "Were you so self-absorbed with what you *could* do, that you didn't stop to consider whether you *should*?"

He raised his chin from his chest, eerily deliberate. "Were *you*? When you decided to cut a healthy heart out of a newborn to advance your career."

Rather than upset her, the harsh comment tugged at her heart as she remembered how he went along with her lie— not for his own profit—but to save Maya and salvage her friendship with Paula and Benny.

"I came to say goodbye." No, she came to see if he would destroy his bioweapon. *Come on Homer*, she waited to hear the words, *beg me to stay like before.*

He was grinning for some reason. "I happen to know you won't leave."

At the end of a long walk to the elevator, the sight of Homer staring vacantly at the churning water hurt more than she expected.

The thing Claudia feared most—a certifiably foul loneliness—had finally found her.

This might be the last time she ever laid eyes on him. Claudia was right, but not in the way she thought.

Chapter 34

Like the water tumbling past the hydrofoil's water wings, Homer's final words to her kept surfacing—especially his unfinished sentence—Dafnis isn't my . . . *concern*? No, he would never feel that. Dafnis isn't my . . . Was it possible the boy was not his son? This was what their driver had said in Syria. If true, a threat to disclose this might be exactly what Claudia needed.

From The Squats' dock, Claudia turned down the stone boardwalk and crossed the road to the orphanage where she found Jaza pushing her son on a swing in the playground. Her sour expression unchanged, she immediately sent him away to play on the slide.

"Dafnis told me about the lab accident," Jaza said as Claudia approached. "So typical. Homer has him crying again."

Great. She had the midwife back onside; it was time to reel her in. "Did he tell you Homer's killing people with stealth drones and bioweapons?"

"I don't know what that is." The midwife squinted. "War and violence, I guess. Now that I can watch the Internet, I don't want to anymore."

"But Dafnis is the one building them."

Jaza shrugged. "Unless he uses them on The Squats, I really don't care." She yelled to another woman to watch her son while she was away and said, "Follow me." Claudia trailed the midwife into the dormitory and down a ground-floor hall to a spacious two-bedroom apartment which smelled of fresh paint.

"Yes. It's all ours," Jaza said over her shoulder while stepping over scattered toys. "I have this place and my son, but I've lost Dafnis. Sad, isn't it?" She went into what looked like a den and came out with something in her hand. "We hardly see each other anymore."

She tossed a magazine onto the dining table with a defeated sigh. "Just after I finished my training, I was on my way to deliver a baby at The Squats camp when I found that thing discarded inside the hydrofoil. I wanted to get rid of it, throw the story overboard or something, but important things have a way of resurfacing, don't they?"

The cover had a headshot of Homer, his island in the distance, and the title "Refugee Saviour—or Notorious Pirate of Body Parts?"

"We all trusted Homer when he said the children in comas were as good as dead, but my midwife training taught me that a coma is not a death sentence. It makes me crazy that I don't know what he did with my family. We were delirious from the cold, but none of us were unconscious."

"Wh—what? Homer said they were lost at sea."

Jaza shook her head in that listless way Claudia had seen so often. "You remember certain things when you're only eleven-years-old. Like the ship that docked every week and stayed for an entire night."

Jaza locked onto Claudia's silent gaze. "I think Homer sedated my family and sold their bodies to whoever was in that boat. There weren't any surrogates or transplants back then, so how else was Homer making money? The only reason I survived is because Dafnis needed a friend."

Claudia felt like she'd come full circle with her early suspicions of Homer. She slammed a palm against the polished tabletop. "Surely Dafnis still wants to escape."

"If he can remember, he might." The midwife let out a tired sigh of frustration. "As long as he's caught up in this plane thing, I doubt he'll help you."

"But maybe *you* can," Claudia said. "I suspect Dafnis might not be Homer's biological son. Get me a hair strand so I can prove it."

Jaza looked sidelong at Claudia, then beelined to a nearby bookcase where she pulled a single sheet of paper from between the pages of a book. "I've always wondered, too."

Claudia took it from Jaza and, seeing what it was, sank into one of the metal chairs around the table. The paternity test from a DNA lab in Malta concluded Homer and Dafnis weren't related.

"*That* is why Homer kept me from my son," Jaza said. "I threatened to show it to Dafnis unless he paid me what I was owed and let me leave with my boy. 'Try it', he said, and I would never see my son again."

A betrayal of this intensity could ruin Dafnis's fragile ego, Claudia thought. The dogged obligation he felt toward his father had bloomed into genuine affection since Syria, and with that—trust. "Dafnis hasn't seen this, has he?"

"Of course not." Jaza grimaced. "Homer knew I could never hurt Dafnis, so we made a deal. If he returned my son and gave us this apartment, Dafnis would never find out."

Claudia flicked the report onto the table. "Why lie about this? I don't get it."

"Homer is desperate for a family, but the worst part is that Dafnis didn't arrive with him. Some of the earliest refugees said Hocking was the only other person here. That means Dafnis and my son might have a family somewhere else. Wouldn't that be wonderful?"

Her almond eyes disappeared behind a pained frown. "Whenever I feel lonely I tell myself it's the same for Homer. Maybe worse." Jaza coasted the report close to Claudia's hand. "Take it if it will help, but please don't show Dafnis."

Damn right it would help. This might be the only blackmail that would.

Chapter 35

Two more days. Time enough to pack, book a flight, and say her goodbyes to Dafnis, Jaza, and the staff of the hospital. Paternity report in hand, her long goodbye with Homer also promised to be an epic dust-up. Either way, Claudia was getting out.

Enveloped in the roiling steam of the staff room shower, Claudia let the water beat her skin raw. If only it were this easy to flush out the worst of Homer's republic. How could she be this exhausted when she hadn't set foot in either the lab or ORs in over a week? Bags's mystery conference might be a lift. If it wasn't about the reinstatement of her license or hospital privileges, it had to be something else equally positive.

The problem was finding a background with all the charm of a sterile Proof of Life hostage photo. While her two bachelor researchers had their generic dorm rooms, Claudia's office was a no-go.

It looked and smelled like a homeless camp in an abandoned building, which was basically what it had become in the turmoil of leaving. Subtle as a skyline banner towed behind a single-engine plane, her sagging clothesline of knickers and socks held dominion over a field of crusty take-out containers and dirty clothes she had planned to wash at home, whenever she got there.

With no windows and white vinyl flooring against a white wall, the deserted hallway outside the lab won out. Laptop on the floor, Claudia settled in cross-legged. Unless they wanted to sink their own careers, the team had better keep their snickers to themselves.

Bags had his monitor off while each member joined the chat, but that didn't mean he wasn't listening in. The team seemed to sense as much, keeping a sparse, guarded tone to their banter until Bags appeared on-screen unshaven, his normally immaculate short straight hair standing on end. The man looked like he'd come off a two-day drunk.

"For almost five months," he said, "I've been dreaming about sitting down with everyone again. I can report that the Johnsons settled out of court, and Claudia has had her license reinstated."

A feeble round of applause petered out under his grim expression. "I only wish it was all good," Bags said. "But today I found out that someone is trying to buy the Thames Heart Institute. They've bid on its patents through a hostile takeover."

Claudia's stomach lurched within the team's chorus of "Who?"

"His name is Homer-something. It sounds like he lives on the same island you were visiting when we held your hearing."

In the silence, all eyes turned to Claudia's image on their monitors. All except the two single scientists left behind at the dormitory, who grinned at each other, likely believing their jobs safe.

"Do you know this guy?" The question from Bags was posed in a monotone voice, free of any rancour.

"Yes. But fucking hell. It's the first I've heard about this."

"That's obvious."

Her shoulders relaxed. Thank God he didn't think she was involved.

"Has the sale been approved by the board of directors?" Jeremy asked.

"Not yet. This guy must be loaded, though. He's not giving up. There's a vote the day after tomorrow. Claudia, what the hell do you think he wants?"

To ruin my entire career, she felt like screaming. Force me to carry on my life's work in the middle of a bioweapons industry. Had Homer not threatened her with, *I happen to know you won't leave,* only hours earlier? Could the man be so vindictive as to sit on the patents and do nothing?

"Oh God," Claudia cried, not realizing at first that she'd said it out loud. "I have no idea, Bags, but I bet I know where he's getting his financing from. Give me a day to try and shut this down."

She caught the fear in her team's eyes. "Guys. I'm going to fix this."

It took mere minutes after she signed off to find out Benny was not the one backing Homer's takeover of the institute.

"Reports are saying he bombed detainees in the north of Syria." Benny said. "What has got into him?"

Claudia headed straight into her lab to soothe her aching heart and try to guess Homer's next move. He was so far ahead, he was about to lap her if she didn't act fast.

Under the spectral blue light of science, and free from the chaos of illogical emotion, she trailed fingertips over the benchtops she'd used for the best months of her life. At the center stood the 3D printer cocooned in a labyrinthine highway of tubes and multi-colored hydrogel syringes. Now idle, empty, and silent.

Through the purchase of her patents, Homer could soon own her future. He was probably doing the Vengeful Vendetta Dance at this very moment.

She stepped inside the inventory closet and lifted the sealed container with the used prototype from its shelf. Within her reflection on the steel door she saw a powerless mother failing to protect her offspring. "Homer. Homer. Why are you doing this to us?"

By the time she came up with a plan, Claudia was standing in a lab ablaze with the setting sun. If he wanted to make this personal, she could, too. Woe be to anyone who tried to keep Claudia from her research.

Unfortunately, her solution might cause a seismic shift in Dafnis's life.

At daybreak the next morning, she started packing. The used prototype would be a squeeze inside her briefcase, but if something went sideways she would need to get to hell out of The Republic of Homer—fast.

In the late afternoon she boarded the hydrofoil to the clinic. Destination—Homer's *de facto* son.

Chapter 36

Dafnis was slurping something called hamburger soup when Claudia burst in with her bribe, and he knew he could never again eat soggy meatballs in the clinic's cafeteria without thinking of the day they plotted against Homer.

He stared at her as if she'd turned into the one-eyed thing called a cyclops. He didn't always like what his father did, but what she wanted was so cruel. Maybe even crueler than Claudia and Homer's relationship itself. In the early days, Homer loved Claudia, but Claudia hated everything about his father except his hair. Now that they finally liked each other, Claudia sometimes seemed to love Homer.

Today—she wanted him gone.

It was hard to figure out those two.

He had a table to himself; the others were buzzing with surrogates eating lunch when he spotted Claudia marching toward him. The bad feelings from the day before flooded in, and he remembered what she told him about a lab accident. The lie hurt, of course, but he decided to forgive Homer because making a mistake and trying to hide it was something Dafnis did almost every day.

She settled in across from him. "I want to give you and Jaza enough money to move to the mainland."

He continued to spoon soup into his mouth. Was this, he wondered, a continuation of a conversation he'd forgotten? Why now, when Homer said what they were doing would make the entire world a better place? It wasn't until she wrote "one-million dollars" on a piece of paper and slid it beside the bowl he was eating from that Dafnis put down his spoon.

She was pressing on the note so hard you'd think she had a dumpster rat by the tail. "You take people's memories," she said, "you take their lives along with it."

As if this was news to him. He took out his notepad and flipped through until he came to an underlined sentence Homer told him to use when someone challenged his job. "The ends justify the means," he said.

It was supposed to help, but it seemed to do the opposite to Claudia. She pushed herself from the table and glared at the cafeteria's surveillance camera. "Damn that Homer. We need privacy. Meet me outside at the playground when you're done."

Minutes later, he found Claudia on the merry-go-round, pushing herself side to side with the balls of her feet. "What makes you think we still want to leave?" Dafnis said, halting the motion with his hand and sliding in beside her.

"Jaza told me she doesn't want your son to be raised in a place selling weapons. Can you blame her?"

If that's what Jaza said, it must be right. He shook his head.

"Then take my offer. But I want you to do something for me in return."

Homer had trained her well. "Of course you do."

"The easiest way to make Homer stop manufacturing bioweapons is to take from him what he's taken from others," Claudia said. "The one thing he deems useless—his memory."

She wanted him to wipe out Homer's memory? Unbelievable. Or was it? Everyone was saying Homer had gone too far this time. What if he'd done that to *their* kids?

"Well?" she asked.

He owed Claudia so much. If he did this thing for her it would be the final chapter of *I Am A Jeep*. Is that what he wanted?

"Jeez. I don't know. I love my son and Jaza. That's where my life should be. Not with a man who's taken advantage of my rotten luck. But I love Homer, too. He's my father."

Claudia moved the briefcase in her lap to the ground, got to her feet and looked him in the eye. "What if I told you Homer isn't your father? You arrived here alone off a refugee boat."

His head snapped up. "You're wrong. I came here from Syria with Homer."

"I'm sorry, but that's a story he made up after you lost your memory. He wanted a family so he pretended you were his son."

"Bulllshit." He was up, pacing with short, agitated steps.

"Dafnis, think about it. Your real papa and the rest of your family might be alive in Syria." She reached into her briefcase and held out a sheet of paper to him. "I'm sick of Homer's lies and manipulation. Aren't you?"

He took it and instantly knew what it was, but when he saw his name beside Homer's, he fought against throwing the paternity report to the ground without reading it. His expert eyes soon found the words—Probability of Paternity—and the number beside it. Zero.

"I can't believe you would do this behind my back." He shoved the sheet into her lap before trudging to the slide where he sat on the metal lip, his head bowed.

As her feet came into focus he raised his head and said, "So I was the back-up plan." A bitter laugh escaped him.

"I'm not telling you to stop loving him," she said.

He caught her gazing over the top of his head, the guilt pouring off her at uncovering a terrible secret that was none of her business.

"Dafnis. You're the one living person Homer truly loves. That part is real. Even someone as vengeful as Homer can be lonely."

He rose to face her. "Well, I'm lonely, too. And tired. But I refuse to be angry. I'm not like him. I don't need to get even."

Claudia suddenly looked like something was choking the life out of her.

If Dafnis knew one thing for sure it was that Jaza was too smart for Homer's republic and that's why one day he would wake up and she'd be gone. And his son with her.

He always knew when the nurses at The Squats got paid because Jaza went into a slump. When would her school debt to Homer end? Never, Jaza told him—"We need lots of money when we leave. I don't want to raise our son in one of those camps on the mainland." Then her beautiful eyes would fill with fire. Such a brave and kind person he would never find again.

It was time for him to prove he was worthy of Jaza.

"The million dollars," he asked. "Was that a joke?"

She smiled. "Do you want it in cash? Or as a bank draft?"

"What's a bank draft? You better give me cash."

He told her they kept an armed drone in the paramedics' shack on the helipad, behind the oxygen tanks. "I could launch from there, but Homer can be anywhere, as long as he's outside."

He didn't mean the playground where they sat, of course, but Claudia started wheeling in a tight circle, inspecting the ground like a dog about to pee. When she finally sat on the bench, her eyes were round and moist. She was hurting. Without much fuss and sooner than she likely expected, their plan was in motion.

"Claudia?" he softly prodded.

He could no longer see her face but her voice was jiggly and quiet. "I can call and tell him to meet me on the beach."

She pulled out the big phone she always carried, but her fingers kept sliding off the numbers, they were shaking so badly. Her face was wet with tears.

"Take your time." When he wrapped his arm around her shoulder, Claudia raised a trembling hand and turned her head from him as if trying to gulp the sobs back down where they belonged.

"How can you be so calm?" she said.

Sure, Homer's latest lie hurt like hell, but he was beyond numb. "Do you remember on our trip when you asked me why I loved Homer?" he said. "And I gave you the dumbest answer in the whole world? 'Because he's my father.' Well, I'm starting to realize that Homer's made me completely dependent on him, but that's not the same as love, is it? I'm like a pet parrot. He keeps me safe and fed inside my cage, and in return I repeat word for word what he says."

Even though his father's republic had gone bad, and Claudia along with it, he whispered, "We need to do this together."

Dafnis grasped one of Claudia's hands and pressed it to his cheek. She came to Homer lonely. Now she would leave even lonelier. Was Dafnis the only one who could see that? Claudia would have been better off to never feel Homer's love at all. And never set foot on Inquisitor's Island, either.

His words low and sweet, he laid out the facts he knew would break her heart. "We've both loved him, but for you, Homer is all you've got."

Her free hand reached for his in a crushing grip. "Tell me what it will feel like for him?"

He released their tangle of hands. "It's like the worst day of fog ever. You can't see anything except what's right in front of you. I don't know how Jaza can stand me sometimes," he said, a touch embarrassed. "Homer won't have any relationship issues, though, because—"

Claudia finished his sentence: "He won't have any relationships." She pinched hard into the sides of her nose and closed her eyes, a defeated thing. "All that brilliance I admired," she said, "gone forever."

This marked the point of no return for them. "Go make your call," he told her. "You can find me at the treehouse."

He didn't expect her to show, but she did—her eyes all puffed-up and red, she kept pulling out her top braid and rebraiding it while she went on and on about Homer trying to buy her artificial heart and how that would kill still more children. "The world needs my bionic heart more than it needs another bioweapon."

He had no idea what she was getting at, but they decided Homer would meet her on the beach at six that evening. "Can I give you something to keep you busy during the attack?" he said.

"Attack?" she said. For one strange second he thought she might ask how to spell it.

"Since I'll be in charge of the Republic after today," he said. "That bastard Hocking will be the first one I get rid of. It was his idea to arm the drones with the aerosol and probably drop it on that camp, too. Now Homer has to pay for Hocking's stupidity. I'm not going to let him sneak off with everything.

"Here's the key you'll need to make the elevator go down to where we make the drones and bioweapon. At the bottom of the stairs," he said, "you'll see a water hose. Use it to flood the computers and control console."

Chapter 37

Since the treehouse was the only place Claudia was guaranteed not to run into Homer, she stayed behind after her meeting with Dafnis. For the next hour, in the skies above the treehouse the chop of the rescue helicopter's blades never abated. Oh, how she wished it would stop. It was like her ghoulish dream of headless cadavers come true.

Forty-five minutes before Dafnis was due to send the drone in search of Homer, Claudia headed to the clinic elevator, glad for something to do which would take her mind off the image of a trusting Homer waiting for her on the beach.

The doors closed, she turned the key and pressed the same blank button the guard had pressed before the presentation. Only then did it occur to her she might find Homer or Hocking standing at the bottom.

The elevator shuddered and stopped. The doors parted. Nobody. Total silence.

Claudia stepped into the connecting passageway, pausing every few steps for any sounds from the factory floor below. Her real challenge loomed ahead—how to get down a creaky steel staircase without being heard. She imagined getting caught with her heavy boots in each hand and decided against removing them.

Two nimble strides would take her to the railing and a crow's nest view of the factory floor.

Chop-Zing-Thud. Chop-Zing-Thud. The metallic racket was enough to trigger a stampede of wildebeests across the Serengeti—but she saw what she needed.

The cavern was bare.

Not a single drone, aerosol missile, assembly line, or biotoxin vat remained. Even the computers and command console she was supposed to destroy were gone. All that remained was a podium and a three-dozen-strong diabolical collection of plastic chairs.

A voice rose from behind the podium. "Is that you, Dafnis?"

Too late to hide.

Hocking stepped into the light and squinted at the top landing. "Oh, it's you, Claudia. Have you come to see our drone factory?"

She was too full of her own questions to answer Hocking.

"Unfortunately, it's all been sold and carted off." He tried a wobbly pirouette, almost toppling from the podium. "I came for a final look-see before I join the new owners."

Sold and gone? This was what she'd begged Homer to do mere hours ago. "Then . . . why the big promo yesterday?"

"I thought that was you I saw down here," he smiled in admiration. "Nothing but a show to confuse adversaries. A condition of the sale. Do you really believe skinflint Homer would waste our precious aerosol on a camp of detainees?"

"Is Homer leaving, too?"

"I should hope not. Who would run the Republic?" The geneticist's eyes flew open. "Oh, sod it. I—assumed you knew since it's your name on the patent."

Hocking jumped from the dais and scurried to the bottom of the stairs. "It seems I've stolen the thunder from Homer's surprise." He plowed on matter-of-factly, spilling the secrets Homer had managed to keep from her for days, possibly weeks.

"Those Thames directors of yours drove the price up far beyond what I felt it was worth. I advised him not to trade a valuable bioweapon for an unapproved prototype, but he wanted you to be happy. I daresay you are."

Homer's final words to her suddenly made sense. He knew there was no greater gift that he could give Claudia than the patent to her bionic heart. She imagined the deliciously triumphant look on Homer's face as he snatched the rights to it from the powerful Thames institute. How she would have loved to be there. She wanted to hear every detail over a bottle of the best whiskey they could buy.

"I've enjoyed working with Homer," Hocking said. "Be kind to the old bugger for me."

. . . The old . . . on the beach. No. No. No. Her watch showed fifteen minutes before Dafnis was due to release the aerosol on an unsuspecting Homer.

She turned and tore through the tunnel.

"Come on, come on." There was a clank and rumble as the elevator began its plodding descent from the upper reaches of the shaft. The beach or the helipad? Inside the elevator, Claudia hit the button for up top, but when she arrived at the shack there was no Dafnis. She pored over the oxygen tanks for the hand-held drone and console, then clawed aside the wetsuits suspended from the wall.

Dafnis and the drone were gone.

Back into the elevator. At the surgical floor, a load of boisterous nurses got in. Exactly the people she didn't want to see. She greeted them then stared at her feet. Through the lobby and main gate, and past the treehouse, Claudia, the surgeon who loved to run, was in the race of her lifetime. At the head of the zigzagging trail to the beach she stopped and bent over, her chest heaving.

Below, sitting against a beached log and looking out to sea, was Homer.

———————◦———————

I'M SURE BUT NOT A hundred percent. You know what I mean? Dafnis wrote in his autobiography *I Am A Jeep.*

If he sat here in his windowless room and did nothing, Homer's idiot son would go on and on as he always had—with one major difference. Whenever Dafnis tried to imagine a life without Jaza he drew a blank. Not a silly old Dafnis blank, either. A fall to your knees and die kind of hole.

He collected the drone from up top and headed out to the beach.

He had just one shot at releasing the toxin before Homer dove into the safety of the sea. Dafnis thought about hiding or making Homer think he was practicing, but that was a Homer tactic. Dafnis was finally going to face his father like a man—a true hunter.

At the beach, Dafnis unhooked the gas mask from the drone and positioned it securely at the crown of his head. As soon as Homer spotted Dafnis coming from the direction of the dock and they were within earshot, he rose from the log he was sitting on and yelled, "Where did you get that drone from?"

"The helipad," Dafnis shouted back.

"Son. You can't practice with that one. It's armed."

Dafnis placed the drone and control console at his feet. "I'm not practicing," Dafnis said right before yanking the gas mask over his face.

Homer side-stepped into the water, never taking his gaze from the drone. By the time Dafnis launched it into the air and had his father within the console's crosshairs Homer was up to his knees in water, his legs driving forward as best they could. Dafnis expected him to plunge under the waves at any moment. Instead, Homer halted, turned, and smiled.

His thumb hovered above the release button. What the hell was his father doing? Go on, dive under. Dive.

Homer would rather die than face up to all the people he killed. When he wrote that in his book, he meant it as a joke. At this moment, Dafnis saw it might not be a joke at all.

Slowly, his thumb sank into the stiff button until it hit bottom. A red cloud wafted downward and Homer disappeared into it.

An image of his father and him long ago sprang to life in Dafnis's mind. They were sitting with their legs dangling from the bridge in the rooftop garden while Homer tried to teach him the flute. Hopeless at it, Dafnis hurled it into the trees. "Someday," Homer said, hugging Dafnis close, "when I'm no longer working I'll have more time and we'll live at The Squats. It's the greatest place on earth."

When the red mist cleared, Homer was staring out to sea in the direction of his creation—The Greatest Place On Earth.

And then he was gone. Homer toppled into the waves.

Dafnis tossed the console aside and ran to catch his father before he drowned. It was done but hadn't gone anything like Dafnis imagined. He hauled a dripping Homer across the sand to a log, his own face awash with tears, then took off running, not bothering to collect the console or drone which was on a downward trajectory far out at sea.

<hr />

"HOMER. HOMER." CLAUDIA called his name the entire way down to the beach, but he didn't turn. Only when she seized his shoulder did he jump and look at her, his face lit with elation.

"I—I . . ." She clutched her stomach with one hand, the other reached for him.

When he stood and clasped her shaking hands between his own, the tears ran down her smiling face.

"Dearest. What's happened?" Homer said.

Words would not release, but that was okay because she was with Homer, where she intended to stay for many years. This amazing man understood better than anyone else what it took to fulfill her. It was what he demanded of his own life—the freedom to soar as far and as fast as he wanted, without the petty constraints of others.

With her cheek pressed to the warm hollow of his neck, she said, "It doesn't matter." Claudia lifted her face to his and kissed him.

"It's so grand to see you," he said, holding her at arm's length. "But where have you come from?"

"Thank you, Homer, for everything you've done for me. You're unbelievable."

He wrinkled his nose, the gleam in his eyes fading. "Who's Homer? Is that me?"

Chapter 38

Republic Island's flat peninsula buzzed with foreign dignitaries, world-famous scientists, and a stream of citizens cycling down from the settlement formerly known as The Squats.

Oh, how she hated that name. One of Claudia's first major decisions had been to close the refugee camp and retire *The Squats* name into history. In place of the rows of shipping containers stood Claudia's H&C Bionic Heart Institute, sparkling white against the blue Mediterranean on its opening day.

At the fringe of the human crush, Bags bent to rest his forehead against Claudia's during a wordless pause in their reunion. "I miss you, too." They hadn't seen each other in over two years. Not since the week Claudia flew off in a panic to Malta.

"Benny's money keeps the production lines going," she said, "but I could always use a top-notch fundraiser if you want to come out of retirement."

"And what would I do for fun in a place like this?"

"You could hang with Jeremy. That's one person you already know."

Bags smiled and squinted at a clique of workers where her lead scientist stood with his pregnant wife. "You know, my sailboat friend is trying to talk me into buying a boat and learning to sail. He keeps the liquor locked up when we go out, and you never know, I might get him to finance a London heart facility for you."

"Oh, Bags." With a hot tear dribbling down, she leaned across and pecked at his lips. "My place is here, now."

From that adored place—the balcony of her house on Republic Island—she often sat in the starry silence and watched dots flickering across the water, inside the Zen garden atop the former clinic, or within the penthouse where Jaza, Dafnis, and their son lived during holiday breaks from her medical school on the mainland.

Surrogates, critical patients, and transplant surgeons no longer roamed the halls—replaced with the hundreds of workers at her production facility who needed a place to live.

Neither was there a strongman at the helm but a strongwoman named Claudia who ruled The Republic of Homer with the same overarching ambition and secrets. Despite the Nobel Prize sitting behind glass in her office, few could guess the trail of ruined lives in its wake.

Some day in the near future, in the glow of their Nobel Prize, she wanted to be brave enough to tell her team everything she'd done here—everything—and what it taught her about true greatness and its close cousin—cowardice.

Chapter 39

"Once upon a time there was a man named Homer."

That's the way Claudia always started the story. Homer would giggle and clap his hands because the story of his life was such a delicious mystery to hear for the first time. And no matter how many times she told it—it was always the *first* time for Homer. She could tell it until the end of time, and it would never be enough for him.

Homer, wiped clean of all memories, was a strange sight indeed. Some days all he did was sit and stare out a window, his brain cortex bone-dry—the sands of his hourglass long expired. Then, without warning, or rhyme or reason, for a precious hour the new Homer would spring to life.

It was uncanny the way he could remember Claudia and his love for her, but no one else from his past—not his beloved wife or brave daughter, nor even Dafnis. Like a warm, contented cat protecting its vulnerable underbelly, his memory cells had curled around nothing but the concept of Claudia.

That's all that Homer carried forward from one day into the next. When she appeared, he was suddenly in love. Whether he'd seen her the night before, or years before, wouldn't have mattered—time was no longer a concept for Homer. Claudia finally had the kind of relationship she could shape to her own ideal, and if it didn't pan out there was always tomorrow. It was understood by everyone that Claudia alone was the master editor, purging the parts that wouldn't serve the two of them.

"Yes, Homer. We have an adopted son and a grandson, too."

"How grand," he said each time, clapping his hands and kissing her like a timid adolescent.

She lived for that moment. Her "family" loved her, and though it took a long time to get used to the idea, she reciprocated with her own brand of truncated love.

Homer didn't remember being strafed by the aerosol or why they were on the island in the first place. In the beginning, she tried to recreate everything that had happened to them, short of the attack. He listened as if it were a movie with a happy ending he knew was coming, but the next time she would have to start the story all over.

Eventually, Claudia stopped trying. Such a strange comfortable relationship they had. Like puppy love or one notch above best friends. And even her brilliant idea to seduce Homer and finally have sex with him didn't go as expected. To say they both got turned on and had one hell of a good fuck was an understatement.

Some might say Homer was living every man's dream because every seduction of Claudia was a new chase for him—the first lay of his entire life, but like Homer's feelings, the sex was stuck in juvenile territory—he couldn't build from the last time.

Claudia refused to grieve the man she'd lost because it felt like she was cheating on the equally precious man she now shared her life with. Whenever Claudia found herself thinking of the other Homer, she imagined he was still there on the arched bridge, playing his flute to his heart's content, satisfied with all he'd created.

Homer was right in the end, the great ones made the hard decisions so others didn't have to—especially when the choice was love.

His aerosol would eventually burst onto the world stage and all hell would break loose, but Claudia stopped checking the news cycle, because short of Armageddon, Homer's cruel weapon no longer concerned their far flung sanctuary trying to do right by humanity.

The End

Don't miss out!

Visit the website below and you can sign up to receive emails whenever Lee Kaiser publishes a new book. There's no charge and no obligation.

https://books2read.com/r/B-A-MKBUE-QMMSH

BOOKS 2 READ

Connecting independent readers to independent writers.

About the Author

Lee Kaiser is a Canadian author who writes women's fiction suspense and thrillers. Her latest stand-alone in the series *Paths Unknown* is a bio-thriller, *Her Artificial Heart*, set in Malta. All three novels follow a plucky group of women adventurers across the globe. While the debut *Sutra of the Pearl* placed her characters in India's underworld, her second, *Towers of the Hungry Ghosts*, was set in a castle in Romania. All three novels are available in both ebook and paperback through any bookseller.

Read more at leekaiserauthor.com.

www.ingramcontent.com/pod-product-compliance
Lightning Source LLC
Chambersburg PA
CBHW021207250626
47155CB00008B/2713